The Judging of Abigail Perdue

Daniel Mallen

For Beth, Viv and Matt

one

Abigail was once of our world, just like one of us. And now she's returned to theirs.

Naked as the day she was born, worn-down weary on an unmade bed, she'd lain there for hours, scared, vulnerable and pleading for mercy. On the Judgment eve none shall sleep. It was almost a law. Her anger rekindled and Abigail, wholly unprepared for time's harvest, hugged her knees to her breast and delved deep into her memories.

She'd found the intractable puzzle ever the same: how can you save yourself, when there's nothing to do, but wait to be processed? For tomorrow they'd vote - life eternal or her life revoked.

Between all this hope, the anticipation, the misgivings, those were her torments now, her agonised throes. Wracking her mind for hours she'd repeatedly come up empty. She'd needed more time. Alas, that most valuable commodity was entirely spent. Tragically it had been for her, at that magical cusp, when the key parts of life had fallen blissfully into place. Yet in our hapless world of the living, it took nothing more than happenstance for everything to change - with no way to warn her.

Abigail Perdue required three votes to save her soul. Three was the minimum. Even in her darkest hours she desperately wanted to ascend. She wondered if it would hurt when the flesh fell from her bones, although they'd assured her it would not.

Once she'd been indestructible, beautifully self-possessed - adorned in the contemporary armour of money and youth. However that was six days in the past, in a life since expired. Now everything depended on the damned verdict.

Three votes to two in my favour, she figured. Numbers that would see her home, yet the harbinger of doubt refused to give her peace.

Unable to sleep, she got out of bed, picked up the cello and placed her thumb between the frog and the leather pad of her bow. She stifled a sob as her mind replayed the infernal day when, unwisely, she chose to take the train.

Six Days Earlier: Lancaster Gate Station. London. England. 7.21am.

She had hurried down to the subway, her coat buttoned high to the neck, soaked through and thoroughly by the raw autumnal rain. Of course to hurry is a more complicated process when you're laden with a big unwieldy box, inside of which was Abigail's love of her life - an outrageously expensive cello.

Not an actual del Gesù, but from one of the lesser Guarneri and purchased for a six-figure sum from Beare's of London - a lavish gift from her wealthy father – who'd wanted to celebrate her accession to the Philharmonic Orchestra. This irreplaceable instrument, a glorious expression of unmatched craftsmanship, was being transported these days in a modern fibreglass case, preferred by Abigail to the dull-black original.

'It's far too heavy, Papa!' she'd cried. But he knew the real reason well enough, it came in pink and Abigail so loved pink.

A taxi would have been more practical in getting to rehearsal, but tortoise-slow in peak traffic. So Abigail Perdue made an arbitrary choice, casually and in the same random way that we all make decisions every day of our lives. For us, most options are mercifully mundane with no major consequence, but wistfully not all of our choices are benign.

Merging in with the moving masses, Abigail opted to save time and to brave the subway. The fading yellowy-purple patches on her skin bore witness to her previous encounters with the city's harried commuters and, as she braced herself for yet more bruising, she wondered, *Why don't I play the violin?*

At the best of times a cello is not the most portable of objects; at the worst it's positively hell, a task of Herculean proportion for one who stands just a tad taller than five foot six. And this morning was especially nightmarish. Carried down beneath the earth amidst this cattle press of humanity, she tipped up on her toes to read the comings and goings on the digitized display, *Five full minutes before the next train!* For Abigail it was an eternity, confined in close quarters, stealing each breath from the mouths of strangers.

'Should have taken the cab,' she sighed.

The ringtone of her smart phone distracted her – Beethoven's Sixth! – It was Katie again. Abigail was undeniably pleased. *No doubt calling me to book the holiday, as if I'd forget!* She had been planning their trip for months.

An influx of late arrivals swelled numbers on the narrow platform to a claustrophobic level, forcing the young cellist further towards the edge. Amidst the impatient throng, she struggled to release her bag, while the polyphonic trilling amplified in volume as it reached the second movement in B flat major. She manoeuvred her Prada with her one free hand, but the barrelling bulk of an acne-caressed youth, deflected Abigail into a violent spin causing the cello to whip-lash from her rain-soaked grip.

Arcing in a blur of pink motion, it tumbled in the air, bouncing twice before landing with a harrowing thud, four feet beneath the red-lacquered soles of her calfskin sneakers. Abigail howled in horror - a guttural noise that erupted up from her core and echoed off the tile-covered walls. Her beloved Guarneri would be smashed into smithereens by the next locomotive. It was well insured, but she loved that cello in the way you love a person, so instinctively Abigail jumped.

Cautiously, she straddled the electrified line. *Is it the third or the fourth?* She wasn't sure. Terrified and pumped full of adrenaline, she calculated she'd at least three minutes - *More than enough time!*

Her baby-pink case spanned the four-feet-eight and one half inch of track and was within a hair's breadth of the live fourth rail. The minute margin between life and death almost bridged.

Ignoring frantic appeals, Abigail went for it, turning from the tangle of arms that beckoned her back to safety. But unnoticed in her haste, its chrome decorative detail now carried 660 volts of direct current around its copper base. Perhaps that doesn't sound like much. But it takes a lot of amps to move a train around and it's the amps that will kill you.

Yet how could she have known? The electrons align and run in silence, losing one atom to another in a cataclysmic sequence for the unwary soul about to conjoin the loop, liable to take the easy short-cut, through metal or bone, back down into the damp earth from where it came. There were no clues for Abigail, no sinister hum or hissing sound, to warn her of the peril at her toes.

Electricity travels along the arteries, racing from hand to head, it passes through your heart, where even as little as thirty milliamps can cause ventricular fibrillation - a heart attack. Abigail bent over and when her moist, slender hand reached out to grab the handle, she may as well have stooped to pet a foul-tempered rattlesnake.

Her unwitting fingers were about to connect when, a sudden strike - an inaudible blue flashed zap - spat life ending current through her stricken frame, as the acrid smell of melting flesh lodged in the nostrils of the transfixed onlookers.

Sweet Abigail Perdue at twenty-six, was gone even before her body hit the floor. In a small mercy, her remains fell into the suicide pit, sparing further desecration when, just 130 seconds later, a train slammed into her priceless cello.

Manhattan, Lower East Side. New York City. 2.20 am.

At almost the exact moment that Abigail Perdue was leaping to the rescue of her antique cello, Michael Roberts, a New York City firefighter, was barely clinging to life on a cold metal gurney being rapidly moved through the ER of the Lower Manhattan Hospital.

Mike had kicked out and struggled in confused panic, but had become more pliant on account of the drugs being pumped through his veins. In the heaven-sent fug of Morpheus, he was vaguely aware of the close press of concerned faces, blurred images of colleagues, friends and frantic doctors. Their muffled commands and urgent prompts went unanswered by the ashen-faced young man with the erratically beating heart.

It seemed mere moments since Mike had been part of a four-man rescue squad, dispatched to a second-alarm at a squalid tenement on the lower East Side. The team made their entry and proceeded quickly to the upper floors, intent on finding the persons reported to be still inside.

They made it up to the fifth, when a clatter of beams came crashing downward in a great ruptured heave. Mike remembers the sensation of falling, his hands and legs flailing through the ether. Being the least experienced he had been the last in the line. The others made it to the safety of the lintel, but in his rookie excitement, Mike had made one small, but fatal mistake - he forgot to connect his safety line to his buddy in front. It's so often the little details that kill you.

The young firefighter, weighed down by 35lbs of breathing apparatus, tumbled some sixty feet onto a mound of scorched steel and rubble. His body lay broken and sundered. His fire crew buddies made heroic efforts to extricate him alive and they succeeded.

Mike was indeed living when they wheeled him into the surgery, but only for moments. He remembers the circles of brilliant light overhead, then nothing. Michael Roberts went into cardiac arrest, his natural sinus rhythm critically disrupted. The defibrillator paddles were primed on command and a shock delivered. Its purpose was to stop the heart, in order that its natural pacemaker – the sinus atrial node - might restore normal rhythm. But it didn't work.

Another attempt was made, twenty five pounds of force again applied by the attending physician. But by then the strident alarm of the electrocardiogram machine was screeching that Mike was in asystole - a state of no cardiac electrical activity - better known as flat-line. Unlike the TV shows, in the real world of emergency room medicine, the crash-cart paddles are not used when a patient flat-lines, because you cannot stop a heart that has already ceased to beat. An injection of the drug vasopressin was calmly administered by the senior medic, while her team commenced a sequence of manual compressions. Sadly to no avail.

In most cases, resuscitation is unlikely at this point. Twenty-eight year old Michael Roberts, of the NYFD, was now clinically dead. Doctor Irene Benrahbi called time of death at 2.36 am.

$$\infty$$

Now I am sure that every human soul requires a small miracle. To emerge unscathed from the ceaseless daily grind of the average life, with all its casual and turbulent inanities, would be an undisputed achievement for any of one of us.

From the moment of your entry into the adult world, you toil at whatever it is you do. If you are one of those rare few, the really lucky souls, you may find a job that you like or even love, but for most people it remains just a means to an end. Then, much sooner than you could ever imagine, here comes that end. Your time is up. You'll find it hard to believe.

So depending on whatever belief system you espouse, where do you go?

They say that the more popular picks range from a strong belief in an afterlife to a nihilistic descent into oblivion. If that's true, then most folks think that you either go nowhere - its lights out, gone forever - or perhaps you believe what the Jews, the Muslims or the Christians have to say: you go to account for your life in front of a supreme being, your maker.

Who knows? Well, I do.

But I can tell you that during my first time here, I was never sure which version was correct. You see the main thing is that whatever you believe or don't believe in, the only certainty that endures is that we're all going to the same place, one way or another. Like it or not. For us poor souls, ours is a same-boat, shared-fate kind of deal. Well at least for the first part - the complicated business of life and death.

By now, I guess, you must be wondering how I've come by this information? I know, because I once lived just like you do now. I died when it was my time and thanks to the benevolence of a preternatural force, I now walk the Earth for a second time.

By a strange coincidence I am once more unsure of my purpose here, but they left me with my memories intact. So I know exactly where we all end up.

The events I write of now, took place during my last days as an Advocate of Souls, in a period of universal time that corresponded with the Judgment of a young woman called Abigail Perdue and five other penitents. This is all that I remember. This is my account.

Room 5. Limbus Stasis.

He glanced down with something akin to despair at the latest bulletins on his desk, each one a grim catalogue - killings in Johannesburg, a mass shooting in Ohio and a commuter jet lost in the ocean. So much human folly and suffering, that resulted in even more souls pouring into the Stasis blocks, each one of them in need of a rep. It never gets dull around here as an Advocate of Souls, that's for sure.

'Are you ready for the next batch?' The woman in the smart grey business suit addressed the burly form of her younger colleague who was seated in a casual sprawl at an unremarkable office desk. The man acknowledged with a semblance of a smile and enquired gruffly in a distinct accent, 'So tell me, who's next?'

'The Scandinavian! You remember, Mister Obnoxious. He seems well on course for an imminent arrival. And...' she paused for effect. 'He's been assigned to you...Tah dah!'

That little piece of information had just made Marcus' day.

A portable TV set was playing network re-runs in the corner, with the sound on mute. The woman distracted, narrowed her eyes as if concentrating, 'Wasn't that the guy who was here last month?' she asked. 'It *is* him. Awesome!'

'I don't think I've seen this one before? Gosh, I do love Oprah. I only wish I had the time to watch.' Returning her full attention to a slim leather folder, she ran a manicured finger down the column of a gold edged page. 'Abigail Perdue, a young English cellist, is on the way and that New York firefighter is not going to make it. I'll take both of those. You can have the fisherman and the eminent doctor.'

This second bit of news was not so welcome. Marcus hadn't cared much for her the first time around, but he nodded in agreement, while rubbing his eyes vigorously. His work schedule here was relentless, punishing even.

'There are the usual variables in play: an unexpected recovery or a last minute change of plan could alter the roster. Lou will let us know when it's all settled.'

'Yet another jolly quorum of six,' he crooned, hands held wide in the manner of Sinatra. His stylishly turned out colleague chuckled and placed three of the files on the desk before making her way towards the exit. 'So I'll see you later, Marcus.'

'Yeah, see you soon Maryam,' he replied, absent-mindedly, glancing once more at the names of those who were provisionally scheduled to be his new clients. One of them was the stand out for sure. 'The Scandinavian,' he muttered, placing one powerful fist in the palm of the other. *I have been so looking forward to meeting you.*

Marcus had been doing this job for a very long time, for more years than he even cared to remember, but he had to admit that it still held occasional attractions. His mind wandered to the small crescent of chairs in Room 5 and to the Judgment seat, almost perpetually in use.

He imagined how this particular fellow would squirm and weep, when it's his turn in the hot-seat. Front and centre, facing five other souls about to decide his fate. No longer the master of his own pathetic world and compelled to grasp fully, one of the more important facts of life - Your own death and what must come after. By then it's far too late to change a thing and most of you can't claim that you weren't warned.

Marcus suppressed his mirth. It was too early in the morning. He took another sip of his bitter-burnt coffee and moved on to scrutinise the next newcomers file.

A certain Mister Nader Khoury.

Somewhere in the Tyrrhenian Sea. Same Day. 9.10am.

Nader Khoury allowed himself another grim laugh, for whomever his predecessor was, he certainly had a sense of humour. Nader knew now, that the 'Mafi Mushkila' was going under. Although a man not given to frivolity, he appreciated the irony. The rust bucket he was trying to pilot was utterly doomed.

After all Mafi Mushkila in Arabic means 'no problem,' but she had big problems now, plenty of them. The most pressing was that his vessel was taking on water, with no working bilge pump. Nader and his unlucky cargo were going into the Tyrrhenian and he knew it. 'What kind of idiot names a boat, No Problem?' he cursed.

What had started as a routine run from the Algerian port of Annaba was now sure to end in high drama. Captain Khoury had that morning, cast off from the dock, then nudged his dilapidated, red rusty Seiner, a short distance due east. Weighing anchor at one of many deserted coves to be found along the 620 mile coastline, Captain Khoury waited impatiently for his cargo. *These things will be the death of me*, he thought, as he dragged deeply on a cigarette and was rewarded with a raucous, chest-rattling cough.

He'd heard the whine of the high-powered outboard engines before he'd caught sight of three skiffs approaching from the direction of the shore. No words or greetings were exchanged only a single nod of recognition to the other Captains, as the consignment was swiftly transferred to his vessel. Forty seven people are one hell of a crowd on the deck of small boat but such overcrowding was certainly not alarming, nor new in this game. Nader Khoury had been part of the clandestine transport of human freight for the best part of a decade. 'Only from time to time,' he'd claim, and besides, he had to do it – *How else could I survive on my meagre earnings?*

They were North African's mainly, but also from the East and the West coasts. The current batch, Nader guessed, was a mix of Somalis, Eritreans and Sudanese.

All in the hands of Allah. For what other twist of fate could have delivered so many innocents to their doom, unless it was his will. Nader sneered as he held tight to the wheel. *Almost there, but still too far from dry land. Where all sensible men belong!*

His thoughts drifted to when the cargo had been transferred and the skiffs had departed. Captain Khoury had hauled his anchor, in what were moderately calm seas. The Sirocco - a southerly desert wind that could alter the going to seriously rough - had begun to blow much sooner than had been predicted. Nader had frowned as he considered this unexpected development. Had he been fishing, he might have chosen to return to port or perhaps to seek shelter. But Nader needed the money - and there was also the fact that you did not disappoint the people with whom he did business.

Once they'd been paid of course, they didn't care about what happened to these unfortunate souls, these people who'd placed their lives in the hands of unscrupulous men. But you never bring them home. They paid for a journey, so they get a journey, but one way only. Many would have borrowed from local money lenders to pay for their passage. Their families, no doubt, would carry the brunt of any default on their investment.

He had heard the rumours, of other crews, who resorted to hurling people over the side at the first sign of trouble. But they were evil men. Nader Khoury was a crook, that he would admit, *But I'm an honest, God-fearing crook.*

The Mafi Mushkila had for more than two hours, hugged the coast on an easterly heading. Confident of avoiding the naval gunboats, Nader then made a turn due north, covering the 182 nautical miles in less than a day, to a point just north of the port of Cagliari.

The Tunisians flocked to Italy, the Moroccans to Spain but the Algerian boats operated in all three jurisdictions. In recent months, the Italian Coast Guard had heavily patrolled the shores of the pelagic islands of Pantelleria, Linosa and Lampedusa. So the risky - more direct - crossing to Sardinia, was Captain Khoury's current route of preference.

His passengers had no prior knowledge of where they would disembark, only that they would reach the shores of Europe. Each of these people now clinging to weathered ropes on the foam lashed deck had paid the traffickers in the region of $1,500 US dollars, to be whisked across the Mediterranean, to a new, more prosperous life. Nader would receive but a fraction of that purse, but one run alone would earn him more than two months of hard fishing.

He also knew well, that the women on-board faced a far more uncertain future. The majority would be sold into forced prostitution, to cover the cost of their fare. But he was not a man given to sentimentality. Life was tough here and frequently cheaper than the rain. He would deposit his cargo in as shallow water as he dared, just offshore from a beach where they could wade their way to dubious safety.

Nader never cared to call her Mafi Mushkila, but had held to superstition - in his culture, it was considered bad luck, to change the name of any sea-going craft. But the fishing in these waters was in serious decline and the now older, more cynical Nader, had succumbed to the lure of illicit money. Approached by a local fixer, Nader had entered into an arrangement. An 'agreement with the devil' he would sometimes joke without laughter.

Nonetheless the income had helped to sustain both his mother and sisters and also his pretty young wife Naira and their children. So Nader continued his half dozen solo voyages each year. Yet easy money doesn't always live up to its name. Thousands of souls perish annually in their dogged attempts to breach the first world.

Nader was certain that the Mafi Mushkila would voyage no more. Her diesel engine choked as the compromised vessel launched itself at another mountainous wave – a solid slab of water that sent another pocket of helpless people over the side. There could be no rescue for them, no about turn in this harpy howling foam-splattered hell. In the old Seiner's wheelhouse, the Captain repeatedly glanced down to where a terrified young woman with a tear stained face, cradled a young child to her breast, a small boy, about the same age as Nader's son. He looked up at the Captain with large hollowed-out eyes that could not contemplate the predicament they faced.

The Sirocco blows fierce along this fetch of open sea and sent yet another lash of iron-grey, hard into the starboard side. Nader tried in desperation to increase power, but his engine was dying noticeably with every response. Each time the Mafi Mushkala rolled with a wave the accumulated water in the hold caused it to shift dangerously. Lurching like a punch-drunk boxer, they plummeted once more down into the deep trough. The Captain had to make a decision. The boat was lost, pitching now at an alarming rate. He could not save the unfortunate souls on the aft deck.

They'd be consumed by the sea, but with the help of Allah, he just might be able to save the woman, child and the others who were huddled together in his wheelhouse. Finally he received a response to his mayday, he knows the Coast Guard were on the way, but there was no chance they could make it in time.

He grabbed the sobbing woman and yanked her up by the hair onto her feet, his hands strengthened by years of hard labour. 'Come with me!' he commanded. The petrified woman obeyed, followed by the others.

The drenched Captain hauled from its storage, a bright orange ball of UV-resistant polyethylene. Pulling a chord he pierced the compressed gas canister which noisily inflated the luminescent plastic into the welcome form of a dome-roofed life raft. A glow-in-the-dark, four person floating sanctuary, unfurled itself in the roaring wind, their last and only chance of survival.

Nader pushed the woman with the child inside and the other two instinctively followed. Only now he realised, that they, were also children - teenagers perhaps fourteen or fifteen years old. Nader, for a split second considered pulling one of them out, but reckoned they were small enough to fit. It should take five.

He closed the entry flap and waited for the next big wave that lifted the life-raft over the gunwale and out onto the broiling sea. Nader planned to follow as soon as he secured his own vest. He glanced one more time at the deck of his now half-submerged boat. There was no one left. Nader paused for a final check, but in doing so, delayed that fraction of a second that may have made the difference between life and death.

The Mafi Mushkila made its death roll, another broadside capsized her, tossing the Captain violently underwater before he could snap closed the buckle of his floatation device. In the tradition of many mariners, Captain Khoury was not a great swimmer, despite having spent most of his adult life at sea. But even the most powerful would not last long in such hostile conditions, without a buoyancy aid.

Nader's last sight above the surface was of a bobbing orange bubble disappearing behind a colossal grey swell, then re-emerging perkily above the onrushing waves.

They have a chance, he thought.

His absolute intention was to have saved his own life, but the capsule had drifted too far and too fast for him to reach. So instead of an implausible salvation, Captain Khoury concerned himself with the practicalities of a death by drowning. He knew the game was up.

Nader had always had a deep, almost obsessive fear of drowning. He had considered that if ever happened, he would most likely die from his heart bursting in sheer panic. Yet instead, with a measure of surprising calm, he accepted his fate. For unlike the trashing portrayed in the movies, a person drowning is unable to shout or call for help, they cannot obtain enough air. Drowning is a silent business.

Overwhelmed by a roller that broke above his head, Nader tries to hold his breath. But his desires are controlled by the outer part of the brain, the grey matter. Those decisions were overruled however by the middle part, the white matter. The increased level of carbon dioxide triggered the breath-hold break.

Although under water he could not stop himself from opening his mouth and attempting to breathe. It is an ancient, automatic response by a human brain in survival mode. Another quaff of water entered Captain Khoury's airway and sent his vocal cords into laryngospasm - they constricted sealing the air tube tight.

The salty water he had ingested was pulled by osmosis from his blood stream into the lungs. Sea water is hypertonic to blood. Its content thickens it and puts pressure on the beating heart. The physiological response to drowning at sea is different to drowning in freshwater but that made no difference to Nader now. For he was underwater, open eyed and going further down, his body and lungs fatally compromised as he sank to the bottom of the sea.

∞

Abigail tried to make sense of what she saw - large swathes of people were being ushered away from the platform by London Underground staff. Most moved along compliantly, following the clear instructions issued by a pair of Transport Police officers, but one passenger had become irate at being delayed for some vitally important meeting.

What's going on? Abigail was curious. She could also see what she believed to be the train driver, being comforted. A blanket placed around trembling shoulders and the offer of a nice cup of tea. *Something must have happened?* She'd figured.

An incident at rush hour she knew could cause chaos for thousands of people, trying to make their way to work. *No one seems to be getting in. They must have closed the station.*

Abigail was unaware that when the driver reported 'one under' a string of protocols immediately came into operation. First, he issued a Mayday call on his comms radio. Then the Line Controller discharged the power to the relevant line, with the train driver also applying safety stops to prevent it being recharged. This cut the juice and prevented another train hurtling into the station at 30mph. With that task complete, the passengers are informed about what has occurred, they're directed to calmly exit the train and alight safely onto the platform, while the Controller summons the Emergency Response Unit.

Some of the carriages were not yet adjacent to the platform so the passengers shuffled their way towards the front, grumbling about their bad luck. The driver opened the doors manually with his butterfly cup and they alighted onto the painted concrete. Most had a resigned expression, as if many of them had been through this before.

Abigail hovered around taking it all in. She heard the cackle of hand held radio transmissions and the words, 'One under at Lancaster Gate.'

She wondered, *One under what?*

Yet more men arrived, wearing yellow and orange high-viz-vests, emblazoned with the letters ERU. They manhandled heavy equipment into place and began slowly jacking up the empty train. They were motioning towards something under the carriage but Abigail couldn't see what it was, from just a few metres above their heads.

She finally caught a glimpse of what seemed to be causing the commotion. *Oh dear, it's a body. Someone must have fallen onto the tracks, poor thing.*

The Emergency workers with great dignity removed the corpse of what appeared to be a young woman, in an expensive, beige, calf-length coat. She had one shoe missing and Abigail noticed the red sole of the other. *Louboutin sneakers - just like mine*!

The girl had brown, gently curling hair, but her longish bangs obscured her lifeless features. When they raised the body onto a waiting stretcher, her hair fell back, revealing a very familiar face. Abigail realised only then, that she was looking down at herself. She recoiled in terror from the scene below, screamed in panic and instinctively floated up and away.

Everything went dark.

two

Gold Coast, Australia. 8.45am.

Per Andersson was in top physical shape for a man in his mid-forties. A combination of wise eating habits, years of Hatha yoga and frequent more robust exercise had given his six foot, four inch frame a svelte, muscular appearance.

The fringe of his carefully styled blonde hair flopped over a deep set of Nordic blue eyes. Per Andersson was indeed a handsome man, but sadly he knew it.

Halfway through his regular morning run, the limber Swede was surprised to feel a sharp stinging pain that radiated from his neck down past the left elbow. He surmised he'd overdone it, at Sunday's mixed doubles match. *A muscle tear perhaps? Nothing serious.*

Satisfied with his self-diagnosis he increased the pace and arrived at his custom designed apartment, breathing more heavily than usual. It gave him an almost sensual pleasure to push his body to the limit. After he'd showered, the Scandinavian towelled-himself dry and stole more than one admiring glance at his reflection in the floor to ceiling mirror.

You've still got it Per man, he grinned.

He grunted his pleasure through pristine white teeth and selected an almost decadent design from a rail of similarly expensive shirts. Per was looking forward with carnal anticipation to his dinner date. A tantalising evening was in store with his new, much younger, Australian girlfriend. She was blonde, buxom and not especially bright, ticking all his boxes.

Per had been married once before, a tiresome and often tempestuous relationship with an older German woman. It nonetheless survived long enough for him to father two daughters, both since departed with their mother.

Modern technology had made it easier to communicate and more importantly at a time that suited Per. He loved having no noisy kids hanging around the place, whining and moaning and basically cramping his style. But he also liked his monthly Face Time with 'his girls' when he got to impart fatherly wisdom to his bored teenagers. It was recorded that he always sent cheques on their birthdays and at Christmas. So as far as Per was concerned, he held up his end of the deal.

On the subject of deals, relocating his web development company to Australia's Gold Coast had been a gem of an idea. As well as the many tax concessions that he'd enjoyed, it also allowed him time to pursue his passions - surfing and beautiful women. The almost ever present sunshine also helped to top up his tan, but not too much.

For although a vainglorious man, Per was nonetheless a creature of high intelligence and was especially careful regarding all aspects of his health. This included being a frequent user of an App that his company had developed – MiRayz.

It was a clever invention, which gave avid sun worshipers the ability to track their personal solar exposure. In a sun-kissed country like Australia, with its predominantly fair skinned population, that little beauty of an idea had made him a considerable fortune.

'Life is good for Per,' was his oft quoted mantra and the Nordic millionaire, a confirmed Atheist, found great solace in the Darwinian concept of survival of the fittest. Per was fit and he would do more than just survive. The handsome Swede was thriving, but his conceited take on life, would soon be put to the harshest of tests.

Mike Roberts opened his eyes, blinked once and blinked again. Something was wrong. A foreign object was lodged in his trachea,

Mike couldn't breathe - he was choking. A violent spasm brought up a sphere of watery-gel from the depths of his throat. Mike stared aghast at the liquid mass as it dissolved on contact with the stone floor. The obstruction cleared, he tried to make sense of his whereabouts.

He had awoken in a foetal scrunch, gagged then rolled onto his back sucking in huge gulps of air. He was lying on the flagstones completely naked.

Where am I? Where's my boots and my kit? I must have fallen into a basement!

There was no hole in the ceiling but when a human brain grasps for a logical response it can often over-reach. The young firefighter looked around with confused eyes and then scrambled awkwardly to his feet. His body felt good, real good, but it also felt new and unfamiliar. He clearly remembered falling and the severe pain that by now had completely disappeared. Neither could he feel the heat of the fire that had licked at his twisted limbs. Oddly, it felt distinctly cold. Mike stood up in a wide stone corridor. Its dry walls chilly to the touch were filled with strange inscriptions, engraved at intervals along its length. He ran his fingers across a mysterious diagram, his curiosity aroused, but he had no idea what they meant.

The passageway had the darkness and ambience of a musty tomb. Lit only by the sporadic throw from open flame torches suspended from its walls. It was almost entirely empty aside from a lone marble table that stood beside a doorway at the furthest reach.

On the table Mike discovered two navy-blue scrubs and a pair of rubber-soled shoes. He felt somewhat self-conscious walking around in the nude, so he'd tried on the pants and the shirt, both of which fitted him perfectly. As he bent to dress himself, he noticed the glint of soft amber escaping from beneath the doorframe.

He turned the unadorned handle clockwise and pushed against the heavy oak panel that began to move without resistance. The inrushing brightness caused a momentary sting of pain to his baby-blue eyes and illuminated the entire space with a phenomenal beam of light, a light so bright it forced Mike to avert his gaze downwards. He stepped through the portal, squinting through the partial shield of outstretched fingers.

What is this?

He couldn't begin to imagine where he was. It appeared to Mike to be a cavernous hangar-like construction. Perhaps he was dreaming or maybe the drugs he'd been given in the ambulance were causing him to hallucinate. *Yeah that must be it!*

The young fireman became abruptly aware of other people, streaming into the concourse but the area was so vast and the light so intense, he could only make out their silhouettes as they also stopped, stared, and looked around in similar bewilderment.

He'd noticed that the new arrivals appeared to be stumbling towards a bank of reception desks that were just about visible, at the far end of the hall. It had felt like he was walking through some giant shopping mall, but one without stores.

There were no lines in view but there must have been hundreds of people here in this unidentified location. The place was so immensely large that all remained quite distant from each other. They were certainly too far from him to make out any distinguishing feature or facial detail, only the shaded chiaroscuro forms of men and women, seemingly all adults, gauging from their size. Mike advanced with a mixture of curiosity and caution, choosing a desk at random.

There was someone in the line ahead but they'd passed through as he'd approached. Arriving at a bright yellow mark imprinted on the burnished floor, Mike halted as if making an approach to an airport immigration check. The official or person seated behind the perspex screen looked up and flashed a welcoming smile. She was brown-skinned, Hispanic looking and she gestured with a casual wave of her hand to indicate that Mike should approach.

'Hello,' Mike began to speak but his voice surprised him. The tone or modulation was weird. For some reason, his voice sounded different.

'Welcome, Michael James Roberts, firefighter.' The young woman greeted him in a friendly manner. 'Michael James Roberts, born New Jersey, March 25th, in the United States of America?' she read aloud, then looked up and gave him another winning smile. It sounded more like a statement than a question but Mike confirmed with an unspoken yes, a single downward nod of his head.

'Excuse me, can you please tell me where I am?'

'All will be explained to you in due course, Michael. Please exit by the door behind me okay? Make an immediate left turn and then enter through the fifth door on your right - Room 5.' She flashed her pearly whites one more time, 'Have a great day,' then lowered her brow to concentrate on the stack of folders, neatly arranged before her.

Mike following her instructions entered into another corridor, this one white and also brightly lit. There was music playing, some Perry Como style crooner lilted 'Magic Moments,' from unseen speakers above his head. He kept to the left and began counting in silence the doors that were evenly spaced along the span of the wall. He arrived at the fifth on which conveniently hung a small sign etched in black with a gold filigree border. Its only inscription was a word and a number - Room 5.

Mike knocked on the door and waited for a reply but receiving none, he turned the handle and went inside. He entered into a compact room, lit only by a single white domed light, centred on the high ceiling. The walls were coloured a pleasant pastel blue and went unadorned without picture frames or any other form of decoration.

Six standard garden or variety waiting-room chairs were lined up about ten paces from the entrance, in a single row that formed a crescent. All were currently without an occupant. The only other furnishings were a run-of-the-mill office desk, manufactured in a plain laminate and a separate, slightly larger chair that stood apart from the others.

Mike waited. Unsure of what to do next, he sat down and waited some more. Still the indistinct music warbled away in the background. He examined his new clothing. It reminded him of surgical apparel. He was pretty sure they weren't his. He reckoned that on any level of strange dreams, this one must be right near the top. *Man, this morphine must be strong.*

After an interminable amount of time had passed and with still no sign of anyone else, he got up and walked towards another door located at the far end of the room. This one was securely locked. He headed back to his point of entry and peeked out.

Moving in his direction, he saw an attractive middle aged woman of slim build and coffee coloured complexion. She wore a tailored grey business suit, matched with a crisp white blouse and clutched an armful of leather bound folders to her breast. Before Mike could react she called out, 'Hi Mike, sorry I'm late. Things sometimes get a little hectic around here,' she smiled amiably.

'Hello, I'm Mike.'

'Yes, I know,' she laughed in a friendly manner and held out a shapely hand to greet the much stronger grip of the firefighter. He followed her into the room where she dropped the files onto the desk and settled into a chair, instructing Mike to take a seat also.

'Please, can you tell me where I am?' Mike was desperate for information, for something that would make sense of his current surroundings.

'Yes of course, I'm sorry, Mike. You're in a place called Limbus Stasis. It's a holding centre for newly arrived souls. I'll explain more as we go along,' she opened one of the files and adjusted her sitting posture.

'Now what have we got here? Michael James Roberts, age twenty eight years...'

'I'm sorry?' Mike interrupted. 'Limbus Stasis? What or where is Limbus Stasis? I guess I'm only dreaming right?'

She sighed, twiddling a pen between her thumb and forefinger. She levelled her gaze to look directly at the young man, 'Mike - you don't mind if I call you Mike do you?'

'No, Mike is fine.'

'Good, well let me tell you what has occurred. Do you recall that you were involved in a rescue in the early hours of this morning?'

'Yes, I remember.'

'Well the good news is that your colleagues made it out safe. The sad news however, is that during the attempt you fell four floors and suffered serious injuries...in fact you were fatally wounded.'

'Fatally wounded, I don't understand?' The young man's voice cracked. She lowered her eyes for a second then began to explain.

'You died from your injuries, Mike, and now you're here in Stasis, for a while.'

Mike attempted to stand up, trying frantically to shake himself awake from this increasingly disturbing nightmare. But he was held in place, as if by some unseen force.

'Look, Mike, I know that this kind of alarming for you right now,' she said. 'And it is a lot for you to take in, but please listen to me. What I am telling you is the gospel truth.'

She got up from her seat and took a step towards the nearest wall. She must have pressed something, Mike guessed, although there were no buttons to be seen. A panel slid open revealing a TV screen. High-definition and backlit, it was displaying with perfect clarity a sequence of recent events: a fire, the emergency response, a building collapse, a man on a hospital gurney. In the ER, doctors and nurses attempted to resuscitate a man, then a close up of his face. Mike's face! Intubated and with pupils dilated and unresponsive.

'Please, I need to wake up now. I really need to wake up,' Mike stammered, panic gripping his chest, his heart pounded like a drum.

'Mike, please try to relax, you are safe here, free from physical pain, free from illness or any other affliction of the mortal world.' She reached out and took Mike's compliant hand in hers. He instantly felt a sensation of peace and calm, as if some form of anxiety relief had been administered to him by her soothing touch.

'Okay, shall we try again? We do have quite a lot of ground to cover.'

The woman returned to her files once more and began poring over the documents within. She looked up and laughed 'I'm so sorry, I clearly forgot introduce myself. My name is Maryam, I'm to be your Advocate.'

'What does that mean?'

'It means that I advocate for you, I will take your part.' Maryam could see that the shock of his arrival in Stasis and the realisation of his passing from the realm of the living were clearly clouding the young man's cognitive function.

'I'm going to represent you, when it is time for your Judgment,' she smiled warmly.

'Do you mean like a lawyer?' Mike ran a broad hand over his well-defined chin.

'Why do I need a lawyer if I'm already dead?'

'Well yes, I guess what I do, is quite like a lawyer, Mike, but not exactly. I'm here only to advise you and to help you present your case.'

'My case? My Judgment? Forgive me lady but I still don't get it?' Mike was perturbed and entirely confused.

'Your *life case* Mike. Every soul that comes here must present an account of their life on the Earth. What they did, or in some cases, did not do. Then based on this account it is decided what happens next,' Maryam again tried to reassure the startled young man.

Mike stared at Maryam. He tried to focus but felt groggy. There was something about her face. You know when someone has had some work done. Your brain automatically registers the image as not quite the way it should be. You can't say why, or what, exactly. But something is telling your mind that something does not sit right.

Maryam had straight, small white teeth, curiously dark eyes but her face did not look like someone who has had surgery. So what was it about her? In fact up close she looked good, although he could no longer be certain of her age. She was quite attractive and Mike was surprised to be having such feelings, even if he was only dead in this absurd dream.

He closed his eyes and tried again to rouse himself, to wake up, even if it was in a hospital bed with a broken back. But when he opened them, he was still in this strange place Limbus Stasis, sitting in front of this enigmatic woman in the nicely cut suit.

Could she be some sort of angel?

Their introductory meeting ended, his Advocate gave Mike directions to his cell.

La Madeline Church, Paris. 8.12 am.

Father Anton Brunet climbed the multitude of steps that led up to the Eglise de la Madeline, rather briskly for a man of his advanced years.

On a bright but crisp Parisian morning, he realised that even after all his time spent here, this imposing structure with its fifty two Corinthian columns and its impressive pediment frieze - a scene from the Last Judgment - still retained the power to take his breath away. Father Brunet as is his habit stopped outside the entrance to the Roman Catholic Church and turned to take in the magnificent views of the French Capital, in particular the Egyptian obelisk that sits at the heart of the Place de la Concorde.

Stepping in from the frigid morning air he gazed around at the interior of this grand old house of worship. Its simple layout of a single dome with three naves and its large bays, had hosted some of the most fashionable weddings of the Parisian elite. Father Brunet could not help but smile at the delightful sound coming from the wonderful fifty-six manual church organ, 'Sebastian,' the old Priest chortled to himself.

Sebastian Dumas, the young deacon just couldn't help himself, but he is hardly to blame when this magnificent instrument has also been played by the composers Saint-Saen and Fauré. Both were once organists in this same church, the very place where Chopin's funeral was conducted underneath Marochetti's marble statue of Mary Magdalene, being exalted towards heaven by two angels.

Father Brunet hummed along cheerily to himself while making his way up along the aisle to the sacristy. The Benedictine cleric noticed that kneeling in prayer by the statue of Joan of Arc, was a familiar parishioner draped in her expensive sable fur hat and winter coat.

Madame Dumond is in early, he thought.

With the loud clip of his sensible brogues announcing his approach, he was surprised that there was no reaction from Madame Dumond, who was normally a sharp witted and inquisitive woman. True he did not know her very well, having spoken together on no more than a handful of occasions, but he did know that she was a retired plastic surgeon of some renown, financially well off and with a reputation for being a high flyer during her prime.

'Bonjour Madame Dumond!' he called out a hearty greeting but there was still no reaction. 'Madame?' He tried again, now somewhat concerned.

Her head was bowed low in prayer her hands clasped tightly together. He touched them lightly but instinctively recoiled on feeling their deathly cold, the blood having long left Monique Dumond's once nimble fingers.

'Sebastian! Come quickly!' Father Brunet called in alarm to the young deacon, although he was certain that there was no need to hurry now. The music droned to a stop in mid-note and the deacon scampered down from his seat, appearing within moments at the side of the more senior cleric.

'Please send for an ambulance Sebastian. Poor Madame Dumond has passed away it would seem,' he addressed the novice priest who obediently headed off in the direction of the sacristy.

This spectacular house of God, which up to a few moments before had echoed with glorious music, had once again fallen silent, other than the sound of passing traffic.

Father Brunet took a seat alongside the corpse. Gathering himself, he looked up at the statue of Mary Magdalene, made the sign of the cross and solemnly began the Latin prayer for the absolution of the dead: 'Domius noster Jesus Christus te absolvat....'

Monique Dumond's earthly remains looked down on the stone floor of La Madeline, but at the same moment the eyes of her new body, peered out from her new skin, and were seeing something quite different - a small sign that simply said 'Room 5.'

Curiously Monique did not look the least bit fazed by her surroundings. Rather she seemed oddly like a woman who has been here before. She straightened her skirt, sighed deeply, then entered the room without a knock.

A swarthy man, with greying closely cropped hair was sitting behind a desk. He looked up when he heard the door open and greeted the new arrival as if he was not in the least bit surprised to see her.

'Ah Johanna it's you!' he snorted, quickly drowning a half-hearted laugh.

'But of course, forgive me, I'm mistaken. It's Monique these days is it not?'

The old woman lowered herself onto a seat.

'Welcome back to Limbus Stasis. We've been expecting you,' he smiled, but his shrewd eyes did not reflect the warmth of the sentiment.

'Hello Marcus,' she said, stealing a furtive glance at the door behind.

Michael Roberts had been scared plenty in his lifetime - when his kid sister got sick, when he was cornered by the Budolski twins at school and lots of times on the job. So what is it that gets your body to do things, when your mind doesn't want to?

It's something that he'd thought about a lot. He remembered long conversations with his Great-Uncle Rick, back when he was alive. Rick had been a Marine during the war in the Pacific. He'd landed on Peleliu and Okinawa. Man those guys ran up beaches in a hailstorm of bullets. *How can you do that?* Mike had marvelled. *What compels you to go into harm's way, like those troops?*

Mike knows it isn't because you're better or stronger. His occupation, like soldiering, draws its fair share of adrenaline junkies and wanna-be-heroes, but in the end we're all just men and women - fragile flesh and bone. He'd come to the conclusion that it was mainly on account of an esprit du corps - you pump your legs and move forward for the man beside you, your friend. It was as simple as that.

There's some primal part of your brain forges a bond with your squad. The thought of letting them down, losing face, is worse than the thought of the pain. Rick said he'd been scared too.

'Nobody wants to die far from home, especially on some shitty atoll.' It had always made him crack up to hear that. Mike liked his Great-Uncle a lot. Strange he hadn't thought about him for years, but his memory seems much more vivid in this place.

He felt a subtle seduction here in Stasis. Everything was cosy and inviting, designed to put you at ease. But Mike knows his history and clever subterfuge was used before, to lure millions to their doom, in killing factories that had prettily painted cottages at their gates. So he didn't know what to make of this place. He certainly felt afraid, but it was a more elemental fear than anything he had known before. The stakes were so much higher than just losing your life. He needed to keep his wits about him and his eyes wide open.

Mike heard at once the first soft knock on his cell door and on opening it discovered a cheerful looking Maryam waiting outside.

'Hello Mike,' I was wondering if you'd accompany me on a little stroll?'

Maryam was wearing the same clothes but Mike noticed that she'd changed her shoes. She caught the direction of his glance and as if reading his thoughts, laughed, 'Sneakers! These are a lot more comfortable for walking. So how about it Mike, are you up for a stretch?'

'Absolutely, that'd be great,' he replied.

The young New Yorker had so many questions that needed answers. Perhaps spending some time with his Advocate would be a good place to start.

Maryam placed her hand on the door directly across from Mike's room.

'Where are we going?'

'I thought some place familiar, might be nice?' she replied inscrutably. She pushed on the door and stepped directly in...

to...Manhattan's Central Park.

'Whoa!' exclaimed an openly aghast Mike, who immediately on crossing through the portal was now looking up and around as if he could scarcely believe what he saw. The simple white door in Stasis had opened out onto the plinth of Cleopatra's Needle, a place that was definitely familiar.

This sixty eight foot obelisk made of red granite was brought to New York from Alexandria in Egypt in 1880 but was carved in the ancient city of Heliopolis in 1450 BC. Its twin column now stands on the Embankment in the city of London, while another similar obelisk, from the temple at Luxor was erected in La Place de la Concorde in Paris, easily visible from the steps of La Madeline church where Monique Dumond had recently passed away.

'Holy crap, that's Cleopatra's Needle! My dad used to bring me here when I was a kid. It absolutely fascinated him. He loved all the history and the hieroglyphs. He told me all about this thing.' Mike ducked under the guard rail and couldn't help but smile as he remembered his father telling him stories about the column; originally built for the Egyptian Pharaoh Thutmose III and inscribed two hundred years later by Rameses the Second.

The first of a trio of obelisks was erected in Paris and the Parisian's quickly coined the nickname L'Aiguille de Cléopâtre. A name readily adopted by New Yorkers and the people of London for their own monuments. Yet these needles had nothing to do with the famous Queen of Egypt. These had stood for well over a thousand years prior to her birth.

The smile evaporated from Mike's face when he remembered his dad and how he must be badly cutting up, having to bury his son. Mike's sister Karen had already passed away from a childhood illness many years ago, at the tender age of eleven.

Why can't I let him know that I'm here? Why can't I tell him that I'm okay, to ease his pain? Mike grimaced.

'Are you thinking about your family?' Maryam asked perceptively, pulling Mike back from his momentary sorrow.

'Can you read my mind?' he asked, his eyes narrowing.

'Mind reading? No Mike, just an educated guess.'

Mike stood on the Greywacke Knoll, located on the Upper East Side of Central Park, a partially elevated area of ground located behind The Metropolitan Museum of Art.

'Let's go over to the Turtle Pond, shall we?' Maryam led the way down the pathway to the much loved landmark. Mike took a deep breath and followed close behind.

'Maryam, I'm sorry. I have so many questions for you,' Mike said on catching up.

'Ask your questions Mike. I would be glad to answer any that I can.'

Mike definitely had the impression that Maryam was someone he could trust and decided to come straight out, 'Are you an angel, Maryam?'

'No, I am not an angel, Mike.' She gave a small titter before adding 'But the Arcs are. You've heard of the Archangels I'm sure, Gabriel, Michael and Raphael.'

'The Archangels - they're for real?' Mike's eyes flared in wild surprise, then he laughed, realising how the existence of angels cannot be anymore strange than his current situation - a dead man, strolling around Central Park.

'Oh yes, they're very real Mike,' Maryam nodded her head for emphasis.

The young man and his Advocate walked down to the shore, stopping as they passed to admire the austere façade of Belvedere Castle. 'Excuse me!' shouted a young couple on bicycles, tinkling their bells, as they hurried by on the narrow pathway.

'Jesus Christ, they can see us!' Mike called out incredulously, turning his head around to look at the cyclists in amazement. They stared back at him, surprised by his outburst and he immediately regretted his choice of words.

'Yes of course they can!' Maryam laughed.

'You've been given temporary custody of another human body, a replica of the one that carried you from birth, Mike. Did you think that we'd be invisible here?' Maryam chortled again. But it was a sincere and not teasing sound and she didn't appear to have been offended. Mike had been so caught up, that he hadn't noticed there were quite a number of people in the vicinity.

'I think there's a performance of Shakespeare at the Delacotte.' She again appeared to have read his thoughts, referring to the open air amphitheatre that overlooked the pond. They skirted around the theatrical space and continued on in a westerly direction crossing the transverse.

'I used to think that God made the judgment on our souls, Maryam? At least that's what we were taught to believe.'

'Well you're partly right,' his Advocate replied. 'The Creator does make the final judgment, Mike, but it's handed down by the Arcs and is for the most part based on the votes of your peers.'

Maryam noticed the confused expression that passed over the boy's face, she thought of him as a child as he was so much younger than her. 'The Archangels have never walked the Earth as human beings, although they have visited people from time to time. So I'm sure you'd agree that, it is better to have other people do the judging. Other souls who understand that same experience, the challenges, the joys, the suffering and the temptation that each of you face during your time on the Earth.'

'I guess so,' Mike murmured.

Maryam continued, 'It's only fair that other souls should come to a verdict on how you lived your life. As such, each of you will judged by a jury of your peers.'

At that moment a young mother pushing a small child on a tiny red and white tricycle passed by and Maryam's face responded with a radiant glow.

'We want you to succeed Mike, each and every one of you. Each soul is an independent and eternal energy that chooses its own path. A few will sadly deviate and become errant. Those that are, cannot be allowed to join with the Great Host in the Heofon. It could have catastrophic consequences.'

Maryam sat down on a park bench and indicated with a pat of her hand on the smooth-grained wood, that Mike should sit also. Mike was dumbfounded by the thought that here he was 'a dead guy' with his feet on the Earth again. In plain sight, on a bench in Central Park and people can see him and hear him. It was an overwhelming sensation.

'You've had a little time to reflect on your passing, Mike. How are you holding up?'

'Still in a world of disbelief, I have to admit.' The young firefighter through his work had been no stranger to death. He witnessed its handiwork many times. He always felt that people were like the great herds of Wildebeest that you'd see on the nature shows. And death was like the Lions who creep up and wait in ambush, thinning us out one by one.

'I guess it was just my turn,' he reasoned.

'I guess it was,' she shrugged.

'So tell me what happens, Maryam, I sit on a chair and spill my guts to a whole group of strangers?'

'Well kind of, there is a chair. But you will be questioned about your life, by a Prot.'

'What the hell's a Prot?' Mike blurted, but quickly gathered himself.

'I'm sorry Maryam.'

'It's okay Mike, I'm used to it. It's been a big day for you.' She touched against his hand and again that welcome feeling of calm came over him.

'Let me explain. The Protatori di Luce are a group of folks on Stasis whose job is to question and get to the essence of every soul. Most of us who work here, know them as Prots. Their name means 'bringer of light' and that is exactly what they do.

They'll probe around a bit and sure, it can make you feel kind of vulnerable. But don't you worry, most of them are nice and the current two assigned to our block, are complete pussycats.'

'So what do I say? Do I speak about the times that I lied or was jealous, like a confession, that sort of thing?'

Maryam guffawed loudly. 'No, Mike. That would take all day. Besides we don't concern ourselves with the smaller quirks that afflict souls in their human form. What is important to us are the things that leave an indelible stamp - propensity to violence, murder or rape, all the machinations of real and genuine evil - the sure signs of a deviant soul.'

Words usually came easy to Mike, but this time he felt their absence.

'Any of these things in isolation will be a barrier to entry into the Heofon, but only when repeated errant behaviour occurs, it becomes insurmountable and that soul must be condemned to die in Gehenna,' she added.

'Heofon, that sounds a lot like Heaven?'

'That's because they're the same thing, Mike. Over long periods of time, men have corrupted the sacred word. People would copy things down then add their own personal interpretations,' the Advocate explained. 'Inevitably the message has gotten garbled, causing a fracture. Which is why these days, so many souls believe so many different things.'

Mike sat back, enjoying the feel of sunlight on his face, listening to this mysterious lady talk.

'Up until the Middle Ages people correctly knew it as Heofon, but it became altered over subsequent centuries. So now you call it Heaven, but that's okay too.' Her face lit up once more. A natural action, that seemed, to come so easy to Maryam.

'And this place you mentioned, where they kill the bad souls – Gehenna. Where's that?'

'Gehenna is not a place, it's the name given to the instrument. It is used sparingly, to carry out dismantling of irretrievably damaged souls.'

'Oh?' Mike was suddenly concerned.

'No need to be alarmed, Mike, you haven't done anything bad that we don't know about, or have you?' Maryam studied his face, her expression at first serious, then she broke into a loud hoot. 'Relax, Mike, I'm just pulling your leg!'

Mike laughed too. It was an automatic response, but he guessed there was not much that this enigmatic woman didn't already know about him.

'How about a pretzel?' she asked, changing the subject.

'A pretzel, are you serious?'

'You're in human form again Mike, you got to eat, remember?' Maryam winked.

'Come on then follow me, I know a good place over by Columbus Circle,' she added, before getting up and heading towards the exit.

three

Gold Coast, Australia. 3.05pm.

Per Andersson casually nudged his Range Rover into park at Duranbah beach. He had briefly debated heading for nearby Snapper Rocks, just around the corner behind Danger Point, but had opted instead to make the short drive from Queensland into New South Wales.

The Scandinavian was no stranger to these northern parts of the state. One of his favourite pastimes was to celebrate the New Year twice on the same day. This is possible because New South Wales operates Daylight Saving Time, whereas its northern neighbour, Queensland, sticks rigidly to Australian Eastern Standard. Thus on New Year's Eve, a quick trip south to the town of Tweed Head, to see in the birth of another wonderful 'Per Year.' Then back over the State line to celebrate again, one hour later, in Coolangatta - the most southerly town in Queensland.

Of course, the New Year festivities would not be complete without the company of his latest conquest and his by now traditional New Year's resolution - to promptly discard *the lucky lady* the very next day, or perhaps a day later if she proves herself to be sensational in the sack.

'Dee-bah' as the locals call it, has consistently high quality surf and there is usually plenty of eye candy lying along its three hundred and fifty metres of sand. Always a bonus, as Per does like an appreciative audience.

The beach's easterly facing exposed it to especially high wave energy and that afternoon the surf was running at almost three metres. Per fixed his eyes on the big rollers and nodded his approval. He then carefully removed his freshly waxed, Newson custom-board from the roof rack before making his way along the beach path. He could see a couple of other surfers out on the water, but as yet it was not too crowded.

Per cracked a million dollar smile. Out here by the wild Pacific surf, he was in his element, at the very peak of his physical powers, and there's not much else that gets his blood flowing like making some top-turns on the ocean. He picked his spot and through his mirrored sports sunglasses, checked out the local beach bunnies, pleased that they were here in reasonable numbers. As he passed by their recumbent heavenly bodies, the Scandinavian basked in what he knew to be their reciprocated looks of admiration.

Arriving at the waterline, Per as was his habit moved his feet vigorously back and forward just as he entered the surf. The splash of his stingray shuffle was supposed to frighten away any rays that may be laying close in to shore. Australia has more than its fair share of dangerous creatures that are capable of killing you. For Per, it just adds to the buzz of living. He climbed onto his board and paddled out into the heavier swell.

The peculiar thing about wet-suited humans lying flat on a surfboard, is that their silhouette when viewed from directly beneath, closely resembles that of a turtle. And there are quite a few things in these Australian waters that like to make a meal of these shell backed amphibians. Unknown to the blonde Adonis, the paddle splashes of his arms and legs had already been picked up by the electrical receptors of Carcharhinus leucas; a large female, Bull shark - three hundred super sleek pounds of fast moving cartilage, muscle and teeth -measuring an impressive ten feet in length.

Bull sharks are opportunistic feeders that favour warm shallows and the brackish water of river estuaries. Dee-Bah beach sits beside the mouth of the Tweed River and this solitary hunter is as always on the look-out for an opportunistic meal. Normally, requiem sharks have a predilection for seals or turtles but they have taken humans on occasion and not always as a mistake. The Bull shark in particular has a nasty reputation as an aggressive and highly dangerous predator.

The Scandinavian had just performed a series of turns and cutbacks and had even managed to accelerate just at the right time to catch the best of a newly-formed tube running from the left. Elated, he lay across his board once again and used his muscular limbs to propel himself over the onrushing waves.

Once again his splashing mimicked the motion of a creature in distress and was picked up by the She-Bull's highly sensitive Ampullae of Lorenzini - the network of jelly ringed pores that are plainly visible as dark spots on the skin around its head. These signals had also been detected by an even larger and equally dangerous Tiger shark, who with its curiosity piqued, moved in at a furious pace from a little further out past the breakers.

The Swede had stepped skilfully to the front of his board and attempted to perform a 'hang ten,' a difficult manoeuvre where the surfer extends the toes of both feet right out at the tip. Unknown to him, just metres below, the Bull shark was preparing for the kill. It came up at speed from underneath, its favoured method for a surprise assault.

Per Andersson was mere seconds from death and completely oblivious of his imminent peril. The female Bull shark, larger than the male and capable of incredible acceleration propelled its body towards the surface. Its jaw when pressed forward protruded the large gaping mouth, with its rows of razor sharp teeth to the fore.

A split second later, Per, could not control his balance and was flung clumsily into the waves. The large Bull launched her attack, repeatedly sinking her teeth into her now catatonic prey; a perfect ambush of a golden brown, Australian fur seal, which she dragged into the depths, to devour.

Per like all surfers, was attached to his board by the length of cord that was velcro strapped to his ankle. He reconnected with the buoyant surfboard and headed for shore. Embarrassed by his dramatic fall, he'd decided to call it a day.

He stepped from the surf just in time to avoid the inrushing Tiger shark, it had arrived just a fraction too late. The totally insensible Scandinavian had escaped death for the second time. Red faced and doing his utmost to ignore the hoots and none too subtle taunts of the 'Emma's' - the name that surfers call their groupies, Per made the short walk back to his luxury SUV, passing on his way an overweight young man in a sweat stained sleeveless shirt, puffing hard on a cigarette.

With barely concealed scorn the bronzed Swede sneered, 'What a useless tub of lard.' The youth was offended, but not fancying his chances against the much larger man, he kept walking.

Per secured the surfboard, exchanged his shorty wetsuit for a designer tee shirt and a pair of pre-distressed khaki shorts, then made the short drive back up the coast. He was sullen and unsatisfied but his thoughts began to turn to his hot date and the pleasure that awaited. Annoyed by the return of the stinging pain in his left forearm, with one hand on the wheel of his imported SUV, he massaged the limb with the other, making a mental note to mention it at his next check-up.

Abigail Perdue was now the soul seated in Room 5, answering questions put to her by her Advocate Maryam. Like Mike Roberts she had awoken to find herself in an unfamiliar stone corridor, curled up naked and momentarily unable to breathe. She had cleared her throat by vomiting up an awful brash of clear liquid.

She'd shuddered when she remembered looking down at her body being hoisted gently up from the rail tracks by careful hands. Dazed and confused Abigail had found some clothing on a marble table by a door that opened into an immense, great hall. She recalls being part blinded by an incredible light. Similarly processed at one of the reception desks, she followed the directions given and tentatively knocked on the door of Room 5.

On this occasion, a lady who identified herself as Maryam, had been waiting for her.

After learning of her untimely death, Abigail took it badly, broke down and wept. Maryam waited with long practised patience and a look of kind concern.

All cried out, Abigail Perdue rubbed repeatedly at her puffy red eye lids.

'So I guess this is some kind of purgatory?'

'Are you Catholic, Abigail?' Maryam enquired, somewhat surprised by Abigail's question. She began flicking through a bunch of documents.

'No, my family are Jewish, but non-observing.'

'Ah yes, I see that here,' Maryam looked up from her file and nodded. 'Surprised that you mentioned purgatory? It is after all, a rather Catholic word.'

'Dante!' Abigail made a weak attempt at a smile. 'I read English at St.Catharine's College, Cambridge University.'

'Yes, of course,' Maryam smiled warmly.

'Mister Dante Alighieri is responsible for quite a lot of the imagery that new arrivals associate with the afterlife. He finds it all quite amusing. But no, Abigail, this is not purgatory. You are currently in Limbus Stasis.'

'Limbus Stasis? Do you mean as in holding...unmoving?'

'Well yes, that is the dictionary definition of the word, if you like, but here it is just the name we give to...this place.' Maryam answered vaguely.

She quickly changed the subject, 'My role is to assist you in presenting your life case, Abigail. All souls that pass over to Stasis are allowed some time to rest and reflect on what has happened. They are then required to give account of their life, in the presence of the Arcs - Raphael, Michael or Gabriel.... This is where I come in. I take your part and advocate on your behalf.'

'So they will judge us then...the Archangels, I mean?' Abigail asked more from curiosity than from fear. A life of education and privilege had bestowed a confidence in her that seemed to carry over even after death.

'The Archangels monitor the Judgment, as direct representatives of the Creator. However it is your peers who will judge you, Abigail. Five other people who walked the Earth at the same time as you did and who died within moments of each other.'

The Advocate paused to take a sip of water from a cup. 'They will listen to your account and record their judgment. They will give their finding and the Archangel will concur, or perhaps not.'

'And then what?' The young English woman was horrified at the thought of laying out her entire life in front of complete strangers.

'There are three possibilities,' Maryam explained.

'One, your soul will be allowed to pass through the door behind me, to join with the others in the Great Host of the Heofon.' Maryam casually pointed a finger over her shoulder, indicating a regular looking doorway.

'Two, you return to the Earth, to be born again, in a different body and in a different situation to what you had previously experienced,' the Advocate explained.

'This is quite a frequent outcome for many and...

...Three, you could possibly be condemned, depending on the circumstance of your life, to be sent to Gehenna.'

Maryam began to elaborate, 'Gehenna is the...'

'Gehenna or Gehinnom, the destination of the wicked in Hebrew scripture,' Abigail interjected.

'Yes, that's right," Maryam smiled, she was very pleased. *This is one bright girl.* She liked her immediately.

'Anyway please don't be too concerned child, for most souls this process is a mere but nonetheless critical formality.'

'Provided you get a receptive jury?' Abigail declared.

'That's very perceptive of you Miss Perdue. Yes you are right, there is that of course.'

'But I must say that in my experience, I have found that most souls who have walked the Earth in human form are sympathetic to the plight of their fellow travellers. I would not be unduly worried in your case.'

Maryam lowered her eyes and began parsing through the open file. 'Abigail Sarah Perdue. Born Geneva, Switzerland, September 3rd. You moved with your father to London four years later. Studied at Cambridge, graduated magna cum laude. Until recently you were a professional musician I see, how nice.' Maryam glanced up.

'The cello,' Abigail offered. 'Stupid thing ended up killing me,' she shrugged in resignation, half joking, half serious.

'Yes, that was most unfortunate, but it is such a beautiful instrument.'

Abigail felt drawn to Maryam. She was friendly, pleasant and most importantly constantly reassuring. Curiously however there was something odd about her face. Her expression, perhaps. Abigail wasn't sure. She couldn't quite put her finger on it.

They continued in conversation for ten more minutes, after which the Advocate excused herself. 'I am sorry, my dear, but I have a lot of appointments today, but we'll talk again later. I'll send for you, okay?'

'So what should I do now?'

'Your cell is across the hallway, turn left when you go out the door and it is the last door on the right. You should rest a while.'

'A cell! Do you mean like a prison cell?' Abigail was startled.

Maryam paused, clasped her hands and spoke patiently as if to a child.

'Not a prison cell, more like a monastery cell. It's a room, Abigail, only a lot more comfortable than the ones monks live in.' She placed her hands on the girl's, which were faced palms down on the desk.

A sudden inexplicable sense of calm came over the young musician.

Abigail rose from her seat, took a few paces towards the door, then stopped and spun around. 'You mentioned being judged by people of different faiths?' She addressed the Advocate who was making additional notes in her file.

'Yes?'

'Well does that mean everyone who dies comes here? Or only those people who believed in God?'

'Everyone comes here. Even the non-believers,' Maryam explained.

Abigail felt somewhat confused. 'So which religion was right? Or were they all wrong? I'm sorry, I have so many questions.'

'That's okay Abigail, it's totally understandable. I don't have much time now, but you can write down whatever you want to ask me and I'll answer all that I can, next time we meet, okay?'

'Yes, sure, I'll do that, thank you Maryam.' The Advocate inclined her head slightly and Abigail turned on her heels and left Room 5, closing the door behind her. The young woman was alone in the corridor.

She stopped to listen to a sombre section of music that was coming from some unseen source, 'Symphony number 2 in E minor - Rachmaninov's Isle of the Dead.' Abigail's well practised ear correctly identified the piece.

'Rather apt, I must say.' She made the short stroll to the last door on the right. Finding it unlocked, she entered into her cell - a large open plan room. Its floor was laid with magnificent parquet tiles of polished mahogany.

Certainly more plush than anything a monk ever spent time in, Abigail approved.

In the middle space sat a bed with white satin sheets, over-sized pillows and a tessellated counterpane. A small glass night stand stood alongside, it had at its centre a white spherical reading light. Directly across the room from Abigail, stood a tall, free-standing locker or perhaps a wardrobe of some sort.

Abigail strolled across the space, marvelling at the enormous curved picture window that encompassed most of the rear wall. The view was magical, looking out over a placid, shimmering body of water that rippled on as far as the eye could see. The window was framed by two towering velvet drapes and placed front and centre was an old fashioned rocking chair painted in a pleasing shade of duck egg blue.

Abigail sat on the rocker and leaned back into the seat, gently putting it in motion. She went over what Maryam had to say and the events of her own death. She recalled the busy platform, the acne faced youth and the failed attempt to retrieve her cello. She couldn't remember if she had been hit by a train or electrocuted but she suspected the latter. Abigail winced when she recalled her last physical feeling; as if some unseen creature had coiled its giant hand around her heart and squeezed it so tight that it could beat no more.

Her mind then wandered to her grieving father, 'her sweet papa,' who must be completely distraught about the death of his precious little girl. She imagined the police arriving at his office, her father's face crumpling. And he still not recovered from the loss of her mother, just three years earlier. She had passed over.

Abigail Perdue was no more of that world. It really was staggeringly difficult to take in. *I wonder if mom is here.* The thought occurred to her. Abigail like most young people had never given much thought to dying and what came after. Now she knows at least part of that story.

The young musician, other than the time she'd watched her mother being slowly eaten alive by cancer, had been far too busy, living a life of diversion and privilege, to ever think about her own inevitable end. And just like most people she avoided thinking about it.

That was until it pushed right up against her face and she was no longer able to ignore it. Finding herself once more on the verge of tears, Abigail recalled the wizened frame of her once beautiful mother, propped up with pillows, dying, incontinent and in great pain.

Where was the dignity? What profound lesson was I to take from seeing the person that I loved most in the world, taken from me in such horrific fashion?

What had terrified Abigail, almost as much as losing her dear Mom, was the horror of knowing that this is what awaits us all. No matter how rich or powerful. No matter how important or young and vital, the cold hand of death unfurls its icy fingers to select and embrace us all, one by one, without mercy or remorse, even when we simply aren't ready to go. Beckoning for the final journey, which each one of us has to make, scared and alone.

She had chastised herself for thinking such depressing thoughts and after her mother had passed, she immersed herself in her music, parties and shopping for the latest fashions. And then she'd found love. A real soul mate, but now that was gone too. Yet Abigail felt unwilling to cry, as if this place itself was somehow soothing her.

Her thoughts wheeled back to her younger years, before they moved into the city. Growing up in that beautiful, grand old house in Golders Green. Her close treasured memories of a happy childhood. A house where in almost every reception room, hung countless black and white and yellowed pictures of largely forgotten relatives and long dead ancestors; Perdues and Rosens.

Yet they'd never made an impact on young Abigail, having little relevance to the life of a modern young girl other than a shared name, as they looked out at her with their strange clothes and their funny hair. What did they dream of? Where did they all go?

Abigail now knew the answer to that mystery. She had made the same journey. Each and every one of them had come through this place, Limbus Stasis.

She rocked back and forth some more then arose to examine the locker that stood opposite her bed, standing much taller than Abigail. A gentle tug on a brass ring opened it to reveal inside; a cello and a bow.

Handsome in all its polished lustre and there on the label she noted, was set the inscription I.H.S. and a roman cross.

'An actual Joseph, a real del Gesù!' Abigail giggled with delight.

Beautifully made over two hundred years ago, by the gifted hands of Bartolomeo Guarneri, in Cremona, Italy; the finest violin maker of the Amati line. It would be accurate to say that Abigail Perdue swooned as if she had just seen her favourite movie star. It was absolute love at first sight.

Removing the instrument with great care, Abigail ran her hands over its purfling and handsome neck that curved like the most elegant of swans, scrutinizing and running her eyes over its proud body. She sighed, cradled it between her thighs.

"A3, D3, G2 and C2," she called out. The cello's four stings were tuned in perfect fifths. She began to play from memory. A piece she'd loved dearly since a very young age. J.S. Bach's, Prelude, Cello suite No.1 in G Major.

Looking out over the hypnotic body of water Abigail, lost in the feel of this beautiful creation, and the glorious tone it imbued on her delicate notes, felt as if she had died and gone to Heaven. She had died, of course - but for now she remained on Limbus Stasis.

Notwithstanding that right at this moment, it was for Abigail at least, not without its consolations.

four

Gold Coast, Australia

The sommelier complimented the Swede on his excellent selection and went off to retrieve the chosen bottle from the restaurant's wine vault. Per looked exquisitely well groomed tonight even by his own high standards. He wore a new shirt by a fresh new designer, one whose name would only be recognised by those who kept abreast of the ever changing trends in fashion. His sun kissed hair was carefully gelled into a tousled, unkempt look. A youthful style that took more than an hour to perfect and his opalescent teeth dazzled in the candlelight.

At the moment the conversation was centred on his most beloved of topics - himself.

His date had a vacant look in her eyes. Either she had tuned out in a state of boredom or she wasn't all that bright in the first place. Per had noticed the slight and usually would have been annoyed, but on the other hand Tamara did look one hundred percent, drop dead gorgeous, so he reined in his ego, just a bit.

Per's eyes were presently riveted downwards towards the inviting crevasse of his girlfriend's plunging neckline. She wore a magnificent cerise blouse that was singularly cut to reveal. *The designer definitely achieved his goal,*

Per for some reason had assumed that only a man would create such a garment, purely for the enjoyment of other males. The Scandinavian felt a stir in his loins at the thought of afters back in his apartment. He'd so enjoy getting to grips with the lissom curves of this twenty two year old lingerie model.

He hadn't picked her up for the date of course. Per never broke that habit of a lifetime, preferring instead to take a taxi to whatever place of rendezvous he'd carefully chosen. He liked to arrive a little early and to have a couple of drinks to get him in the mood, in spite of his fitness regimen he did have a weakness for more than the occasional single malt.

His date would have to make her own way, but he would allow her to share the taxi ride home. Of course he'd take care of the fare when she was hastily dispatched in the early hours of the morning, for the Scandinavian had always been a man who preferred to wake up alone.

Tamara ordered a tossed salad of selected seasonal greens with an extra light balsamic dressing whereas her date had chosen a starter of oysters. He wasn't entirely convinced of their aphrodisiacal properties, but he understood that it sent out the appropriate signals.

Chatting about Tamara's modelling career, the Swede's mind frequently wandered back to his favourite surf spots. *Maybe tomorrow I'll head over to Surfer's Paradise.*

His date kept waffling on about some photo-shoot for Victoria's Secret. Per didn't really care a jot and had smiled inanely. But he was cunning enough to occasionally flash a smile or drop in a 'for sure,' or some other verbal pretence that he was a good listener.

The Maîtres d' of Chez Henri, always looked after Mister Andersson personally - he was a good tipper. Not of course that he was generous by nature, but it was requisite part of his man-about-town image - independently wealthy, eligible bachelor. A status he was in no hurry to relinquish, for Per Andersson was having way too much fun.

Over a main course of coq au vin, that the young model permitted him to choose for her, most likely because she couldn't understand the menu, he thought, as it was printed only in French. Of course if he had bothered to enquire after her academic accomplishments, he would have been more than a little surprised to know, that as well as being an attractive model, Tamara was a high achiever with designs on a post-graduate degree. But such matters rarely entered the equation when the Swede was in the zone.

'Jesus!' Per slammed his oversized glass down on the table, sloshing some of the delectable Proprietor's reserve, onto the crisp white linen. A sudden breath-taking surge of pain had exploded on the left side of his neck. He managed to stifle a cry but stared maniacally at the ravishing Tamara who looked on all busty and uncomprehending.

He attempted some version of a twisted smile but it evaporated when instead of his delectable date and her highly desirable cleavage, sitting directly across from him was the fat guy from the beach, still pulling hard on a cigarette. Per's mind was clearly in meltdown, shuffling ridiculous random images between the lobes of his brain. He sat up rigidly stiff with a frenzied stare, the pulse in his neck sky-rocketed. This ugly fat fuck, he prayed, would not be the last image his bright blue Nordic eyes were ever to see.

Where in God's name are those beautiful breasts? Ah there they are! A final stupefied smile crossed his face. She was back. *Hurrah!*

Per Andersson in spite of the great care he took with his body, the careful low fat diet, the yoga and all that rigorous exercise, was now falling victim to an enemy from within, an attack from a source that would have never entered his expensively coiffured head - his inherited genes.

At 9.25pm. Australian Eastern Standard Time, at the most exclusive French restaurant in town, Per was dying from Hypertrophic Cardiomyopathy, a disease that affects the heart muscle commonly due to a gene mutation.

Poor genetics had sneaked up and prematurely hurried the Scandinavian's demise. It is perhaps better known as Sudden Cardiac Death. Often the left ventricular heart wall has thickened without any known cause. It's the thing you read about in the newspaper, when a high profile athlete or otherwise healthy young person dies suddenly. Now the very same thing had done for, the unarguably handsome Per.

His by now unseeing eyeballs rolled up into his skull and his face crashed down into his bowl of Coq au vin, splashing his designer shirt and the ample bosom of his now screaming date, with the juices of braised chicken, lardons and pearl onions.

Nader Khoury clearly remembered going under and the agony of breaking his breath hold. His futile struggle ended with too much water ingested, his respirations ceased. It entered his lungs and it burned him like hell, the pain had stopped only after several eternal seconds. Then everything went black as Nader's body dropped like a stone settling gently onto the dark bed of the sea.

Nader's salt stung eyes shot open by some miracle, after an intense spasm of coughing, he was once again breathing air. *But how?*

He could sense its sweet taste on his spittle covered lips as a strange brackish liquid dissolved in the sand beside his prone form.

He lay perfectly still for several minutes, watching in disbelief and even childish delight as his lungs expanded and emptied their precious cache in visible patterns. He took another satiating breath before finding the strength to raise himself to his knees.

I'm not alive, in the name of all that's holy I cannot be?

He was no longer in a watery grave that was for certain. But his eyes sent signals back to his brain that were impossible to interpret. To his astonishment Nader Khoury was once more on dry land, but which land?

His present whereabouts, a tented structure, its canvas sides buffeted and snapped sharply in the billowing wind. *Have I been plucked from the sea, revived and taken to a hospital?* His mind was in turmoil. *But if so, why am I naked?*

He made his way to the far end of the unfamiliar shelter. Laid out on a small wooden table he discovered a pair of sandals, a carefully folded shirt, trousers and a burnoose; a one piece traditional hooded cloak. Nader donned the garments then tugged the canvas door open, becoming temporarily blinded by a powerful beam of light.

Disturbed yet captivated by his new surroundings, Nader Khoury more stumbled than walked to the distant bank of tables, arrayed along the far reaches of this titanic hall.

There he was greeted in a cordial and welcoming manner by a handsome young man with deep set eyes, possibly Iranian if Nader had correctly ascertained the accent. The unidentified male instructed him to continue to this place where he finds himself now. Standing outside a plain white door on which a sign says Room 5.

Nader didn't knock but turned the handle and entered unannounced. He was greeted by the sight of a chiselled jawed man, of good height and greying hair, who was sitting in a laid back manner; legs stretched forward, hands clasped behind his head. A powerful man with a military bearing.

'I think I may be lost?'

'You are indeed lost.' The man replied.

'I'm sorry, I'm not sure if I am in the right place?'

'And what place do you seek?' the unnamed man answered in a not unfriendly tone.

'My name is Khoury, Nader Khoury.' It suddenly occurred to the fisherman that he had no idea know how to describe where he had just come from. The man at the desk looked on expectantly. Then breaking the silence, he sat up and began reading from a slim file - one of three that were laid open on his desk.

'Nader Khoury. Born in the city of Beirut. Occupation: Fisherman. Is that correct?' The man raised his gaze to take in the dark eyed man standing before him, who was nervously entwining his thick calloused fingers.

'Yes that is correct. I am Nader Khoury, I live in Algeria now, close to Annaba. Well I used to live there, as I presume that I am dead now?' Nader shrugged in resignation.

'Yes that is correct Mister Khoury, you are indeed deceased. It says here that you drowned.'

'I was fishing,' Nader answered, being more than a little economical with the truth.

'Fishing... Hmm I see.' The man smirked and seemed rather amused by Nader's response.

'The thing is Mister Khoury, you are here to be judged, so best not to tell lies. You'll find the truth to be the best way, in fact it's the only way.'

Nader could feel the flush of embarrassment race up from his neck to his wind burned cheeks. The man identified himself as Marcus and said he was to be his Advocate.

Nader could clearly make out his muscular profile through the pale linen jacket that Marcus wore over a dishevelled white shirt. *Not a man to be trifled with*, he concluded.

Marcus explained to the startled fisherman and part time smuggler that he was now dead to the human world and was temporarily in a holding block called Limbus Stasis.

He would remain here for the next six days. Then on the seventh day he would be called to account for his life, before a jury of peers, five other recently deceased souls who will listen to the tale of his life's journey and who then will record their verdict.

On hearing this unwelcome news, Nader became visibly nervous. He had after all not lived a blameless life and there were, when he thinks back to his time on Earth, several episodes that would cause him concern.

Who are these people who will judge me? he wondered. *Maybe I could make allies with them?* Nader Khoury had always possessed an agile mind.

As if reading his thoughts, his Advocate told him that he'd meet the other five tomorrow, but for now he should go to his cell. A look of surprise crossed the fisherman's face but Marcus explained it was merely a room, someplace to lay his head while he waited his turn.

He provided Nader with directions and said that he should reflect on his life and on his previous deeds, 'A little reflection and whole a lot of repentance. Always a good plan when you find yourself in Stasis.' Marcus added while stretching and yawning.

A bemused Nader Khoury prowled the confines of his cell like a caged animal. A room that was identical in almost every detail to that of his immediate neighbour, a young English woman named Abigail Perdue. But he was as yet unaware of her or any of the other recent arrivals to this section of Stasis.

A fiercely pragmatic man, in life, Nader had never given much thought to the subject of death, other than on the occasions that he had encountered it. He retained some semblance of his Muslim religion but was in no way devout. The prosperity of his family and at times, their very survival had occupied most of his time.

Born in Beirut, Lebanon, Nader had moved to the city of Algiers with his family at the impressionable age of sixteen. His father, who was a very capable engineer, had found lucrative work in the booming oil industry. But just a few years later, during the vicious civil war that had plagued this desert nation, he was brutally slain in a car-bombing.

The death of Abdullah Khoury had plunged his young family into a bind and an uncertain world financially. Abandoning his nascent academic career to support his mother and two younger sisters, Nader, by then well into his late teens, had drifted into the fishing industry. Working long hours, often in arduous conditions, he eventually saved enough to purchase his own, albeit well-used, boat, the Mafi Mushkila.

All was irrevocably changed and his own existence was now overriding. No longer able to help his family, they are once again on their own. The very thought of this brought a needle sharp pain which made Nader wince. He was filled with remorse and regret, but it was much too late for that now. Pacing back and forwards across the room, the fisherman contemplated his predicament and was a gravely worried man. For that is what Nader Khoury does, he works problems over in his mind.

Over and back and inside and out, nimbly searching for an avenue of opportunity or escape, but this time his dilemma appears to be intractable. He will soon be called to account and then judged, probably harshly, he expected.

The very word alone made him shudder, judged, by five other men, perhaps women too? It did not augur well. When he reveals that he is in fact a smuggler and in particular a smuggler of people, it is unlikely to elicit any great sympathy, especially from those who come from a world where they would not understand the type of life that men like Nader are compelled to live. He feels unlikely to be chosen by the Almighty.

He accepts this, but right now what he really needs, is to avoid having his soul condemned to this place that his Advocate had rather too casually mentioned, Gehenna.

Perhaps at this stage, his best hope is to be reborn, to have a second chance at a human life. Marcus had explained to him the process of *The Selection*. He spoke of the three options, the only sentence available to each panel of jurors. Three options to choose from and at least one, was truly horrendous. *Which one of these will become my fate?*

He had also told him about the Protatori and how these inquisitors would delve into his personal history. They thought of it made his new skin crawl. The Advocate then made a comment that Nader hadn't understood and he had been too afraid to ask. Something about him being lucky that his Prot was not *the Prince*, or something like that?

This capable fisherman had honed and sharpened his survival instincts from the day his father had been murdered. He knew he would need all his cunning and skill to extricate himself, from this looming judgment. *But how do I achieve this?*

He cannot come up with an answer. 'Allah is merciful,' he whispered to himself. *He will surely understand*. Nader Khoury prayed more in hope than belief.

Captain Khoury's thoughts were ripped away from his self-examination on hearing a blunt double knock on the door of his cell. He called out, 'Who is it?' For in the world where Nader Khoury had lived, it was not wise to open a door without first knowing who was there.

No reply was immediately forthcoming, so Nader sat quietly and waited, but once again, came the rap of knuckles on wood. He reached for the door handle, a simple brass object devoid of any decoration and turned it slowly anticlockwise, revealing a tiny gap, just enough to allow him to see. His eyes fell upon a stocky, balding, dark skinned man, holding a tray of food.

'Hello Mister Khoury, I have brought you something to eat,' he said, his smile displaying a jagged row of off-white teeth. 'May I come in?'

Nader opened the door fully but did not speak.

'I'll just leave it here for you, shall I?' The man carefully set the tray down.

'Thank you,' Nader replied and in a cautious tone said 'May I ask, who you are?'

'My name is Lou,' the older man answered cheerfully.

'Do you work here, Lou?' Nader instantly realised the ludicrous nature of his question considering his present whereabouts.

'I guess you could say that,' the man chuckled softly. 'I mostly clean up the mess around here.'

'My name is Khoury, Nader Khoury.' The fisherman bowed and placed his hand on his heart, he quickly realised if he was going to begin making allies then there was no time like the present.

'Yes I know,' the shorter man took the extended hand offered to him in greeting.

'Lou, what can you tell me about this Judgment? Do most people usually go to the Almighty?'

Lou pursed his full lips. He pondered the question for a moment then replied that, as far as he knew, most people did not go forward at the first attempt.

'They require you to have certain qualities that have to be acquired during your time on the Earth. They need to ascertain this before they allow you to enter the Host of Souls,' he said, scratching a crescent of tight curls that curved above thick folds of chocolate coloured skin.

Nader frowned at Lou's reply but remembered his manners and asked him to sit for a while and to share his meal. Lou, politely declined, explaining he had other meals to deliver. Nader noticed that this fellow had a very human face, nothing seemed other-worldly. He was to all intents and purposes a normal, friendly, old guy.

The Attendant smiled amiably once more and told the fisher-man that they would surely speak again. Once Lou had left, Nader examined the food. It smelt glorious and for the first time since his arrival, he realised that he was ravenous with hunger.

'Braised lamb and couscous,' he marvelled. Each bite was mouth-watering, every morsel infused with the flavours of herb and eastern spices, He was further surprised that it tasted exactly like his mother's recipe. A simple jug of ice cold water accompanied the meal.

Well it appears I have made one friend, at least, he returned his attention to his dinner, which he devoured with relish.

The Advocates Room, Limbus Stasis.

The small annex adjacent to Room 5 was identified as Room 7, but was universally known by those on Stasis, as The Advocate's Room. Inside Maryam and Marcus were on a short break.

'So what do you think?'

'About which one?' Maryam was flicking through the pages of an old magazine.

'All of them!' Marcus was curious about Maryam's take on the new arrivals. He had been working under her wing for centuries and in his opinion there was no one - in any of the Stasis centres - who was a more astute judge of character.

'The English girl, Abigail, she's a sweet little thing, but other than the passing of her mother, she's never had any serious test. So I'm not sure yet. Life has gone marvellously easy on her,' Maryam said, distractedly chewing on a pen.

'My gut-feeling is she's a good soul, but you know I can't risk the future of the entire Host based only on my intuition, Marcus. I can't be sure how they'll vote but I would guess that Gabriel may want her sent back, to get a bit more experience, and most likely in more modest circumstances.' she added.

'It would be hard to imagine Little Miss Moneybags growing up in some sinkhole housing project,' Marcus laughed.

'Oh come on Marcus, that's unfair and you know it. It's not Abigail's fault that her family were wealthy.'

Marcus clapped his hands gleefully together. This was typical Maryam. She so loved each of her souls and would go to bat for all of them, if she had to. He knew also that his more senior colleague, constantly interceded with the Arcs if there was some doubt or indecision about what to do with a particular soul. Maryam would always wade in with a list of their positive qualities, supporting their case. No one here worked harder than Maryam. Marcus was filled with admiration for his boss, but couldn't resist teasing her about her beloved souls.

'You know what he said about the rich, easier to pass through the eye of a needle.'

'Yes, I know, but this girl may yet be an exception.' She pretended to be miffed and indeed was sometimes exasperated by the younger man's edgy sense of humour. But she knew that Marcus had lived a hard life on the Earth and he still retained some of his old flaws. Besides he was a very capable Advocate. One of the best - in her opinion.

'What about the quiet one?'

'Miyu Tanaka? She is a hard one to figure alright,' Maryam mused. 'She doesn't say a lot but you can see there's a bright intelligence at work.' By now most of their quorum of six souls had arrived.

'You do know that the Arcs won't let her in after...well you know.' Marcus made a gesture with his hand, raising his fingers in the air then letting them flutter slowly down.

'You're right, they possibly won't!' she agreed. 'But she was treated appallingly in the final year of her life. I'm going to speak with Gabriel. We'll have to do something for her.'

Marcus got up and poured himself another coffee, 'Want one?' he asked, but Maryam declined.

'What about the hero then?' he began stirring the spoon in lazy circles around his cup.

'You mean Mike?' Maryam guffawed. 'My, you are especially caustic today, Marcus. You must be in an extra good mood.'

'But seriously Maryam, is he too good to be true?'

'Mike is a good guy. I think he is a real good bet for the Heofon.'

The door opened and a bearded, older man stuck his head around, 'Hello Maryam, hi Marcus,' he greeted his fellow Advocates with an almost toothless smile.

'Sorry to disturb you, I think I left one of my client files here?'

'Is this it?' Marcus reached over and produced a folder that was lying on the side table. He glanced at the name, printed on the cover.

'Wow is that the football player?' he asked.

'Yes it is - drugs overdose. Quite sad really, he was very talented,' the older Advocate replied, gratefully taking the folder from Marcus.

'Catch you later. Busy day today,' he quipped.

'Aren't they all,' Marcus groaned.

'Bye Ezekiel,' Maryam said, focusing back on her colleague she enquired about his charges.

'The fisherman, Nader Khoury. It's looking bad for him, Maryam. I mean human trafficking? You know that won't go down well. Mind you, that one thing he did at the end. That's a game changer. You know how that kind of stuff impresses the Arcs. I guess he could have an outside chance, but he's a longshot.' Marcus scratched at his scalp absent-mindedly.

He began wiping at a coffee stain that he'd dropped on his shirt.

'Darn it, I can never keep these things clean,' he grumbled.

'There's the genial doctor, of course. I told you I had a really bad feeling about her. They went far too easy on her the last time. Those poor kids!' Marcus shook his head from side to side in disgust.

Maryam shrugged. 'He sees much more than you or I and you should know that better than anybody, Marcus.'

He felt a dull throbbing in the back of his head on being reminded. Even after all these years the shame was robust and alive in him. He knew she was right, of course.

'What do you think they'll do with her this time?'

'I don't know.' Maryam said. 'I honestly don't know.'

'Best get back to work, I guess. My Scandinavian is due in about now.' Marcus finished his coffee, washed out his cup and gathered up his paperwork.

Mike woke from a full eight hours of restorative sleep. In fact he could hardly recall ever sleeping so well. He felt unusually energised, fit and strong. Mike gripped his right upper arm feeling his thick veined bicep flex beneath his shirt. He had always taken good care of himself. He rowed crew on the Harlem River and was a regular in the small but well equipped firehouse gym.

He remembered last night, that nice old guy called Lou, had arrived to his cell with a tray piled-high with a fourteen ounce New York strip loin, done medium well, sides of fried onions and mashed potatoes and lashings of rich gravy, his absolute favourite. And to wash it down, a pint bottle of incomparable craft-beer, with a tonsured monk on its label.

He didn't however recall falling asleep, but noticed that the few uneaten morsels were no longer on the table. Mike did remember Lou joking when he'd asked him about his role on Stasis.

'I just take out the trash mostly,' he'd chortled.

The young firefighter sat on the edge of the bed, rubbing his eyes and yawning loudly with outstretched arms, as he accustomed his eyes to the changing light. Lou had mentioned to Mike that when he awoke he should return to Room 5. When Mike asked about what time he should be there, Lou just said, 'Whenever you wake up, will be fine.' Then he went and Mike was left to enjoy his meal and his slumber.

He got up from the bed, entered the adjacent shower area and examined the contents of the cubicle's single cupboard: a toothbrush, a tube of toothpaste, a bar of soap and a bottle of an unidentified liquid, which Mike examined and concluded to be some sort of shampoo or shower gel. Mike enjoyed a lei-surely soak and while drying himself afterwards, he examined his reflection in the small washroom mirror. He was surprised that he didn't appear to need to shave, as usually after the elapse of a full day or so he would have an almost full shadow going on. *That is so weird!*

Leaving his cell, he bumped into Lou who was whistling a tune as he mopped the floor. 'Good Morning, Mike!' he called out to the fireman with a hearty greeting.

'Morning, Lou. Thanks for the great food, I really appreciate it.'

'You're very welcome young man, glad you liked it,' Lou answered affably then returned to his whistling. Mike Roberts made his way along the corridor, arriving once more at Room 5.

He knocked before entering and was surprised to see two young women sitting at either end of the semi-circular bank of chairs. They both looked around as the door creaked open. One of the women was oriental, in her late teens. The fringe of her dark hair partially obscured a pair of what Mike thought were sad look-ing eyes. The other was a good looking Caucasian woman, middle to late twenties, Mike guessed, but it was hard to be sure. Before he could speak, the brunette stood up, smiled and introduced herself.

'Hello, I'm Abigail Perdue and this is my new friend Miyu.'

Mike caught a glimpse of a dark head of hair bobbing down in a quick bow, but she didn't speak or look directly at him. He approached Abigail and extended a hand in greeting,

'Mike Roberts. Nice to meet you both.'

Abigail lightly gripped Mike's hand with her long fingers and returned the handshake eagerly, but the Asian girl merely gave the smallest sliver of a nervous smile and did not offer her hand or a single word.

'So Mike, what happened to you?' Abigail was immediately curious, 'How did you end up here with us dead folks?' she laughed.

Well at least someone is happy to be here.

'I was working with my crew, trying to rescue some people. I'm a firefighter or at least I was,' he offered by way of explanation. 'Building was years old, the extreme heat must have caused the steel girders to buckle, next thing I know, I'm a goner and I end up here,' he grimaced. 'How about you folks, what's your story?'

'Oh I'm here on account of a stupid cello!' Abigail giggled. 'I should have stuck with the violin or even a bloody trombone!'

Mike was a little confused and smitten by this pretty girl with the strange, rather cute accent. His puzzled expression prompted Abigail to say more.

'My cello got knocked onto a subway line.' Abigail had gone with the American vocabulary. She guessed that the yanks would have no idea what the Tube was.

'Some dumb klutz in a hurry. It was worth an awful lot of money, I don't know I just kind of reacted, jumped down to retrieve it and I guess I must have got electrocuted or got hit by a train. I'm not sure which? Anyway, no matter, here I am.'

Mike offered a sympathetic smile in return. He guessed that her upbeat demeanour, disguised an element of nervousness. *I mean shit, everyone's got to be nervous here.*

'You're from England, right?' he asked

'That's right. I'm a London girl.'

'What about you?' Mike turned his attention to the defiantly silent Miyu.

The Asian girl lowered her eyes to the floor and in a barely audible voice said, 'Forgive me, I'd rather not say.' Mike looked at

Abigail who made it clear with a pulled face that she didn't know what happened to Miyu either.

The awkward silence was abruptly ended when the door was opened by a swarthy looking man of medium height and strong build.

'Hey someone else! Welcome buddy,' Mike called out a friendly greeting.

The man who was Middle Eastern or perhaps North African in appearance nodded a terse hello and closed the door behind him. He approached the others cautiously making his way to the seat beside Mike.

'Hello, my name is Abigail, this is Miyu and this is Mike,' she smiled pointing to each of the seated people in turn.

'Khoury, my name is Nader Khoury,' he replied gruffly and did not offer his hand. Abigail Perdue studied the new arrival, a good looking man gone just a little to seed, not so young, but whose face had the lines of someone older than his years or somebody frequently exposed to the elements. He sat in a self-conscious manner, head slightly lowered and with his strong prominently veined fingers, wringing together like those of a man in some deep torment.

'How did you get here?' Again it was Abigail who pierced the silence. Nader turned his deeply tanned face in her direction and said only two words in reply – 'I drowned.'

Just a deflated 'Oh!' escaped from the young woman's lips.

Once more the door creaked open, this time admitting an elderly woman, attired in an expensive grey jacket with a white, high collared blouse and immaculately done hair. She had a thin mouth, darting eyes and a hard-to-read expression. She scurried over to the one of the two vacant seats and sat down, carefully adjusting her pleated skirt as she lowered herself gently onto the chair. She gave only the merest nod of acknowledgement before fixing her gaze on the door at the rear.

Abigail guessed, correctly in this instance, that it would be futile to engage this particular lady in conversation. Something about her suggested that she didn't much care for small talk.

Miyu Tanaka surreptitiously stole a quick glance at each of the recent dead. The British girl, Abigail, seemed friendly enough even if she was also a bit brash, an over confidence that Miyu guessed permeated from a very privileged upbringing.

The American called Mike, he had kind eyes and sat straight backed in his seat but his confidence was forced and did not have the natural, effortless poise exhibited by Abigail. Miyu had always been an astute watcher of people.

The Middle Eastern guy, she guessed correctly that Nader was from the Levante, the near east and was not North African. He was much harder to figure out. His coal black eyes flickered around the room but his facial expression gave little away, expressing neither curiosity, nor anxiety. The language of his constantly twisting hands however was in marked contrast to his show of calmness, betraying him as someone with a troubled mind presently in active overdrive. Then there was the shrew like older woman, diminutive in stature but there was something in her countenance that prompted in Miyu a sense of fear. This woman for some unknown reason deeply unsettled her.

Miyu Tanaka had the day before made her way out to the plush Roppongi Hills district. The capital city of Japan is in the Kantō region on the South Eastern side of the main island Honshu. Tokyo is the world's largest metropolitan area, home to almost thirty five million souls. Nineteen year old Miyu had been one of those.

She had been working for over a year as a domestic worker in one of the many large houses in this swanky division. There her former employer and lover had barred her from entering his home. Pressing an envelope crammed with money, into her child-like hands, he ordered her to never return and to dispose of the bastard baby that Miyu was carrying. Coming from a poor family that nevertheless retained strong traditional values, she was too ashamed to return to the tiny apartment that she shared with her mother and younger sister, in one of the less salubrious wards of Tokyo.

Instead the distraught young servant made her way, in a blur of tears to the fifty-fourth floor observation deck of the city's fifth largest building - the Minato Miro Tower - almost 780 feet above the ground. There the slight figure of Miyu Tanaka scaled the security barricade, she took one final look at the twinkling towers of the metropolis and uttering a brief prayer for the care of her mother to Hotei, she flung herself into the ether, falling at 9.81 metres per second.

Miyu Tanaka thankfully passed out long before her tiny body hurtled hard into the concrete pavement, killing both her and her unborn child instantly. A confetti shower of currency fluttered loose from its envelope falling silently over the shattered corpse.

Making her way to Room 5, on that first occasion, she was greeted by the welcoming embrace of the woman called Maryam. Now she finds herself beside this confident young British girl, an older lady of unknown nationality, an Arab man and an American. But there is still one empty chair in their semi-circle. She was suddenly aware of the presence of her Advocate with another man by her side. She smiled at Miyu. Something about her made the normally timid youngster feel immediately at ease.

'Hello everyone, we are very pleased to have you all with us today,' Maryam gave a beatific smile to each of the group in turn. 'Some of you will have already met my colleague, Marcus.' All eyes took in the broad-backed man who sat at Maryam's right hand. The taciturn Advocate did not speak but waited for Maryam to resume.

'As you are aware by now, each of you has passed over from the mortal world, your most recent life there is over. Although it is possible, depending on the outcome of your individual judgment that some of you may be sent back to start anew.'

Mike and Abigail each had a hand raised.

'If it's okay with everyone I won't take any questions at this point,' Maryam looked directly at the faces, all wore visibly anxious expressions.

'Please be patient,' she said. 'It is of course completely understandable that you have many questions. However it is better that I first explain to you the process. Then later you can address your queries to your assigned Advocate at your individual meetings. Is that okay for everyone?'

Miyu found herself analysing the Advocates. Maryam, had a complexion that seemed to her practiced eye to be almost imperceptibly blurred, like an ever so slightly out of focus photograph. Whereas the male Advocate did not. Miyu had been an avid photographer. It was her great passion. Something about how the light fell on Maryam's features compared to his was not quite right. But what exactly it was she could not say.

'We will assemble here in a few days, for your Judgment. As you know by now each of you in turn will be required to give an account of your life, in front of this group of people who will form the jury. In attendance will be Marcus and I, the Prots and at least one of the Arcs.'

'Will the Archangel be the judge?' Mike uttered. 'Oh I'm sorry, couldn't help myself,' the impulsive young firefighter cringed with embarrassment.

'That's okay Mike, but please do try to bear with me,'

This time it was Marcus who spoke, 'The Archangels monitor the judgment but it's you who will be the jury and it is your judgment of each other that will prevail, well at least, that's how it will be in most cases,' he explained.

'Our role is to guide and prompt you. However it should be well noted, that the Arcs do have the final veto and the very last word.'

Even though they had each been given this most important piece of information when they first arrived in Stasis, Miyu saw the look of unease and dread spread quickly. As if on the previous occasion it hadn't sunk in, but hearing it now, in the presence of the others made it all the more real and imminent. Her eyes darted again to the one empty seat. Maryam must have noticed, as she added, 'There is one more soul who will form part of your jury. As he is arriving a little later than we had expected, he will be brought up to speed in due course.'

So we each will decide, what happens to the other, Mike mused. *Well that's certainly not something they ever taught at Sunday school.*

Mike Roberts had been raised an Episcopalian, something that when asked, he would always refer to as Catholic-Lite.

five

Nader Khoury took a glorious deep breath of air, the wonderful cypress-scented air of his homeland, a place he had not set foot in for many years.

After their meeting, the jurors returned to their cells to find some light refreshment awaiting. Nader wolfed down his turkey sandwich. He had always believed that you should eat food when it is on offer, as you never know when it may be your last. There was a distinct rap of knuckles on his door, Nader again hesitated, but thought, *What the heck! Who is going to harm me here?* Waiting outside was Marcus.

His Advocate had called to enquire if Nader would care to accompany him on a short journey, to which the fisherman readily agreed. They strode along the corridors of Stasis without speaking a word, the Advocate leading with Nader in tow - two paces behind. Arriving at a plain non-descript door, Marcus opened the portal with one hand while gesturing with the other for Nader to pass through, which he did, emerging on the other side onto a bustling street.

The very first thing that had bombarded his senses was to Nader, a wonderfully familiar noise. 'Rue Gouraud!' Nader exclaimed with boyish wonder.

He was in Rue Gouraud, a half-residential, bohemian hub in Gemmayzeh, a neighbourhood in the ancient Achrafieh district of Beirut. These were the streets of Nader's childhood and he knew every inch of them.

'Do I get to come back to stay here?' For a moment his heart pulsed with excitement at the prospect, but it was quickly dashed by Marcus' gruff response,

'Of course not Khoury, the Earth is only for the living and you my friend are already dead.' Despite his disappointment Nader rapidly regained his good spirits.

To be here once more, for even a single moment, is a miracle! He had not dreamt of the Lebanon for a very long time, it had hurt too much. They were happy days for the most part. They two men ambled south, through narrow winding streets to the Stair of Saint Nicolas emerging onto Rue Sursock. 'Why did you bring me here, Marcus?'

'To help you prepare for your Judgment. Bringing you some-place familiar, I thought it would help you to relax.'

'It has indeed. Shokran.' Nader automatically reverted to the Arabic word for thank you.

'In my day this town was called Birot,'

'When was your day, Marcus?' Nader asked, genuinely curious. He knew that the city's name in old Aramaic was Birot.

'A very long time ago but we're not here to talk about me,' his Advocate replied.

'Would you like to stop for a drink? A little shade would be nice,' Marcus said, changing the subject.

'I'd love one, how about over there?' Nader pointed towards a small cafe with a few tables perched on the pavement beneath a tattered blue awning. They each ordered strong coffee from the waiter while Marcus proceeded to explain more about the pro-cess of the Judgment. 'You and your new friends,' he began.

'They are not my friends. I don't know these people,' Nader interrupted.

'Well then, maybe you should get to know them,' his burly com-panion responded in kind.

'For you Nader Khoury, all may depend on it. They hold your very future in their hands.'

'Yes of course you are right. I am sorry for my rudeness,' Nader's pragmatic side reasserted control and he moderated his tone accordingly. He guessed that he'd downplayed the role of the Advocates.

Maybe they have a lot more influence on things than he lets on?

He realised that Marcus could be an important ally, so he reminded himself not to piss him off again. Besides he liked this man: he was brusque but he was straight forward, traits that Nader greatly admired.

'You have children Khoury, yes?'

'Yes, I have two. My son Abdul, and also a little girl Mina.'

'And your wife, do you still love her?'

'But of course,' Nader replied and he had meant it.

Marcus laughed, 'In my time, love was lust and was considered a temporary fever of the blood. Real love was the bit that remained when all the passion had passed.' It was such a long time since Marcus had been with a woman, he could no longer remember how good it had felt, a fact he wasn't about to share with this lost soul.

They finished their coffee in silence gazing at the people who passed by their little mosaic table. Shadows were short and large numbers were in the small square selling their produce at Souk el Tayeb. Nader remembered that Saturday was the day the farmers came to this part of the city. His Advocate talked about how the Arcs had no interest in the trivialities of life.

'So you lied, so what? Everyone has done that. Even if you cheated, not such a big deal, but better for you that you didn't cheat on your wife,' he laughed.

Nader had been instructed in the words of the prophet ever since he could remember, but in his adult years he had drifted and he had not much time for religion. He was far from a righteous person. He only attended the mosque infrequently, but he did at least believe. Well he had done mostly, in his own personal way. He hoped that this at least would count for something in the eyes of Allah.

The two companions continued in a northerly direction to a reclaimed sliver of land called the Corniche. Nader had always loved the sea. True it had ended his days, but it also had provided for his family. For Nader the sea was life.

Marcus said, 'What the Arcs want to know about, is the pivotal moments of your life - the events and choices that made you the person you were. Who you helped or didn't help and if you didn't, why you didn't.'

'So what should I say?'

'The truth is the only way Khoury. What is done is done. You cannot change a single thing. You must account for your life with only the truth. If you lie it is most likely they will find out and in that case it would not go well for you,' Marcus cracked a rather unnerving smile.

As they arrived at a small beach - uncrowded even though it was a weekend - the sun was now at its zenith and the day was blistering hot. The fisherman slipped off his shoes, rolled up the legs of his trousers and waded into the surf. Marcus did likewise. 'May I be allowed to swim?' he asked the Advocate.

'I don't see why not,' Marcus slapped Nader's back. 'I may even join you.'

Nader swiftly unbuttoned his shirt and dived out into deeper water. Marcus followed him in, surfacing some twenty seconds later, to swallow a great lungful of air.

He noticed for the first time that Marcus had a tattoo carved into the flesh of his left arm, a line of single letters - S P Q R.

'What is this then?' Nader asked pointing at the tattoo. It looked familiar to him but he couldn't place it.

'What, this thing, S P Q R?'

Nader nodded.

'It's Latin. Senatus Populusque Romanus. It means the Senate and People of Rome.'

'That's it!' Nader remembered that abbreviation now, he had been keen on history in his student days. 'You were a Roman soldier?'

'Yes, I'm a Roman, although my home town is Ravenna. I was a Questionarius in the Legio X Fretensis. My full name is Marcus Caelius Agrippa.' He gave the short armed Roman salute as he said this bringing his forearm straight across to touch his chest.

'What's a Questionarius?'

Marcus had turned and walked back to shore, plopping down to sit on the sodden sand, his feet still stretched out in the cooling breakers. Nader followed Marcus, his curiosity now heavily piqued.

'I was an interrogator,' Marcus answered truthfully.

'So you hurt people then?'

'Yes, I hurt lots of people.'

Nader was amazed that Marcus could say this as a simple matter of fact, without the slightest grimace of distaste or discomfort.

If Allah can forgive a torturer, then maybe he may also forgive a poor smuggler, he thought. A glimmer of hope had flickered in Nader's chest.

'Where and when was this?' Nader probed further.

'Almost two thousand years ago. The Tenth Fretensis were assigned to the Province of Judea. I had an acting rank as an Optio commanding the Cohors Sebastorum.'

'What is this Cohors?'

'You sure ask a lot of questions Khoury,' Marcus feigned annoyance. 'A Cohors was a local unit of Samaritan soldiers.'

'Astounding! You've been in Stasis for about two thousand years. That's a really long time.' Nader let out a low whistle. 'Why so long?'

'I'm paying my dues, helping new arrivals like you prepare for their Judgment.'

'What did you do that was so bad?' he knew he was being impertinent but he had to know.

'I had a man scourged and I placed a crown of thorns upon his head,' Marcus said.

'Under the orders of the Prefect Pilate I ordered my men to crucify him and to drive nails into his hands and feet. Marcus lowered his eyes momentarily.

'The man was named Jesus of Nazareth.

So I expect I'll be stuck in Stasis for quite a while more,' he looked up with an anguished expression.

Nader Khoury stared at the Advocate, as if seeing him for the first time and he felt a solitary moment of terror pierce his heart.

Gaius Agrippa came from modest means and farmed a small plot with his wife Licia, on the outskirts of Ravenna, a farm that had been allocated to him when his legion had been disbanded. His son Marcus had grown up on tales of the great campaigns but for now he was content working the land.

The bashful Marcus had met a girl named Cornelia, they fell in love and planned to marry. Nevertheless fickle fate intervened to change all plans. A wedding was not to be. Cornelia, when out walking, was confronted by two bandits, who mercilessly raped and murdered her. She was fifteen years old, two years younger than Marcus. The distraught boy swore to Nemesis that he would have vengeance and tracked down the culprits.

Marcus, like many boys of that era, had spent endless hours drilling with wooden swords and small arms. He shadowed the two men and followed them to a tavern and waited until they were well in their cups. Intercepting them – as they drunkenly stumbled out of town - at a lonely trail that passed through a copse of woodland, the two debauched misfits were no match for the burly youngster. He quickly overpowered the larger one, then settled down to have fun with the other.

A dark malevolence had grown and festered in young Agrippa's heart and had twisted it until all the compassion had been squeezed out. Pitiful screams rang out through the night, but there was no one coming to help. Marcus discovered that he had a talent and an inventive mind for devising ever more painful punishment for the men who had desecrated his beloved. When their mutilated bodies finally gave up, Marcus left their corpses to rot or be feasted on by birds and wild animals.

Everything had changed, he never returned home again and without any word to his family he took the long road to Rome intent on joining the legions. He swore the oath, accepted the brand and was taken into the Legio X Fretensis.

It was ten days before his eighteenth birthday. But taking revenge for Cornelia could not abate the pain that had cursed him nor soothe his troubled heart.

Marcus spent the next several years drifting from outpost to outpost, putting down a rebellion here and fighting small wars there. A senior soldier had noted a fierce brutality encompassed in the sturdy frame of the legionary Marcus. He recommended that he receive training as a Questionarius - a role that would involve the use of torture and other dark arts for extracting information from prisoners and the enemies of Rome.

The now twenty-five year old Agrippa held an acting rank as an Optio commanding the Cohors Sebastorum, when his company was assigned to the troublesome Province of Judea. One day he was summoned by the Governor. The Sanhedrin, a local rabble of religious leaders, had brought in a young trouble maker whom they wanted punished. The man was handed over to Marcus and his unit. The soldiers tied him to a post where the skin was scourged off his back, his buttock, thighs and calves. One of the men had heard of this fellow and how some called him the King of the Jews.

This greatly amused the on-looking Marcus who concocted a crown out of razor sharp thorns and jammed it hard onto his head. But the Sanhedrin were not to be satisfied with torture alone, they demanded his death.

Later that night, following some drunken urge, he went down to the cells to look on the disfigured body huddled in the rancid dungeon. He mostly remembered his eyes - piercing, brown - that seemed to look right through the Roman officer. Grinning wickedly, he proffered his cup of wine to the wounded man, who declined.

Through smashed teeth and clots of dried blood the man said, 'I forgive you for what you have done and what you will do, tell me your name and I will remember you.'

For some inexplicable reason, Marcus felt compelled to answer, before he could stop himself he said, 'My name is Marcus Agrippa.'

Angered, he flung his cup violently into the cell, turned on his heels slammed the door and shouted, 'I am an officer of the Tenth and I do not require your fucking forgiveness!'

The following morning the badly wounded and dehydrated man was dragged from the cell by pairs of rough hands, his manacles were removed but instead he was burdened by a large wooden cross. At a hill known as Golgotha, the place of the skull, crudely formed spikes of metal were hammered into flesh and bone, pinioning him in agony to the unyielding wood. Marcus Agrippa stood back and admired his men's handiwork.

It was there that he first saw Maryam, peering out from among a coven of other shawled women, her face, creased with pain, her dark eyes flooded, mouth twisted and trembling, but yet there was a sense of stoicism and acceptance. There was something else about her that drew his attention. He could not know it then, but they would soon meet in vastly changed circumstances.

His task complete Marcus left the hill and walked back down into the city. He allowed the men some free time to wonder among the drinking dens and rank brothels while he himself returned to camp. The execution had gone off well, with no trouble from any of the onlookers. It didn't shake the composure of the young Roman officer in any particular way. Marcus had participated many times in such killing - a gruesome but necessary business.

Marcus Agrippa, lost his Earth bound life some eight years later, when an arrow pierced his lung. He mostly remembered the strange sensation of pissing himself as he drowned in a puddle of mucus and blood. When he reopened his eyes, he lay struggling for breath outside a temple in Ravenna. A place he knew well from his childhood.

When he entered he was met by someone who introduced himself as his Advocate. Six days later he sat along with five other penitents and was judged. A druid from Hibernia voted him to Gehenna and the others followed suit. Nearly two millennia ago, people were not so forgiving.

Marcus remembered the Archangel Gabriel standing up to pronounce sentence, sure to concur with the jury and the stocky Abyssinian called Lou hovering ever closer by his side. From the back of the room he heard a voice.

The same voice he had heard before, it said,

'I promised this man that I would remember his name and that I would forgive him.'

Marcus recalled how his knees almost went from under him when he saw the face of the man who his men had crucified - the Jewish preacher named Jesus. For the first time since the death of Cornelia - Marcus Agrippa wept.

The Advocate Maryam stepped out from the stall of a ladies toilet block, in Waterloo Subway Station. She was followed by Abigail. They had both passed through the Stasis portal and emerged on London's South Embankment. When they came up from beneath the Earth, they found the day inclement and overcast. Persistent rain laid a pattern of rippling puddles on the sodden pavement. While a plodding stream of passers-by sheltered beneath umbrellas of every size and hue.

'People think we control the weather,' Maryam joked, 'but it's nothing to do with us.'

Abigail smiled. It was nice to be back in her hometown. The two women strolled in the direction of the London Eye - a gigantic Ferris wheel, which stood on the bank of the River Thames, across from the famous vista of the City of Westminster.

'Do you know,' Abigail remarked, 'despite all the years I lived here, I've never been up.'

'Really, well then we shall have to go on,' Maryam said. 'Besides it will be a good place to escape from the rain.'

As they approached the Eye, a substantial line of tourists had already formed, but Maryam walked directly past both the queue and the ticket booth and nobody batted an eyelid. They stepped into one of the rotating capsules and the door immediately closed behind them.

'How did you do that?' Abigail laughed gleefully.

'Oh...mind over matter,' Maryam winked.

Maryam had mentioned that there were two issues most likely to be examined by the Prots. The major one they had already covered extensively and the minor was the fact that Abigail had never tried to help anyone less well off than her.

She had lived a life where for the most part, she was unaware of the suffering of others. After the death of her mother, her father - Jacob, saw to it that his beloved daughter's every wish was fulfilled. His money and influence had opened door after door for young Abigail. But these connections can't open the doors that matter in Stasis.

Living in London for most of her life, the squalor and poverty of some boroughs should have been evident to Abigail, but her eyes went unseeing and she never volunteered or offered to lend a hand. When images of famine or disaster came on her television screen Abigail would reach for the remote, before a world full of sadness killed her buzz. She would from time to time, donate sums to charity, but it was small change and non-committal for this wealthy young lady and she never really tried to get directly involved.

As they rode up to apex of the ride at over four hundred feet, they looked out across the river towards Big Ben and the Houses of Parliament. Abigail could not recall a single event, where she made a personal difference to a fellow soul.

She felt dreadfully ashamed, despite the encouragement of her Advocate.

A marvellous pair of breasts! What he liked to refer to as his 'Per of tits.' No doubt they were cosmetically enhanced by silicone implants, but nonetheless to his covetous eyes, they were a magnificent sight. This was the ridiculous last recollection of the middle-aged Per who found himself alone on a trail in the midst of a dense Nordic forest.

He'd no idea how he'd gotten here. Had he got too drunk and someone had dropped him off in the middle of nowhere? He remembers getting sick after waking up.

Someone's idea of a practical joke? Some schoolboy prank? But who were they?

Which of his few acquaintances could pull this off?

Jake, the pro at the golf club was a real practical joker, but why would he bother? Per and he had never exchanged more than a couple of jokes and some sordid stories and they certainly wouldn't be described as buddies.

Or what about Philip? he thought.

Philip Weldon was the second in command at the company.

Not that happily married, emasculated sap! He wouldn't have the cojones for this!

Could one of his many ex-girlfriends have plucked up the nerve to extract some sort of stupid vengeance? The thoughts kept spinning through his head.

Per couldn't make out where he was. The tall, dark impenetrable firs on either side shepherded him along towards a clearing in the near distance.

Why did he think this was Sweden? Something about this place seemed uncannily recognisable, but not immediately so.

Whatever had happened to gorgeous what's her name? he wondered.

Never mind there's always more where she came from. There's plenty more fish in the sea. For Per it seemed a never ending supply of pretty young girls was always on tap when you had the cash, but he was about to be proved, dead wrong.

He looked down at his feet that crunched on the compacted snow and the accumulated layers of hoar frost that covered everything in this frigid landscape.

So very strange?

The Swede didn't recognise the clothes he wore, a white cotton shirt, a dark pants, no socks and to his revulsion, cheap canvas shoes. He'd found them in a pile, close to the spot where he had woken.

Per was also spooked by the revelation that he didn't feel cold. Not the least bit frozen which was odd as the ice crystals that dangled from the branches were evidence of a temperature well below freezing.

Light was fading fast and the forest took on an even more ominous aspect. A shot of fear entered his mind that was further compounded when he arrived by the shores of a frozen lake, encircled by a towering wall of pine. Per's heart almost stopped again. He knew this place well.

'It can't be possible!' he muttered. But right on the edge was his father's hunting shack, a log building that lay deep in the vast wilderness of Northern Sweden.

'I'm dreaming this, I must be,' Per laughed out loud but inside he was afraid.

He had gone out this evening for dinner on the Gold Coast and he now found himself back in his homeland.

A drug induced hallucination! If that chef slipped me some magic mushrooms, I swear his ass is so fired when I get home!

His sudden pique of anger summoned his remaining resolve and he headed for the shack. Per had not thought about his father for many years.

His dad, Søren Andersson, was a politically well-connected industrialist who controlled extensive mining interests throughout Scandinavia. Danish by birth he had settled in the city of Malmo with his Swedish wife Frida - a submissive woman with a timid nature whom he also controlled. The product of an expensive education and a privileged upbringing, his father however was as emotionally hard and unresponsive as the rock that his workers excavated from the deep earth.

Per had once overheard his mother remark to her sister, after one glass of Chardonnay too many, that Søren had at a very young age been molested by a step-uncle and the trauma had crushed any incipient happiness that was developing in the boy.

The incident had been hushed up, for fear of a scandal, that would tarnish the family name and the old uncle was ordered to take an extended holiday abroad. Of course her husband had never whispered a word of this to his spouse but the contrite wife of the abuser had contacted Frida to express her deep remorse, for what had happened under her roof - albeit without her knowledge. She had wanted to get it off her chest before she died.

Listening unseen from upstairs, he heard Frida confide to his aunt, that Søren had, many years ago, swapped human affection for the thrill of making vast quantities of money - more money than he could ever spend. However the man was now a soulless wretch and she pitied him. Through insipid tears she confessed how she had settled for the worldly comforts that his great wealth could buy and the more than occasional bottle of Grand Cru.

Per had vowed that he would never permit anyone to pity him, ever.

Desperate for any sign of affection from his mostly absent parents, the teenage boy naturally rebelled and tried his hand at securing the wrong kind of attention, if nothing else was on offer - bad attention being better than none. Pulling off one outrageous stunt after another, he was expelled from school. His father tired of paying for his only son's antics and Per gradually tired of reaching out to his parents. A compromise was reached that saw him hastily dispatched to a prohibitively expensive institute. Short ineffectual trips were made home for Christmas and the holidays but his father's love was an impregnable fortress that he never could breach.

Over the following seemingly short years, he grew to be tall, handsome and as cold and ruthless as his old man. Sharing his father's business acumen, Per established a firm that tapped into all aspects of internet activity. It found a particular niche in the development of applications, that no one really needed, but Per's real talent, was in convincing the world that they really did. A not inconsequential ability that made him considerably wealthy by the time he had reached his late twenties.

He had met his German ex-wife Patti, when she was working in a Berlin nightclub. He'd been there attending a bachelor party with college friends and was immediately taken with the striking looks of the tall blonde hostess, who was bringing them a steady supply of champagne. He asked her out, whisked her off to Sweden and soon after, felt a short-lived desire to settle down.

They married and within twenty three months had fathered two daughters, Pia and Franziska. The restlessness soon returned however and consumed him. When finally having grown irrecoverably tired of her husband's indiscreet dalliances, Patti Müller restored her family name, packed up her belongings along with her dignity and moved with her daughters back to her home town of Wernigerode close to the beautiful Harz Mountains of Saxony Anhalt - a place where she worked hard at being a good mom to her girls and leaving the sham of her first marriage, as far behind as possible. Of course being financially secure, helped her to do this.

Per was more than happy with this arrangement as in one fell swoop it had resolved a number of awkward personal problems that he had been fretting over for some time. This was the clean break he needed, especially as he had long been planning a new life in Australia, somewhere he could cut back on the demands of work and enjoy its more convivial climate.

The bonus for him was being free of his erstwhile unwise commitment, he could instead indulge more time to his passions.

It was a win-win. Noted in his file too was that despite being self-obsessed and unrepentantly vain, he was surprisingly unselfish with his money. He gave his former wife a very handsome settlement. In fact, quite a generous one, the truth be told, perhaps in an effort to soothe any sign of a budding conscience. But being miserly was not one of his many flaws. After all it was only money, and money was something that Per had plenty of.

He'd planned to stay in regular contact with his daughters, even have them over for the holidays. However after one stupendously bad trial run, he packed them off home, a week ahead of schedule. Each, with an extra suitcase stuffed with expensive gifts and cuddly toys, he accepted the fact that sometimes life just gets in the way of even the best made plans.

Now standing on the steps of the veranda, Per steeled himself and with growing trepidation snatched at the handle, yanking open the weather-beaten door of the cabin.

The place never contained anything of value, so was left unlocked at all times. Also due to its location in the deep wilderness, barely anyone was ever seen in the vicinity of the lake. It stood alone, isolated and remote, just like the son of its owner.

Per almost jumped out of his skin on seeing the man who was gently rocking in his father's old chair - a sturdy block of a guy with a chiselled jaw and close cropped hair. Before Per could marshal a word, the man looked up, fixed his gaze on the tall Swede and introduced himself.

'Hello Per. My name is Marcus and I regret to inform you that you are recently deceased.'

six

They were definitely screams that he'd heard, Nader was sure of it. There were other voices also, some sort of commotion taking place, but he couldn't say for sure what was happening.

Nader had been outside in the gardens checking out his new home when a shout rang out. He hurried in the direction of the river but was stopped in his tracks when he rounded the bend.

A broad shouldered man with his back to the shoreline was holding something under water, just a few feet from the edge. Whatever it was, it was no longer struggling. The guy bent low and cradled his load and with a great heave it came to the surface.

Nader paled and was unsure what to do, the killer hadn't seen him yet. Should he shout or should he run? The man looked solidly built and bundled the body over his hip with considerable ease. Even from this distance Nader could see it was human.

Nader's impulse was to run before he was spotted, but as he spun away he ran straight into his Advocate. 'Marcus thanks be to Allah that you're here. I think that man just murdered someone.'

'What are you babbling on about, Khoury?'

'The guy over there he's got a body!' Nader was pointing to a spot some thirty yards away.

'I think he drowned him,' the fisherman exclaimed. 'I heard shouting.'

The Advocate scrunched his brow and took a long hard look at the scene before him.

'That's Lou!'

Nader was puzzled. Lou was the guy who had brought him his meals.

'He didn't kill him, he's retrieving a body, you fool!' Marcus growled.

'That guy, he drowned himself. He was a drug dealer who reckoned his Judgment wouldn't go well. What an idiot,' the Advocate guffawed.

'But why?'

'Because seconds after he tops himself, where do you think his soul's going to go?'

'Right back here to Stasis?' Nader guessed.

'Now you get it,' Marcus sneered. 'There's no escape from here, Khoury. You can't avoid the Judgment. No way, no how.'

Marcus called across to the man who had loaded the corpse onto a trolley. Nader stayed back watching in astonishment. It wasn't the first dead body that he had seen but he hadn't expected to see one here in Stasis. The Advocate and Lou were laughing, no doubt at Nader's expense. His face flushed red. Marcus finished his conversation and headed back in the direction of the fisherman.

'So what happens now?' Nader asked.

'To that moron!' Marcus pointed to the corpse. 'His soul goes straight back into another human shell. He'll be on the chair tomorrow as expected.'

Something about the way he had said *The Chair,* sent a shiver through Nader.

The Advocate placed a meaty hand on the captain's arm and led him away from the river. 'It's not so bad you know.' Marcus had an unnerving smile.

'People on the Earth, they look at famous people as if they've some magical insight or ability. That's a crock of shit! Those folks, grapple with the same doubts and insecurities as the rest of us.'

Nader looked at his Advocate, not knowing what to say.

'The chair, it's the great leveller, Khoury. It's where the little guy gets to shine. All you need to have done is to have led a decent life. The powerful and the mighty all come through here with no more rights than you. Doesn't matter if they were a King or a President, they get no extra favour. And if you're a billionaire, you'd better have done a lot of good with all that money!'

After the meeting in Room 5, Doctor Dumond returned directly to her cell without engaging in conversation with any of the others. In fact everyone there seemed reticent apart from the brash young American but that, she knew that was to be expected.

She reached a willowy hand into her double-lined jacket and removed a set of red coral rosary beads, a gift from her dear departed husband. He had been a Professor of Philosophy at l'Universite Paris-Sorbonne, up until the time of his unexpected demise from a short, mysterious illness.

Gradually she lowered herself, with some difficulty, to her knees. The hip operation had improved things considerably but still the physical restrictions of old age were a constant source of frustration and annoyance for Monique. Even this new body had its kinks.

She remembered a time when she was young and beautiful, a brilliant student, ambitious and determined. Her whole life mapped out in front of her. Once she moved amongst the great and powerful but old age had now reduced her to this sad, wizened crone.

'Growing old, how you humble even the greatest,' she complained.

Still she made the best of every situation. She glanced up at the picture window that dominated the far wall of her cell, Monique Dumond began to recite a decade of the rosary working the beads through practiced fingers, asking the Virgin Mary to intercede on her behalf. She continued praying in her native French, then in Latin which came easy to her and which proved useful during her medical studies. She even added some short prayers in German, that she vaguely recalled from her younger years. Monique had studied for a time in Munich, that wonderful Bavarian City which held an unknown attraction in her heart.

Towards the conclusion of her prayers Monique's thoughts drifted to the others who had gathered in the room, waiting to be addressed by Maryam and the curt Marcus.

He doesn't like me much, she guessed correctly.

The Japanese girl, she could not remember her name – *Mizu, or something oriental sounding?* She made a mental note to learn it properly, for she was very young and surely could be influenced by a more mature woman such as herself.

The British girl, Abigail, was a much more confident and assured creature but Monique was certain she could also be swayed over to her side. That leaves only the men. Monique allowed herself a complicit smile.

Although much older than her prime, Monique had always been adept at managing the men in her life - well most of them anyhow. Her dear father, the handful of suitors and dear Albert who had won her heart, they were all so easy to bring around to her way of thinking. Dear Albert had been the easiest of them all.

She had cleverly convinced him to propose to her, all the while allowing him the illusion that the idea had been his. He probably would have proposed anyway, but Monique was never prepared to wait for what she wanted. She'd continued to use her maiden name Dumond, throughout her most recent life. Never for a moment had she considered taking the surname of her husband - Dreyfus. *So grey and so dreary.*

Madame had earned a good salary as a surgeon specialising in the increasingly popular field of cosmetic procedures. A very good remuneration package with a host of benefits ensued from the finest private hospital in Paris, but it was Albert's inheritance which had topped it off nicely and had permitted her access to the finer things in life.

'Yes, indeed,' she once again cracked a paper thin fissure of a smile. The power that she had always felt inside could persuade a man to do anything for her. She was sure of it.

'So what about my new friends,' she muttered to herself.

The young American would no doubt have a boyish naivety that she believed could be worked on, whereas that surly Arab animal would no doubt be an altogether more difficult prospect. The former plastic surgeon recalled there was to be one more individual added to the group, man or woman, she wasn't sure. However, no matter, she would work her wiles on them too. She badly needed allies if she was to have any hope. She had always been good at collecting acquaintances, *you never knew when they could become useful* and now would be no exception to that. *Especially now!*

Why was that other person not there in the room with the rest of us poor souls? Was it always thus? she pondered.

Madame Dumond chided herself for allowing this distraction from her prayers and promptly resumed with the Glorious Mysteries, working the beads deftly through her once nimble fingers.

'Ave Maria, gratia plena, Dominus tecum,' she whispered in Latin. After which she raised herself, painfully, to her feet once more.

The Mother would help her surely in her hour of need. She would be forgiven once more.

'Watch this!' Mike said, getting up gingerly from the bench that he shared with Nader Khoury. After their individual meetings with Maryam and Marcus, they had been told that they were now free to move around almost anywhere in Stasis.

Almost meant any door that will open or, as Maryam had explained,

'If you find a door that won't open, then it's not for you.'

Mike and Nader had been walking through the gardens and the meadow area that Maryam had called the Elysian Fields. There were other small clusters of people visible, gathered in pairs, sitting, engaged in conversation or the occasional individual who went off alone, most likely to reflect on their current situation.

The Elysian Fields were laid out in the manner of large informal gardens, divided and sectioned by trees and by tall rows of hedging. Pathways took you west towards a wildflower meadow of incredible fragrance where unknown multitudes of blossoms clambered upwards, as if drawn to some unseen attraction. Eastwards brings you to the shores of a small river called the Lethe. River is possibly too grand a label as it barely spans more than a dozen paces even at its widest point.

'Something that the classical Greeks got correct,' Marcus had laughed.

'Souls that were going back to start a new life on Earth were first immersed in the Lethe's waters which erased the memory of their previous life,' he said. 'Definitely do not drink from it,' he warned, 'It will leave you completely unintelligible at your Judgment.'

Nader had spotted a woman who had detached from the nearest group and had strolled deliberately in their direction, until she was no more than the length of a football field from the two men. He could only tell that she was a dark haired woman of indeterminate age.

She stopped and stared at them both, eventually raising her right hand to give a hesitant wave. Both Nader and Mike made the involuntary response of waving back, self-consciously.

Mike began striding purposefully towards the woman, who had also increased her pace. But at about fifty paces, his stride began taking him away from her. He tried to correct but to no avail. He noticed she had also diverted from her course and was going in the opposite direction.

Both of them came to a halt and the woman cupped her hands and appeared to shout something, but neither Mike nor Nader could hear any sound she made. Mike shrugged in an exaggerated gesture and waved at the woman, who smiled, in resignation and then turned away as if suddenly realising the futility of her actions.

He made his way back to Nader who had been looking on intently.

'It's totally weird man. It's as if out of the blue, torque is applied to your feet and steers you away from where you want to go. It's the strangest sensation.'

'A magnetic dipole field is repelling you apart from each other,' a deep resonant voice chuckled from behind them. Nader turned to see the smiling figure of the caretaker who was wheeling a barrow chock full of what seemed like leftovers.

'Just taking out the trash,' he said by way of explanation. 'I guess I should say recycling. Nothing on Stasis is ever wasted.'

'Hey Lou, buddy, what's going on here? Why can't I go talk to that lady?' Mike asked, pointing in the direction of the nearest group.

'You can't, Mike. It's made that way. You can only meet with and interact with your own group, the Advocates and the Arcs.'

'But why don't they let us talk to the other people here?'

'Well I guess it's because you are in a sense the same as a jury panel that's been sequestered. Until your verdicts are heard, you only get to speak with each other,' he explained.

'I had better get on with my work. Catch you guys later.' Lou walked off porting his barrow and whistling a tune that Mike who played some guitar recognised as something by the Stones.

'I'm not sure about that guy,' Nader whispered.

'Lou? Why not?' Mike asked, looking after the broad figure of the caretaker who vanishing behind a hedgerow.

'I don't know why. I'm just not sure that I trust him. He seems far too pleased with himself.' Nader remembered Lou with the body at the river, but didn't speak of it.

'You don't trust anyone!' Mike joked.

'And that policy kept me alive for a long time, my American friend,' Nader responded with no hint of a smile.

The two men had taken a stroll after their meeting had concluded. The friendly, talkative firefighter and the reticent and mostly silent smuggler sat on a bench, quietly mulling over what they had just been told. The first time that they met, Mike had extended his hand which Nader hesitated before taking. Both had a firm handshake. Nader had even applied a little extra pressure on the squeeze but the young American matched it readily.

Nader was impressed. His hands having been toughened from years of labour, were powerful instruments, so this young American was also a fairly strong guy.

Mike wore an easy smile on the type of corn-fed face that was open and worry-free. Nader although not many years older looked out from under a furrowed brow and lines in his skin that had been etched out by too much worry and exposure to wind and sun.

They talked for a while - well Mike did most of the talking with an occasional input from the fisherman. Despite his initial first impression of the firefighter, Nader found himself warming to the guy.

'I think I may be in some trouble, Mike,' Nader interrupted.

Oh why's that?'

'It's my job.' Mike could see that Nader was struggling to get the words out.

'Your job? You were a fisherman right? That's not so bad.'

'I did some smuggling also,' Nader said and lowered his head into his upturned hands.

'Oh, I see!'

I trafficked people too.'

Mike looked askance as if seeing him for the first time but kept his silence.

'I smuggled many people, over a very long time, making lots of money for bad men. Which I guess also makes me a bad guy too. Being here now at this time in my life, before I have the chance to make amends, could go very poorly for me.'

Miyu Tanaka was at her favourite place on Limbus Stasis. Maryam had earlier shown them a room that was called, 'The Mirador,' a portal that when opened allowed you to enter a random landscape so unremittingly beautiful and entrancing that it was hard to break yourself away from it.

When they had arrived with the Advocate they had found themselves at the base of El Salto Angel - The Angel Falls in Venezuela, The waterfall drops over the edge of the Auyantepui Mountain in the Canaima National Park. Looking up at the world's highest waterfall, with a drop height just shy of a thousand metres. The image felt so real that you would swear that you had actually been there. 'It's a place for contemplation and reflection,' Maryam had remarked before leading the group off to see another part of their temporary home.

As soon as the Advocate had departed, Miyu had quietly slipped away from the others. She doubled back to the Mirador and what awaited her inside brought tears to her eyes. She placed her face and hands against the domed glass barrier and looked out at the absolute desolate beauty of the small blue sphere that stood out above the ink black horizon.

A solitary view 237,000 miles in the making - Planet Earth.

'You're here you know?'

The unexpected voice startled Miyu who hadn't seen the elderly doctor standing inside the doorway.

'Remarkable isn't it. And it's not a projected image. You're actually standing on the surface of the Earth's moon.'

Miyu was astonished by the old lady's words. She lowered her eyes and noticed her feet. Her sandals were coated with the same grey lunar dust as outside.

'The place they call the Sea of Tranquillity, where the American Astronauts, Armstrong and Aldrin landed, is visible there to the South. But this protective dome is necessary my dear, as we are in our human bodies, we still need to breathe air,' Monique added, before taking one of the seats that were fixed to the rear wall.

'If I was outside this dome what would happen to me? Would my blood boil or my head explode?'

No my dear, that's just in the movies. If you stepped outside into the vacuum, the air in your lungs would be expelled out of your mouth, your body would go through the motions of trying to breathe, but there is no air to take in. So you would just die of oxygen starvation,' the doctor explained.

'So Limbus Stasis is on the moon,' Miyu said in open amazement.

'No, my dear. Limbus Stasis is exactly wherever they want it to be.'

'But..' Miyu was puzzled, '...I don't understand? How can they do this?'

'They created everything, so they can make it do whatever they want, and be wherever it needs to be.' The older woman tapped her fingers on the adjacent seat to indicate that Miyu should join her.

'I am Monique, Monique Dumond, from Paris and you are?'

'Miyu Tanaka from Tokyo.' The younger girl bowed respectfully to acknowledge her senior. 'You know a lot about Stasis,' Miyu said shyly.

'Only what my Advocate has told me,' Monique was of course being coy.

The older woman continued to lead the conversation. 'Do you know that the human body, despite its frailties, is the absolute perfect vessel for the transport of a soul? It was designed specifically for that purpose, Miyu.

The soul is carried in a part of the brain called Ammon's Horn. It is quite tiny.' She gave the young woman a thin lipped version of a smile before continuing, 'Where was I?'

'The human body! Yes, of course. It can suffer from trauma or disease and will eventually fail. However it is an impeccable design nonetheless.'

Miyu was about to interrupt but Monique anticipated her question and said, 'I was a surgeon, down there on the Earth. I was quite a good one too, if I may say so myself. I specialised in Plastic Reconstruction. I helped many people recover their lives after being disfigured by car wrecks or serious burns.' The doctor's speech was intended to impress the young Asian girl, a calculation that proved entirely accurate. Miyu stared up at the older woman in awe.

'So you helped many people. That is so wonderful for you,' she clasped her slim hands together between her legs, which dangled back and forth like a child on a swing, returning her attention once more to the bewitching blue orb enveloped in vast swirls and wisps of white cloud.

'The Earth is really so beautiful,' Miyu whispered.

'It is indeed, and it's the only one of its kind in the entire Universe. Created entirely for us - or at least for the testing of us. It is their little soul laboratory,' Monique added cryptically.

'Who are they?' the petite girl asked, choosing the wrong, but more obvious question, as she looked up at the face of the impressive doctor.

'God and the Archangels my dear. They made and control everything including that little body of yours.'

Per had rocked back on his heels after hearing Marcus' words. He struggled to catch his breath only succeeding when his Advocate, as the man had called himself, had touched Per's hand bringing a sudden sense of relief to the confused Swede. But it wasn't to last.

'I can't be dead...I eat healthy...I exercise...I even do yoga! I'm a very healthy man for Heaven's sake, I'm in really good shape. This has to be a mistake!'

'Take it easy, Per man. Relax!' said Marcus.

'Take it easy! Relax! Are you fucking nuts? You've just told me I'm dead. How do you suggest I relax?'

Per pulled himself up to his imposing full height of six feet, four inches, a good three inches taller than the Advocate. The Swede aggressively pushed him on the chest. Marcus barely budged and merely raised both palms outwards in a show of non-violence and smiled.

'I know it can come as a shock, but you are dead man. You really can't change it, so be a good chap and calm down a bit and come with me eh?'

'I'm not buying it. I'm not playing your game. I demand to go back and I'm not fucking going anywhere with you.'

'Please don't Mister Andersson, I must warn you.'

Per felt a surge of false courage building, stoking the feeling of impotent rage at learning of his apparent death. An ugly sneer contorted his normally handsome face. Once more he pushed hard against Marcus' solar plexus.

The Advocate of Souls took one crisp step to the side, gripped Per's wrist and bent his thumb back at an angle, sending a spasm of excruciating pain shooting up the hyper-extended arm. The former Roman Soldier then applied a little more pressure forcing him to his knees. The Swede at this point was staring, eyes blood-shot and bulging and screaming for mercy at the Advocate, who mumbled, 'Sorry about this.'

He slugged him with an expertly aimed punch to the right temple. Per's eyes rolled back in his head and he collapsed to the ground in a crumpled, compliant heap.

'There always has to be one. Fuck, he's a heavy bastard,' Marcus grunted while exerting considerable effort to pull the long frame of the unconscious man up onto his shoulders. He stumbled at first, but correcting his balance the compact and burly former Optio of the Tenth Fretensis, made his way to the rear of the hunting cabin. Turning the handle he walked out of the back door and into the great concourse and the blinding illumination of Stasis Arrivals.

Marcus Agrippa had of course done this before, many times in fact. When you consider that on average 150,000 souls pass through Stasis everyday you're always likely to get the occasional awkward customer. Marcus didn't enjoy punching anyone, at least not since he came to Stasis. But in the case of this guy, Andersson, it wasn't an entirely unsatisfactory experience. He waddled unsteadily with his unconscious burden towards one of the arrival desks.

'Hey Marcus, how are you today?' A young lady with a fantastic smile greeted him warmly.

'I'm good, Rachel, thank you.'

'So who is your friend?' She inclined her head to the side to get a better look at the recumbent giant. 'He's a good looking fellow, who I guess wasn't behaving himself,' she gave a brief chortle then called out

'Per Oskar Andersson. Born in Uppsala, Sweden, most recently resident of Queensland, Australia.'

'The very man! I'll bring him straight up to 5,' Marcus grumbled as he readjusted his stance. He was beginning to feel the full weight of his long limbed cargo.

'Oh dear God, it *was* a dream. I'm alive!' Per uttered these very words when he came around and found himself slumped across three chairs, part of a group that formed a small crescent. He rubbed the right side of his head. It throbbed as if he'd taken a blow from a hammer. The look of sheer bewilderment that crossed his chiselled features when he saw Marcus sitting opposite, well an uncharitable soul might have reason to laugh out loud, but there are not too many souls devoid of charity in Stasis, considering what is at stake.

'Yoouuu?' he stammered in disbelief. I don't understand this! I don't understand what is happening?'

'Look Mister Anderson, we've gotten off to a bad start. My name is Marcus. I apologise if I was somewhat abrupt in the manner that I informed you, of your recent passing from the mortal world. But please listen to me. You are now in a place called Limbus Stasis. It may only be a temporary stay until your Judgment is heard.'

'My what?'.

'Your Judgment, sir,' Marcus had reckoned that exaggerated politeness might result in a better response from this guy. 'You have died and as you will know, you are now required to give an account of your life.'

'No, I don't agree to this, I've never heard of such a thing. It's utter nonsense!' he moaned.

'It says in your file that you were raised in the Protestant faith - Presbyterian to be precise.' Marcus waited for a response but none was forthcoming. Per remained rocking back and forward, his fingers tapping out a rhythm on his skull, so the Advocate continued.

'You'd have read the Bible in your formative years. So you should be familiar.

I refer you sir to Hebrews 9:27 - And as it is appointed unto men once to die, but after this the Judgment.' Marcus offered his best smile. 'Also Corinthian's 5:10, if you'd like a second opinion.'

The Scandinavian was rallying. He had raised his head and had straightened himself up on the chair. 'So, how is this going to play out?' He let out a hollow laugh that dripped with derision.

'I'm going to sit on a chair someplace and give account of my life in front of God, is that it?' Per Andersson stretched out his long legs and folded his arms in as haughty a manner as he could muster. Marcus was rather amused by his new client's bluster.

He smiled grimly as he replied, 'Not exactly Mister Andersson, you will sit on that chair,' Marcus pointed to the solitary seat that faced the other five. 'And I regret to inform you that you won't be judged by the Creator, well not initially. You'll be judged by two men and three women.'

Per Oskar Andersson shot to his feet in alarm, 'Three fucking women! You have got to be shitting me?' The internet millionaire momentarily considered lunging for the smirking man sitting opposite him. He so badly wanted to shove his smug grin back down his throat but he remembered the pounding he took earlier. His attention was distracted when the door opened behind him and a short, stocky black man stuck his head around the jamb.

'You okay in here Marcus?'

'Yes, I'm fine Lou, thanks.'

'Okay I'll get back to work.'

'You do that Lou, you do that,' Marcus replied, but Lou didn't immediately move off.

'Now Mister Andersson, I've got a lot of information for you. We've much to speak of. Oh and I would recommend that you moderate your language and drop the profanity. As someone soon to be judged, I think you're smart enough to realise that's a good idea.'

Per wanted to scream but something about the way the black guy was studying him with his coal dark eyes, made him close his mouth and keep it shut tight.

seven

'Wait for me Abigail,' she called.

'Hurry up darling we'll be late for your party,' Abigail slurred her words. She'd had a bit too much champagne already and the full effect of their recent little top up had yet to kick in.

'We're having fun, aren't we Ru?' She encouraged her onwards, a pair of expensive platinum bracelets dangled from the wrist of her beckoning hand.The petite and pretty dark haired girl stumbled forward, her high heels clacking on the tiles, her tightly fitted skirt restricting her free movement.

'I...I don't feel so good.'

She attempted to regain her balance, her hands reached out parallel to the floor, like a tightrope walker on an invisible line. Then she stopped,

'Abi...Abiga...aaaaah...' a stream of liquid came gushing from her mouth in a steady brown flow. The hematemesis was not bright red highly oxygenated blood, but a dark coffee ground colour that stained the front of her party dress. She stared first at Abigail then down at her dress, startled, uncomprehending.

Then her eyes rolled and she collapsed in a convulsing heap, her clutch purse still gripped in deathly pale fingers. Abigail screamed at her friend to call an ambulance. Then she sat with Ruth on the cold floor, her cocktail outfit a white centrepiece amidst the petals of a reddish brown expanding puddle. Cradling the young girl's head in her lap, running her hands through her hair, muttering between pitiful sobs,

'It's your birthday Ru! It's your birthday!'

Abigail sat up in alarm. It was on her second night in Stasis that the dream had returned. The exact same nightmare which had tormented her back on Earth - a recurring dream which had required eighteen months of happy pills and therapy at a Harley Street clinic, to expunge from her subconscious mind. It was back!

But why now? she fretted tearfully.

'Abigail, Abigail, you can't say you weren't told,' her mom's words, spoken years before, echoed back from a distant time, further unsettling her. Her home-spun sage, rattled out a warning like a fire-bell. But the mocking voice was clearly her own.

'You know your angel will have the truth of it,' the old girl had been fond of saying, still, this timeworn chestnut held a scrap of prophecy. Something that Abigail had overlooked.

Unable to settle and feeling restless, she dressed and went to explore the parts of Stasis she'd not yet seen. She'd considered calling to see Miyu, but on a whim she chose to carry on alone. She felt a strange compulsion to head out to the gardens, onto the meandering paths, all of which converged at a great central mound. Following the trail she was surprised to see that the others were already gathered by its grassy slopes, encircled by incalculable blooms that ran back towards the meridian like the mathematically perfect spokes of some great wheel.

Standing at its hub was an enormous spire of obsidian; a deep black volcanic rock, sharp and brittle like glass which had been worked by some creative mind with gifted hands into carvings of mesmerising beauty. All assembled were listening to the Advocate Marcus who turned towards the newcomer and said, 'Ah Abigail, I'm glad you're here, you just made it in time.'

'In time for what?' Abigail laughed. Her sorrow at her premature death had by now almost receded to the point of inconsequence as she felt more and more excited about her new surroundings. She desperately wanted to go to the Heofon.

'You'll soon see,' Marcus said as he excused himself from the gathering.

'Miss Perdue I believe?' The much older lady extended a hand in greeting, accompanied by a sliver of a smile. Abigail automatically took it, but the skin felt cold and unwelcoming.

'Doctor Monique Dumond,' introduced herself. 'Eminent Plastic Surgeon from Paris, recently deceased,' she laughed at her own joke, but Abigail noticed that her eyes didn't align in synch with the upward curve of her mouth.

'Enchanté, Madame Dumond. Je suis Abigail Perdue.'

Abigail nonetheless always had impeccable manners. And although not entirely fluent, she was a competent speaker of both French and Italian.

Madame Dumond reached out with her free hand, gently cupping Abigail's elbow. 'It's so lovely to meet you my dear. It fills me with great sadness that you passed so young.'

'Oh that's sweet of you,' Abigail blushed. She was about to speak again but her conversation ceased in an instant, at the first detection of that sound.

When we hear something, especially something unusual, the stretched membrane of the eardrum passes the vibrations through the hammer, anvil and stirrup into the thousands of cilia of the human ear. Abigail's auditory canal sent the signals to the cortex of her brain, which from years of musical training had become highly sensitive and reactive to sound.

She later would describe the experience to me as one of hearing, an intense susurration followed by the long low drone of an instrument, a sound like the booming of sand which coalesced and unleashed a massive wave of acoustic energy...

A sound once heard, that can never be forgotten, always anticipated, always longed for.

A double sonic boom exploded overhead as the unrestrained reverberation of pure joy echoed through the Elysian Gardens, audio waves of millions of voices: singing, laughing, in unison, calling out to each other. Every soul in Stasis stopped dead in its tracks and looked towards the horizon.

Daniel Mallen

On the eastern flank of the fields, far beyond the waters of the Lethe arose a planet-sized sphere that pulsated and moved in the erratic manner of a huge murmuration of starlings, suddenly dipping and advancing with implausible speed and then turning back the way it came. The naturally sullen countenance of Nader Khoury was lit up with a sparkling smile. Miyu Tanaka fell to her knees chanting out loud in her native tongue, her eyes rapt with glee on the fast approaching orb. Abigail, eyes opened wide, pupil's fully dilated, felt Monique Dumond clutch nervously at her hand.

On it came and it was colossal, the voices ranging from booming bass to soaring trebles. It was at once both terrifying and magnificent.

If you could have ripped your eyes away from this phenomenon, you would have seen hair rippling out on its very ends, bulging eyes and the facial muscles of every human present, oscillate wildly with each vibration of the sphere, as if affected by some manic palsy. A feeling of mild nausea and dizziness was common to all, as the waves spun the fluid in the ear, causing the cilia to dance, resulting in total confusion for an organ unable to process such a magnitude of raw sound data.

Nader Khoury mouthed the words of the Muslim prayer Al-Fatiha,

'Praise be to Allah, Lord of the worlds, the beneficent, the merciful. Owner of the Day of Judgment.'

The sound wave preceded the arrival of the Great Host. On it came until it was directly above, almost blocking out the sky with its vastness, its mass so immeasurably huge.

Every soul in Limbus Stasis felt the same overwhelming desire to be joined with their brothers and sisters at that moment. Even the recently atheist found a prayer on their lips. Those who had been raised in a faith reached into their subconscious and recited almost forgotten words they had not heard since childhood. People of different religion and of none at all realised they were one indivisible core, the children of the Creator.

Abigail began mumbling the words to a Hebrew prayer from the Siddur,

'Barukh ata Adonai Eloheinu, melekh ha'olam. Blessed are You, Lord our God, King of the universe. But it was impossible to speak coherently with the uncontrollable movement of her face. Her heart was overflowing with the sensation of supreme love as The Host passed overhead and dipped down and disappeared behind the outer western limits – the sphere was gone.

'What the hell was that!' A beaming Mike shouted, he was the first to gather himself after the tumbling orb had passed from view. He pressed his hands hard on his cheeks to halt their waning quaver. He found himself giggling and grinning from ear to ear.

'Not hell, my friend, in fact the total opposite. Your eyes have just seen and your ears have just heard The Great Host of Souls – The Heofon.' The words were spoken by a young man.

He had approached from behind the group unheard in the commotion and the ensuing clamour of excitement. A man with brown eyes and olive hued skin, who appeared to be in his middle or perhaps late twenties, it was hard to say.

And just like with their female Advocate, it was difficult to focus for any length of time on his features. The same ever so slightly blurry quality surrounded him.

'It was the Heofon, you are blessed.'

'They were the voices of Puresouls, rejoicing in their happiness and acclaiming the Creator. Hopefully you may go with them soon. I can promise you, that you will be very happy if you are chosen.' The young man brushed his longish hair away from his eyes.

'I'm sorry but who are you?' Abigail asked.

'Forgive me, I am Manny,' the young man gave a polite bow. 'I am Maryam's son.'

As Maryam made her way out into the corridor she knew by his disquieted look that something was wrong. 'What is it Marcus? What's up?'

He didn't immediately reply but instead thrust a document towards Maryam.

She took it with more than a little foreboding and as she scanned the text her jaw slackened, 'No, no, no' she mumbled, closing her eyes, she pressed her back against the wall and groaned.

'Yeah Nicky Mac is back in town,' he said, his grin soured to a grimace.

'The Prince,' she said almost in a whisper, as if to give voice to it would spoil the air.

'But what about Robyn and Ishmael?'

'Gone back to the Host, both of them. Lou just told me. It was their time,' Marcus replied.

'My word, has two centuries passed already? How time flies,' Maryam was genuinely taken aback.

Marcus shrugged, 'What can you do? Although I'll miss Ishmael and Robyn, they were nice.'

'You'll miss them because they were easy.' Maryam raised an eyebrow.

'Anyhow, we now need to prepare for an entirely different experience. Gather them up Marcus, get them into 5, soon as you can.'

'Will do boss.' Marcus was already making his way back to the accommodation block.

'The Prince,' Maryam sighed once more. 'It's been a long time Niccolò. But it would be better if it had been a bit longer.'

City of Valencia. Spain.

In the modern La Fe hospital on Avienda de Campanar, Tomas Esposito lay motionless in his ICU bed. An intermittent bleep from the diagnostic monitor was the only sound that escaped from this quiet, sterile room. He had no family there to watch over him. Apart from a sad old Padre who attended once a day to pray for his soul, Tomas was completely alone. His aged and mottled hands lay open and unheld.

Airlifted from the cruise ship where he worked, before his sudden collapse several days earlier. He was brought from a location thirty miles off of the coast by a Sea King helicopter to intensive care, in Spain's third largest city. He was unconscious throughout.

Fifty two year old Tomas Esposito was drifting ever closer towards the realm of the dead. Despite his Spanish sounding name, Tomas had no Hispanic ancestry. His family heritage was Chinese. His surname is the peculiar result of an old colonial decree that ordered the mandatory and systematic implementation of the Spanish naming system on the entire population of the Philippines irrespective of their origin.

Born on the island of Luzon, Tomas had a mainly poor but resoundingly happy childhood, growing up with his parents and his older brother in the Marinika valley. A pleasant, good natured boy, he was always willing to lend a helping hand. When he was nineteen he moved to Quezon City in search of work. A year later he had the great fortune to meet the love of his life, his beloved, Gloria.

Both Tomas and Gloria worked long hours in the hospitality industry. It left little time to be together and he had begun to lose hope. But an employer impressed with his work ethic offered Tomas a job at his new venture in the popular tourist city of Baguio. Tomas eagerly accepted and Gloria accompanied her new husband, to the mountainous regions of northern Luzon. There they found a cheap but cosy apartment and also a job as a chambermaid for Gloria.

The Esposito's were deliriously happy and looking forward to a long life together. They were not yet blessed with children but that would come in good time, Tomas was sure.

It was on Monday, July 16, 1990, however, at 4:26 pm local time, that the densely populated island was struck by an earthquake. And it was a big one.

With a 7.8 surface wave magnitude, it produced an almost 100 mile ground rupture as a result of strike-slip movements along the Philippine Fault and the Digdig Fault. One of the more prominent buildings destroyed that otherwise innocuous summer's day, was the Hyatt Terraces Hotel, where more than eighty employees and guests lost their lives.

Tomas rushed to the scene, distraught and desperately searching for Gloria amidst the chaos. His search was in vain. Three people were later pulled alive from the rubble but sadly Gloria was not one of the lucky ones. The earthquake had taken down more than tall buildings it had toppled the cherished dreams and hopes of a man named Tomas Esposito.

Unable to bear to a single night in their apartment without her, after the funeral he packed up his few belongings and returned to the city where he found work with a shipping line. And at sea he would remain.

After several years Tomas moved to work as a waiter on a Mediterranean Cruise Ship, conveying the fortunate and the well-heeled from port to port. Filipinos were cheap to employ and had a reputation in the shipping industry as hard workers.

Tomas was one of the shadow people, countless millions who operate in the background of our lives, serving food, cleaning rooms, eking out a meagre existence, far from home, their families and the familiar. They survive by working long days, barely escaping crushing poverty and scarce opportunity. Yet, by some miracle they retain both dignity and their joy.

Tomas enjoyed his work but never remarried. He said a life at sea was not conducive to holding down a relationship. But the simple truth was that under the veneer of his easy smile, and charming ways, Tomas Esposito, this slightly built, gentle man was still broken hearted and no one could ever replace his Gloria. Other than occasional phone calls to his mother, Tomas had never returned to his homeland. So today Tomas Esposito would die alone, far from where he played happily as a boy.

A young Filipino nurse from Mindanao who worked at La Fe said a quiet prayer for his soul in his native Tagalog language. Then, quietly and without struggle, Tomas Esposito passed away. His employers would arrange for his mortal remains to be transported back to the care of his brother. Tomas had been baptised a Roman Catholic but had ditched his faith in his despair. There could be no God for Tomas Esposito now.

At the same instant that the hospital registrar pronounced Tomas Esposito deceased. The Filipino reached for the sides and spewed out the unknown contents that were impeding his airway.

Reopening his eyes, he had initially struggled for breath, but he felt much better now as he sprawled on a boat crossing a lake. 'I know this place!' he croaked, his throat parched.

Burnham Lake in Baguio was a place that Tomas indeed knew well,

It must be Panagbenga; the flower festival.

Beautiful blossoms were in riotous assembly everywhere.

Strange, there are no people here? Tomas' last recollection was carrying a tray of used dishes to the ever busy kitchens of the cruise liner '*Bountiful.*' He must be dreaming, he figured. His small craft carried itself effortlessly across the mist shrouded lake. Tomas could scarcely believe his eyes. Standing on a wooden pontoon, was a girl, small of stature, shoulder length black hair and deep dark eyes. She was smiling and waving ecstatically. She beckoned with a wave of her hand for Tomas to follow her.

'Gloria, wait!' Tomas Esposito cried out.

The Pivot is the event or occurrence in an individual's life that sends them hurtling toward a different path or fashions a vastly different outlook from previously held views. For Abigail it was simply her choice of cello case and the decision to cancel her taxi. For Miyu it was accepting the job at the Sato house.

For some it is a change for the good, but sooner or later, most will experience the jarring realisation that something, perhaps even everything, has altered - death, profound loss, new birth or new love, each can be a catalyst for such a change. Losing your flimsy grip on an almost forgotten religion or having a burgeoning awareness that you are quite simply alone in this world. All can unhinge the most stable of minds.

The landscape that yesterday seemed romantic and inviting now appears bleak and remote to the lacerated and bruised soul, and yet tomorrow it could be worthwhile again in the heart of the more resolute optimist struggling through the onset of later years - the forfeit of precious youth and even more damaging the permanent loss of the youthful armour of invincibility. Your devil-may-care attitude has abandoned you and has left you residing in the lair of diminished options and unfulfilled potential. Only the charmed and most fortunate of us will progress unscathed, blissfully unaware. For few are those eternal summers.

Resorting to the perceived security of what you had learned as children, from parents once strong but whose strength has now withered before your eyes. The bedraggled soul searches for the way back home. Emptied out and weary, no longer as innately curious or as easily impressed. Mortally afraid that all you strived for might be in vain, all for nothing. No longer do you have the ability to defend or to protect those you love.

For everything will pass, everything and everyone you have ever known and you yourself. Less vital, less required. Even the strongest of us must fail. So what is the point of it all?

Why do we go on? Only to fall and get up again. How can a spirit so gravely hurt and routinely wounded respond so readily to the slightest chance of salvation, the vaguest hope of redemption? Only the soul can remember where it came from, and weathers all storms on its journey home. Even when it appears all is lost. All can be won again. Heofon knows how.

eight

'They don't care about us at all. At least they don't care about us when we are living down there on the Earth, as humans,' Doctor Dumond had said to them both.

'Whatever do you mean?' Abigail asked the older woman.

A few moments earlier she had felt so very happy, the vision of the Host had filled her with such a feeling of euphoria that it lingered long afterwards. She had come to the Mirador expecting to find Miyu but instead the American guy, Mike, was sitting there, completely lost in a vista of the Sahara that lay in front of him, around him and down to the grains of desert sand that lay beneath his feet. Abigail really liked Mike, she had the feeling that he was a really good person, someone who could be trusted and relied upon. She guessed also that he was a little bit sweet on her too, which was cute but not very practical.

She'd have to speak to him about it at some point or maybe not, perhaps things will just play themselves out naturally. Anyway for now she enjoyed his company. Mike told her how he had always wanted to see the great African deserts. He told Abigail, how his dad and he loved to watch the old movies together when he was just a kid, the epic *Laurence of Arabia* being a particular favourite. Their moment of intimacy was soon interrupted by the arrival of Monique.

As she entered the room she declared, 'Ah Abigail I'm pleased to have found you and you too, Mister Roberts,' but she allowed her smile to drop when addressing the young man.

Without warning a bright burst of light made all three people shield their eyes with their hands. When it had passed the

Mirador's setting had changed from the rippling sand dunes to the grey dust and craters of the lunar landscape. The Earth suspended in the distance just above the Moon's horizon.

'It's so awesome isn't it?' Abigail was transfixed by the radiance of the small blue planet that turned amidst the vast blackness of the galaxy.

'Yes, it is beautiful my dear, exactly as it was designed to be. It's their testing ground for souls. The Earth is their factory floor.' Monique pursed her lips as she said this, emphasising her disapproval.

Abigail was speechless but Mike was alert.

'What do you mean by factory? I don't know what you're getting at lady.'

'What do you see when you look out there young man, apart from that solitary blue orb?' the older woman pressed her point.

'Some stars and a lot of empty space, I guess.'

'Empty space and darkness! That is right, Michael.' Monique did not care for abbreviations.

'It's no accident that there is only one planet like the Earth out there. In all the inestimable enormity of space, this one single life supporting planet exists. A coincidence you may think? Well I can tell you, that I don't think so.'

Spurred from her silence Abigail asked 'What are you trying to suggest Madame Dumond?'

'The very existence of the Earth, when you think about it, it is absurd, Abigail, entirely illogical, in an ocean of emptiness and vast tract of nothingness. It shouldn't exist, but it does! People get out of their beds every morning oblivious to the fact that their lives make no sense. Why are we here? Do they ever stop to ask?'

She paused for effect than added, 'The Earth is a quality control facility my dear. Created with the single purpose of testing each and every one of us,' Monique narrowed her eyes and stared at the blue sphere, which was imperceptibly turning through the ink black of space.

'But surely you're mistaken Doctor Dumond, why would they need to test our souls? Who are they anyhow?'

'Why the Arcs of course, my dear and the one you refer to as God,' Monique replied.

Abigail Perdue and Mike Roberts both shared a look of wild disbelief.

'But why do they need to test our souls?' Abigail asked for the second time.

Monique took Abigail's hand in hers, she felt envious at the touch of her fresh young skin, 'Because a human soul just happens to be the greatest power source in all the Universe, my dear. We are the ultimate building blocks, Abigail. Millions of souls bound together release immense waves of raw energy, powering absolutely everything you can see. The planets, the stars, solar systems, everything.'

'So you're saying that the Heofon is like one great big battery pack for the Universe?' Mike guffawed.

'You can choose to disbelieve me if you wish Mister Roberts but without the constantly rejuvenated output of human Souls everything would simply go out.' Madame Dumond transformed her disapproving glare from the young man back to an insipid smile for Abigail.

'But how do you know this?' she asked.

'Because they told me, well more or less,' her mouth creased with a harsh cackle of laughter.

'They create souls which are then sent to the Earth to be tested, inserted before birth in the flesh and blood capsules that we call our bodies. The soul lives a lifetime determined by however long its host body can survive, no matter the duration. If it lives a good existence it is deemed to be Puresoul, which they can use. If not it goes around again to iron out any kinks so to speak. And if it proves to be bad, well that's another story.' The old lady made a telling gesture with a single index finger pulled straight across her throat.

'A new soul has to be tested to be put through a quality control process before it can be moved into the Heofon. That is why each of us is here, and the only reason why that planet exists,' she said, pointing towards the Earth, that had but moments before seemed so wonderfully tranquil and welcoming but which after Monique's startling revelation, had inexplicably taken on a perceptible degree of menace.

Monique stood up with some stiffness, declaring herself to be a little fatigued, she excused herself leaving the two young people in a state of alarmed confusion. But before leaving the Mirador, she said in a soft, controlled voice, 'We need to look out for each other in this place, be supportive of one another.' She let her words sink slowly in before continuing. 'The Arcs don't care about us, so we need to mind each other well, my young friends. I'm sure that you'll agree that it makes common sense.'

'Stick together?' Abigail, was unsure.

'Yes my dear, in the voting on Judgment Day. No matter what we hear about a soul, we must ensure that we vote to send everyone to the Heofon,' Monique said. 'Well, all except that Arab fellow, he's a shady character,' she laughed in a disturbing manner, 'We could leave him out!' A much more defined smile, like an ugly pink slash cut across the retired surgeon's face as she retired.

Mike and Abigail made their way back out to the gardens. Abigail was still reeling from what Monique had told them.

'Mike, do you think she's telling the truth?' she asked with a tremble in her voice.

Since she first arrived in Stasis, Abigail had quickly found her feet and had rejoiced to discover that there was an afterlife. The sight of the great gathering of souls in the Heofon only served to reinforce her contentment and she had quickly lost any concerns about her past life on Earth. Now all that had been shattered by the ramblings of the mysterious French doctor.

'Don't take any notice of her, Abigail. She's bat-shit crazy! A harmless old kook,' Mike wanted to comfort her, but inside, he also was discommoded by the doctor's revelation. The problem as he saw it, was that some of what she'd to say added up. Life on

Earth - it simply has no context when you compare the billions of empty lifeless planets and moons.

Why Earth? Why did we exist? Certainly her belief that our souls are some sort of energy is as valid an explanation of anything he had previously heard in church or otherwise.

That's the big problem, Mike thought. *It always sounded too much like a fairy tale, all of us being children of an all-powerful, benevolent creator, waiting for us to come to a Heaven where hosts of winged angels play harps and stuff like that. It's nuts!'*

Yet here Mike finds himself, his consciousness still exists after the death of his body. That he has a soul is now beyond doubt. No matter how absurd the idea, there is an afterlife - well Stasis anyhow - and whatever happens in the Heofon, if you get there. From what he could see, the sphere that had come blazing across the sky, gave off only a sense of harmony. Mike decided to keep an open mind, perhaps he'd ask Maryam when he next had the chance to speak with her.

As they went out into the gardens, Abigail and Mike spotted a new face. A tall man was sitting on a bench, arms positioned on his knees, his head cushioned between both hands. He looked up at the young man and good looking woman who had stopped a couple of paces from where he was sitting.

Maybe things are beginning to look up! Per smiled.

'Hello there!' Mike approached the stranger and offered his hand in greeting,

'Mike Roberts, from the United States,' he said cheerfully.

Oh Christ not a bloody yank, is there to be no end to my torment, Per concealed his innermost thoughts and delivered a well-practised smile. 'Hello to you. Per is my name, I come from Sweden by way of Australia.'

Abigail stepped forward and also offered her hand and a warm smile,

This guy is quite a dish.

'Abigail Perdue, from England. Call me Abbie if you like.'

Abigail's reaction surprised even her, she never asked people to call her Abbie and yet here she was acting like a schoolgirl and going all doe eyed in front of this very attractive man.

'I do indeed like, Miss Abbie Perdue. Now aren't you the most delightful looking thing that I've seen since arriving in this Godforsaken place.'

The Scandinavian stood up to his full height and towering over the young woman, took Abigail's hand while touching her forearm. 'Delightful indeed, there must be a Heaven after all. I'm convinced,' he gave Abigail his best smile but his eyes read lechery.

Oh don't tell me he's a creep! The smile quickly evaporated from her pretty features as she promptly extricated her hand from his.

'So, how long have you been here in Stasis?' Mike asked.

'Not very long, I hope to get back to my old life soon.' Although speaking to Mike, his eyes never moved from Abigail.

'You want to go back! Are you nuts? Why would you not want to go to the Heofon?'

Per flopped onto the bench and stretched his long legs out. He placed his hands behind his head, adopting a nonchalant pose. 'It simply doesn't suit my plans Abbie. I belong down there. I don't want to be up here flapping around, wasting my time. It would be far too boring - well unless it was with you, of course,' he said, with a wicked smile.

She didn't return the sentiment. *Gosh, he has great teeth, pity he's such a dick!* Abigail was even more annoyed at her clumsily attempt to flirt with him.

What was that about? Abigail had never been much into guys. She tried to make eye contact with Mike, to urge him to move away from this odious person. But Mike was engrossed with the new arrival and continued talking,

'So what happened to you Per? What got you?'

Per decided to indulge the American for now and replied 'I think it was a great big set of boobs actually.'

'No way!' Mike laughed uproariously.

'It's true!' Per allowed himself a little chuckle. 'I was enjoying dinner with this gorgeous creature, the very last thing I remember, is looking at her breasts. Next thing I know I'm in this fucking place, meeting with some aggressive bloke with a bad accent and a crew cut.'

Mike and Abigail shared a look of surprise, *Marcus!*

Mike was having too much fun to stop, 'The sight of them big boys stopped your old ticker eh? Then bang!' he laughed slapping the Swede playfully on the back of his head.

'You sly old dog you.'

Per was close to losing his temper with the younger man, mostly for his injudicious use of the word old. He reminded himself however, of what Marcus had told him,

You will be judged by a jury of your peers. Perhaps this young clown is part of that jury, so better to keep my cool for now and make some friends,' he reasoned.

Abigail was a little surprised at Mike's barrack room banter with the Scandinavian but she put it down to the alpha-male environment where he had worked at the fire house. She hadn't known him very long but she was sure that Mike was a good soul at heart. She still felt confident that she could rely on him.

This new guy however, he was completely full of himself, *A big set of boobs huh? Serves the arsehole right that he got a heart attack! They can mark that down as another uncharitable thought!*

'So do you have this freak Marcus as your Advocate?' Per asked.

'No, we've both got a nice lady called Maryam,'

'You're lucky there mate, he's a nasty mongrel. Can you believe he actually punched me? I didn't think there would be any violence permitted in Heaven. I'm going to make a complaint to his superiors,' Per added sullenly.

'We're not in Heaven, Per. We're in some sort of limbo in between,' Abigail interrupted.

She's a bloody know it all too! Granted she's a looker but she's going to be a royal pain in the ass.' Per imagined. *Still, if she's the*

best of what's available around these parts, I may have to let it slide.'
He smirked and decided he'd enough of the American and the
pretty woman for now.

'If you folks don't mind, It's time for my yoga,' Per announced.
Abigail raised a brow at their rude dismissal, but was actually
quite glad to be going, she grabbed Mike gently by the arm and
said, 'Come on Mike, let's take a stroll by the river.'

'Yeah okay, nice meeting you buddy,' Mike automatically held
out his hand but was left hanging as the Swede arranged his limber frame into an asana - a complex yoga posture. He merely
grunted a curt reply 'Yeah! See you around pal.'

When they had moved far enough out of earshot, Abigail who
had unconsciously linked arms with Mike said, 'What a first rate
tosspot that guy is!' She laughed but felt a rage surge through her.
She couldn't help but to glance back but he was staring directly
at Abigail and gave a little wink.

'I caught you! Can't resist a bit of Per now, can you darling?'

'Dickhead!' she huffed.

'You're being a bit unkind Abigail, or shall I call you Abbie?' Mike
teased her.

'I am not! He's a…., oh I don't know, but that guy is not a nice
person, I can tell. You can call me Abbie if you like? Abigail sometimes makes me feel so old.'

'We'll never be old Abigail! If you don't mind, I'll stick with that.
It's a fine name. We're as old now, as we'll ever be.'

'Gosh, I hadn't thought about it like that?'

As they walked along the banks, they fell deeper into conversation. Mainly it had to do with their most recent meeting with
the Advocates. Maryam had explained about the new Protatori
they'd been assigned. She'd not appeared as assured as usual, so
as soon as she'd left, Abigail collared Marcus.

'So what's the problem with this Prince fellow?'

Marcus pulled up a chair, collected his thoughts and said,
'The Prince is actually an okay guy, a bit pedantic, but not so
bad. However, some of the more mischievous souls on Stasis

have stuck him with a rather unfortunate nickname - The Angel of Death.'

Mike and Nader exchanged a disconcerted look.

'Listen up, he's not an Angel, he's not even a Prince. They call him that on account of a book he wrote back in the day. It was quite infamous, you might have even read it,' Marcus said.

'So why Angel of Death?' Abigail pushed.

'Because Niccolò has had an unfortunate run of 100 straight, where a soul got sent down to Gehenna!'

'What?' came a chorus of groans.

'It's just a coincidence. With the numbers here, it was bound to happen, sooner or later and it happened to him,' Marcus deadpanned. 'The powers that be wanted to avoid any fuss, so they promoted him sideways. He ended up running the Prot-school but as Maryam explained, with Ishamel and Robyn returned to the host and a real shortage of Advocates, he's been pressed back into service. But look guys, you don't have to worry, just do as we've told you. You don't have to worry about him.'

'What about the other one, Jocelyn?' Nader asked.

Marcus got up from his chair without speaking, headed to the exit, turned and said, 'You didn't hear this from me okay? Jocelyn Wu is a bit of a bitch. But hey that's just my opinion.'

The memory of the Advocate's words still rang clear as a bell. Mike remembered something that Lou had told him, 'There are some flaws in the system. You could get through an entire life without doing much wrong, but don't mean you've got a kind heart.' He also mentioned that the Arcs are always looking out for souls that have particular skill-sets, talent spotting for new Advocates and Prots. Both were so engrossed in their conversation, that they didn't hear the soft footsteps that had gained on them.

'My friends, how are you, on this glorious day?'

They looked back in surprise and for a split second there was an awkward silence. Something about this young man's presence left both Mike and the normally chatty Abigail, speechless.

'Do you mind if I stroll along with you?'

'Not at all, please do,' Mike had once more found his tongue.

'So what do you do here, Manny?' he ventured.

'I help around the place.' Although his response was vague, Abigail noticed that he answered with no hint of evasion or insincerity. Recovering her composure, she came straight out with what was on her mind, since the unpleasant meeting with the doctor.

'Is the Earth, just a testing ground for souls, Manny? Are we just some kind of batteries?'

Manny let his head fall back and guffawed, Abigail felt the soft burn of a blush race across her cheeks. His laugh was not intended to be hurtful and he noticed her discomfort immediately.

'Please forgive me, Abigail. I didn't mean to cause you distress. Your words, they caught me by surprise,' he apologised.

'Why don't we sit here for a moment and I'll try my best to answer your questions?' He pointed to a clump of flagstones set back from the river's edge. Manny was a striking man, although of average height and perhaps not conventionally handsome, he had a great smile and intelligent eyes, but there was something about him, charisma maybe? Abigail was unsure but felt completely at ease in his company.

'So please, ask me again?' he said when they were all seated.

'Is the Earth just some sort of testing ground for souls?' Abigail desperately wanted to know the truth.

'Okay let me see, how best to explain this to you? When a soul goes to Earth, each one is placed in a human body - its soul carriage. The Earth was created for man and woman and yes to be honest with you, living life on Earth as a human, is a form of test,' Manny noted the cloud of doubt that was beginning to form over Abigail's pretty features.

'Please don't be scared, Abigail. A soul is the most precious entity in the entire Universe. It was created in the Heofon and wants to return there.'

'If I may offer you an example, do you know that feeling of unrest you would sometimes get, when you were on the Earth? Even when you had all you needed to be content, you still felt like there was something missing. That was your soul, longing to come home.'

Abigail was listening carefully to every word, but still appeared pensive.

Manny continued, 'The soul retains a memory of where it was born. Like a salmon always returns to the river of its birth, the soul always wants to come home too. I can assure you there is nothing sinister about what happens, it's an entirely organic process.'

'But why if we are born in the Heofon, do we not just stay there?'

'That is perhaps the most pertinent question Mike. Why do we not all just stay in the Heofon after we are born? Why go through the trials of a human life? Well the short answer is, when a soul is created it is a completely unknown quantity. There is no way to tell if it is Puresoul or not.' Manny leaned in closer and spoke reverently.

'A soul is basically a combination of love and intellect. But it is a delicate balance. To achieve Puresoul, the balance must be just about right. To place an errant soul in the Host could cause a propagation that could lead to irreparable failure. As such every soul must go through a highly supervised process of quality control. What a person does during their time on Earth is recorded - all of it,' he added.

'So these bad souls are what exactly?' Mike asked.

'An errant soul gives itself away by the seriously bad choices it makes in the course of its human life.' Manny looked directly at Mike. 'Decisions made in the certain knowledge that it may hurt people. When these deviant souls lose their carriage and come to Stasis, what they have done is established at their Judgment, where they are frequently sent back to try again, in different circumstances.'

'But if they are deviant, why not destroy them right away? By sending them back, won't they just harm and kill other innocents?' Abigail asked. 'Are you not just postponing the inevitable?'

'It is of little consequence in the overall scheme of things, Abigail, they may kill the human body with their misdeeds, but they cannot destroy another soul. Quite often with a life on Earth, there are many influencing factors; how a child was raised, its experiences, good and bad, they colour and contribute to its actions.'

Manny's voice has a quality that held your attention. 'A child who grows up in dire poverty, may learn to steal merely to survive, that doesn't make it bad. Circumstances matter. Children who were raised in warrior societies such as Spartans or Samurai, they believed that to die in battle was the most honourable death achievable. That did not make them deviant. So everything needs context.'

Mike and Abigail found themselves nodding in agreement.

'So now I'm sure you'd agree, it's only right that you should have more than just one chance to get home,' he smiled.

Mike looked across at Abigail, he could see that Manny's words were hitting their mark, in the way she inclined her head with the points he was making. He had also impressed the young American.

'So the meaning of life is simply to get through the tests, be good and you get to go home,' Abigail shrugged.

'Not quite. That is only the path, Abigail. The meaning of life is love. And the way to that meaning is through acts of kindness, as it always has been.'

'What happens then if we're sent back? Will we remember anything of our time here?' Abigail was intensely curious about this, as she reckoned it was a real possibility for her.

'A returning Soul is immersed in the waters of the Lethe, it will forget almost everything of its previous human life and its time in Stasis.' Manny explained. 'A small semblance of memory may remain, but this will manifest as dreams for the most part. Although sometimes you have people who feel they are in the wrong body or even the wrong sex. It may be that they retain a trace of their previous life.'

Manny reached out and took Abigail's hands in his, 'You are a child of the Host, Abigail. Do not be afraid of anything.'

Abigail looked at Manny and tears began flowing. Not from feelings of pain or sorrow, but of joy at finally knowing what her life was about, even if she is made to forget, for now at least she knows it has meaning and it is beautiful.

'I would like to return home to the Heofon, I want this with all my heart,' Abigail whispered.

'And you will, Abigail. One day soon you will be safe home for all eternity.' And with that he stood up and bade farewell. 'We will talk again soon.'

'Manny?'

'Yes, Mike?'

'Is my sister in the Host?'

'No she's not. Mike, Karen was too young when she passed. She has a new life now. She's a really good person.'

'Why does the Creator allow kids to die?' Mike could no longer restrain himself from asking the question that had been burning in him since his arrival in Stasis.

'Mike, you shouldn't!' Abigail tried to intervene.

'No it's quite okay, Abigail. He needs to know.'

'Mike, the human body is one of the most marvellous of the great creations. It is incredibly complex, every single one unique and none exactly perfect. Sometimes one of the billions of cells can mutate in a dangerous way and cause sickness. Sometimes that sickness cannot be repaired and the soul will pass here to Stasis.'

'But know this....' he paused briefly.

'Sickness is not a test for the person who suffers but it is not the will of the Creator that any child should die. It was not placed on them or was not by design. Nonetheless how the person who cares for the sick, how they cope, well that becomes a test of their spirit, even if it came about by fault and I know that such tests are very harsh.'

He stayed silent for a moment, contemplating his next decision. 'Follow me. I'd like to show you both something.'

They could scarcely believe their eyes when they saw him raise a hand vertically, then across horizontally, before repeating the motions in the opposite direction. And with these simple movements Manny had somehow formed a door where they had previously just been air. At his bidding, they followed him through the portal.

Both covered their eyes, shielding them from the change in light. They were inside another colossal hall, similar to the one they had arrived in. Yet this one was subtly different. There were no reception desks or lines of people threading their way through. In its centre was a clear domed tunnel that extended the length of the concourse.

The furthest reaches of the glass-like-corridor were in darkness emerging gradually into a more crepuscular glow.

Abigail gasped. From the gloomiest part of the tunnel emerged a figure, a small blonde haired child in pyjamas. She was holding the hand of someone in a human form, but both Abigail and Mike knew instantly that it was not human.

'Angels,' Abigail whispered in amazement and turned to look at Manny.

'Yes,' he smiled.

'Welcome Sarah,' he said as the child passed by. The little girl gave a wave of her tiny hand. She was about three or four years old and was smiling radiantly. Her guardian, who had a female form, turned her head towards Manny. She didn't speak but inclined her head in acknowledgement. She was almost luminescent in her appearance.

Serene and perfect.

'The souls of children just know,' Manny turned to address Abigail.

'They are completely unafraid when they arrive here. They know they are safe, that it's okay,' he explained.

'Where are we?' Mike asked. He couldn't help but imagine his own sister passing through this strange place.

'Limbus Infantum. It is from this name that you got your word, Limbo. But there is no Limbo for children. They are cared for briefly by the guardians and then they go back to start again.'

Abigail was touching her face and palms against the tunnel as one then another young child passed from the darkness into the light. Some were small babies carried in arms.

Abigail felt like her heart would burst. 'There's no need to be sad, Abigail. These children are loved, without sickness or pain and will have the chance to start a new life.'

'But what about their families? If they go back they'll have new parents, and they won't remember the ones they had, the ones who'd loved them,' Abigail felt close to tears.

'They will know them in the Heofon. Know them and love them for all eternity, like atoms that attract others. I promise you. Do not grieve so.'

Abigail waved at a small boy who was happily bounding along, his guardian barely able to keep up with his enthusiasm. The boy smiled and waved back.

'We should go. The Seraphim are not overly keen on humans being in this section,' Manny headed towards a door. Abigail and Mike followed behind unable to speak another word.

Abigail when she considered this later believed that Manny has brought them there, only because they were both singles - with no kids. No parent she felt, would have the heart to stand in Limbus Infantum.

Mike opened the locker and caressed the guitar. A wonderfully made instrument, solid spruce top and rosewood neck with mother of pearl inlays on the frets. He sat it across his knee and stretched his fingers over the fretboard in a series of rapid arpeggios. It was perfectly tuned with a nice, not too low, action. His dad had taught him his first chords at the age of twelve and Mike had practised almost every day since. He couldn't help thinking of his pop and the sorrow he must now be feeling. He felt an intense stab of anguish.

He remembered the little girl in Limbus Infantum and he could picture Karen, his beautiful kid sister, coming through the same transparent tunnel, with her guardian watching over her. He missed her terribly and now she was back on Earth.

'As long as she is okay, then it's okay,' he had been repeating this like a mantra, ever since he got back.

Monique had until now, avoided opening the locker in her cell. She was mortally afraid of what it might contain. However curiosity getting the better of her once more, she gave into temptation and immediately regretted that she had.

She recoiled in shock on first sight of the only object inside - a framed photograph of six children, all smiles and pretty hair. *How could they do this to her? It is too cruel.* Monique grabbed the photo to her chest, slammed the door shut and fell slowly to her knees. She let out a keening sound that came right up from the pit.

Monique knew she wasn't an easy person to like, her dedication to her craft, the time spent constantly improving her skills had left her impatient with people who were not inclined to better themselves.

After all what she did was for the benefit of all mankind. Her techniques would be learned by student doctors all over the planet, who will in time improve on them, continuing man's constant march towards increased scientific knowledge. She may not be the warmest of souls, but she was a good person, she fully believed that. She would try to make friends here, but it's never easy for an old woman.

She was born the only child of a successful Jeweller named Bertrand Dumond and his wife Margot. The family lived in a large apartment on the Invalides Eiffel Tower. This exclusive address - one of the most elegant in all of Paris – is situated in the seventh arrondissement. The gardens of Champs de Mars extend through the neighbourhood but Monique confessed to her childhood being somewhat lonely in a city that was slowly emerging from the war.

A studious girl she'd set her heart from an early age on becoming a medical doctor. Always openly ambitious, she remained unsure throughout her life if that was a blessing or a failing. Her early years were uneventful until the tragic death of her beloved

Papa from cancer of the oesophagus, brought on no doubt from many years of pipe smoking.

Bertrand's jewellery business on Rue de Rivoli had been a profitable enterprise and after his passing, the money that accrued from its sale was more than sufficient to keep Margot and Monique in a comfortable lifestyle for years to come. But her Mama, retreated into herself, becoming reclusive and no longer caring for the company of friends and neighbours.

The corporeal wilting of Margot Dumond ironically corresponded with the blossoming of her daughter who had been accepted to study at the renowned Sorbonne. Monique's drive and ambition propelled her to the top of her class and while not a conventionally handsome woman, her razor sharp brain and acerbic wit did get her noticed.

A thoroughly modern woman of the times, Monique had her fair share of lovers including a fiery and hot-tempered affair with one of her professors. All were short lived however and some more unkind soul might claim that her partners were changed in direct proportion to the advantages that they could offer Monique.

Nevertheless she conducted her affairs and her life in general with the utmost discretion and secrecy. Parisian polite society never got a sniff of scandal regarding her public demeanour.

It was in the circles and echelons of the city's elite that the increasingly well connected young woman moved with the ease of a serpent in the trees. She confessed a lingering sadness that she spent little time with her *Mama* throughout this exciting period of her life.

She'd been greatly disturbed during one of her infrequent visits that her mother had shrivelled further through lack of nourishment and had progressed into early stage dementia. The now fully qualified, Monique had her consigned to a care home. To be fair she spared nothing in making sure that she was provided for, but that care would be provided by someone else and not Monique.

The young doctor was now at a delicate stage of her development, fully immersed in her post-degree studies and her progress towards becoming a surgeon. She exhibited a special interest in reconstructive surgery. There is no doubt that Monique worked hard to gain what she had achieved in life. The body of work involved in her study and the erstwhile attentions of two possible suitors filled every moment of her days and nights.

Fashionably thin, she'd cut an impressive figure, attired in black, at her mother's well attended funeral and her more than modest inheritance and rising star meant Monique had finally arrived. She'd had two lovers during that period – Albert - a slightly older, newly promoted University Professor and Alain - a dashingly handsome, army officer who had regrettably limited prospects.

Both suitors were kept carefully apart, each blissfully unaware of the other. Alain was undoubtedly the more accomplished lover but in the end she opted for good natured Albert, who although a little portly did make her laugh. It helped that his family had access to the prime movers in French politics.

Monique and Albert were married ten months later in the very same Saint Madeline Church where more than forty years later, she was to pass from her Earth-bound life to Stasis. Theirs was a childless marriage by design. Whenever she found herself feeling broody something deep inside Monique reminded her that, it was not a good idea. Besides, there were the parties and her career to consider.

Per had opened the locker in his room when he'd first arrived. Inside there was nothing. It was just a big empty box apart from an old tarnished mirror attached to its back wall, it's coating cracked with a thousand spidery lines. In an undamaged section he took in the reflection of his trim and tanned body.

'You must be the best looking dead guy ever!'

Once he had gotten over the shock of being in Stasis, the Swede began analysing his situation. It was one of his great strengths, being able to compartmentalise stress and isolate problems and using logic to overcome or resolve them.

He was certain of one thing - he did not want to go to the Heofon. He was having far too much fun on the Earth. He would plead his case to return. He figured that most of these saps would be begging to get through the Pearly Gates. So a request to go back is likely be unusual. *Who knows, they might agree?*

In the meantime he had better use all his guile and charm to get on the good side of the other suckers. After all, Per was well aware, that he'd done many things that he was not so proud of. But he wasn't a bad guy either, was he?

Why did they put an empty locker in here anyway? What use is it? For each day all of the new arrivals awoke to find a fresh set of clothes laid out for them.

When they arrived back in their cells, the bed was made up and the used clothes had been taken away. *It was like staying a top class resort, but without the booze and the chicks,* he snickered.

Per realised that there was not much time left before the Judgment, but maybe there was enough to get to know that posh wench a little better, before he heads back.

Man this will be some story to tell over brandy and cigars. But he knew he'd never tell anyone, they'd only think him insane. His rambling thoughts were disturbed by a rap on his cell door. He opened it to find a stocky, grey haired black man standing outside with a tray of food. The same guy who'd disturbed his meeting with the Advocate.

What the hell was his name again, Lenny?

'Your evening meal Mister Anderson,' he said cordially but without a hint of pleasure.

'You can leave it over there Leon,' Per pointed to the table feigning disinterest.

The man laid the food on the table and turned to leave the room without saying a word.

'Thanks Leroy,' he sneered as the waiter closed the door behind him.

'Well now, what do we have here?' Per lifted the metallic cover. Underneath was a lightly seared tuna steak with tender stem broccoli. *Not bad,* he thought. His mood improved further on noticing a carafe of a blood-dark full bodied wine. Per was an unabashed wine snob who enjoyed the best of vintages. He slowly poured the red liquid into the glass and took a sip, letting it run a across the tip of his tongue, checking the level of tannin, grasping for the subtle nuances of flavour and appreciating the bouquet.

It was magnificent, pure velvet, a first-rate Grand Cru Bordeaux, was his educated guess.

A decent looking bird to seduce, and a great bottle of wine. Not too shabby a day after all. Maybe I should stay a while longer?

He swallowed another mouthful and once more checked his reflection in the mirror. He had been a fit man when he was alive but this new body was something else. He felt invincible.

I wonder if they'll let me keep it when I go back?

Abigail Perdue sat with her cello nestled against her thighs and resting on her calves. Only the modern cellos have the long endpin on which to balance. But the warmer tone from the older Baroque instruments in her view was unsurpassable. She had played for what must have been a couple of hours, but it was impossible to keep track of time here. Abigail could not shake the thought of the young man they had spoken to by the river. Manny had made her feel so convinced that all was as it should be. The old doctor's frightful admonitions no longer held sway in her heart. She was just a crazy old lady. *Mike is right.*

After all, Abigail had passed into the afterlife, it existed and it was good. The people who go into the Heofon would first shed their human skin, 'It is not painful,' Manny had assured her and there they would assume their natural form - *Puresoul.*

They'd be home. They'd recognise their loved ones, not by their familiar human appearance, but by the love they had for another during their life together - a unique and individual signature that every soul possesses.

Manny had also cautioned Abigail, that not every soul is deemed Puresoul on the first pass. Sometimes it can take several attempts and that it was from this occurrence, that some religions formed their belief in reincarnation.

Souls go back to Earth when they're not quite ready for the Heforn, but most eventually find their way home and they don't go back as creatures or animals. He had smiled when he said this. All living things have a proto-soul, the spark of life, and all should be respected, but only the ones that humans carry are immortal.

Abigail felt comforted after speaking with Manny. She replayed his words over in her mind. She wondered if he had been Jewish in his lifetime. Abigail readied her bow and resumed playing.

nine

When Per opened the door, he was taken aback to find the solid bulk of his Advocate standing there. 'What do you want?'

'I thought you might like a couple of hours back on Earth?'

Per's mood brightened instantly, 'Back to Earth, really? Yes indeed.'

'Well follow me then, Mister Andersson.'

Marcus headed to a doorway a short distance from Room 5. The Scandinavian followed just behind. It was a broom closet with a coat rail. He removed two heavy coats from inside and handing one to the Swede said, 'Put this on. You'll need it where we're going.'

Someplace cold! Maybe Sweden in wintertime, Per guessed.

Marcus closed the closet and both men donned the weighty fleece-lined jackets. He reopened the same door and indicated with a sweep of his free hand that Per should enter.

'What? You want me to go into the closet?' Per asked, sure that his Advocate was joking with him. 'Actually, you know what? I've changed my mind, I'm a little claustrophobic.'

Per folded his arms defiantly, although he'd learned to behave a little better in the presence of this Advocate, knowing only too well that he was a tough customer.

'Well, if you want to get back on Earth, this is the way,' Marcus replied, completely nonplussed.

Per's forced bravado crumbled. He desperately wanted to go, even if only for a while. 'Okay then!' he growled defiantly, pushing past Marcus into the cloakroom and emerging head first into a raw blast of Atlantic wind.

'What the f..?' Per was astounded. 'Where the hell are we?' He looked around to see his Advocate, step out from the doorway of a derelict lighthouse.

'Welcome back to Earth, Andersson.'

'You've tricked me Marcus! You evil prick. We're on a fucking rock in the middle of the fucking ocean, that's what you mean!' Per was furious. He placed both hands on his head and turned three-sixty, taking in his surroundings, utterly disgusted.

Marcus ignored his cussing and pushed past him, starting down along a walkway that ran the perimeter of this jagged wall of limestone that reared up sheer from the crashing swell below.

'What did you expect, Andersson? Cocktails by the pool, some dancing girls, maybe?' Marcus glared at the Swede who had rushed to catch up.

'Well dancing girls would be a vast improvement,' Per found his dark sense of humour overcoming his anger. But his Advocate who had turned to face him wasn't smiling.

'Listen up you asshole! You just don't get it, do you? In a matter of days you will be judged on your deeds and actions while you were here on the Earth. I've seen your file and it doesn't make for pretty reading. If I were you, I'd seriously start thinking about repentance.' Marcus turned away to continue down along the path.

'Well you're not me,' Per shouted after him. He was doing his level best not to be cowed by his Advocate, but the reality was he found him hugely scary.

'Besides,' he continued, 'Angels are surely not allowed to go around calling people assholes?'

Marcus stopped in his tracks, when he turned he had a half-formed smile, something between a leer and an ugly grin. 'They're not, I guess! Then again, I'm not an angel, Andersson. So I get to call you whatever I like. Now quit yakking and follow me,' he snapped.

Marcus increased the length of his stride as the sulky Scandinavian followed a few steps behind. Something seemed eerily familiar to him about this place, but only when they rounded the corner and he saw the automated lighthouse, did the penny drop for Per.

'I've been here before,' he marvelled.

He paused for a moment, checking landmarks in his mind, before scurrying once more after Marcus. 'Hey! Wait up! I know this place! Wait up!'

But the former Roman soldier kept moving down the narrow path hewn from the rock-face and didn't bother to reply. Marcus was struggling to find anything to like about his charge. The pathway plateaued into a wider space at the foot of a visible line of ancient stone steps. There were hundreds of them, peeking out from mossy ledges, like a twisting amphibian of damp glistening rock slithering up towards the high peaks.

Marcus took the steps at a steady pace but Per - who was fitter - overtook him, calling out as he passed, 'I know where this is, Marcus!'

The Advocate still didn't speak. They ascended this remote island in a silence, broken only by the occasional shrill call of an Arctic Tern that wheeled overhead in a series of acrobatic tumbles and dives. It was the only sound that accompanied the waves that threw themselves against this near vertical wall, falling spent into eddies of white water and whirlpools. A ceaseless turbulent assault that feasted relentlessly on the rock-face, carving out temple-tall arches and spectacular caverns over countless years.

Climbing up past a large jutting rock he remembered the way. A hundred more paces brought him to a stone wall with a crooked low entrance. He turned to see where Marcus was before ducking under. When the Advocate emerged into the long abandoned settlement, he found the Swede sitting alongside one of circular stone huts.

'You remember this place?'

'Yes, I remember,' Per replied.

Inside the abandoned monastery they were sheltered from the worst extremes of the wind. The clouds were parting just enough to allow shafts of sunlight to penetrate to the deep silver waters below. A real life weather phenomenon, lifted directly from some Hollywood Biblical epic. The Scandinavian stared out to the east towards a smaller, stubbier, mountain top that lay a half mile from his vantage point and some eight miles beyond that to the mist shrouded ridge of the mainland.

'We're in Ireland,' he murmured.

We're out on the Skellig Rock. He was about to ask Marcus why he had brought him to this wild and remote place but he was distracted by the sudden tap of a long forgotten memory.

My father brought me here when I was fourteen.

They'd stayed for a week in an old farmhouse rental a few miles from the provincial town of Cahersiveen, clung to the side of Sive's mountain, at the most westerly point of Europe, its forlorn fingers of headland crawling out into the ocean amidst a lingering pall.

They walked on the lush hills and deserted beaches, just the two of them, mostly staying in by evening playing cards, or strolling into town to purchase newspapers and magazines from the quaint bookstore that doubled as a grocery.

Per recalled it as quiet country with loud weather.

It rained most of the time. But on the second last day of their vacation, an explosion of sunlight subdued the persistent damp, bathing the landscape in rich chromatics of blue and green - seamlessly and perfectly intermingled. Once the cheerless shroud of mist lifted, it was no exaggeration to claim that this place sparkled like paradise.

Per remembered his normally distant father being ecstatic on that particular morning. Søren Andersson did not have many passions in life, but one he did hold, was the study of birds -ornithology. Birds captivated him. They took a boat trip together, father and son amidst a dozen or so other pilgrims who were travelling out in a little converted fishing boat with a Gaelic name; 'An Beal Bocht.'

The skipper was erudite and talkative. He had kept his passengers entertained with tales of this little-known place. Before embarking onto the island Per recalled they had circled the smaller rock - The Skellig Beag - home to 30,000 pairs of nesting gannets. The noise was horrendous, but he didn't care, as his father clapped him gently on the shoulder, excitedly calling to his son, the different names of seabirds that surrounded their little tourist flotilla.

He was happy, and to a young boy accustomed to a father not much given to outpourings of affection, this place seemed like heaven. It had been many years since father and son made their way up together, along steps formed by the bare hard hands of resolute men.

This vertical island was also awash with cute black birds with brightly coloured beaks, *puffins!* - another flash of recognition.

Per recalled great flocks of them, comical looking creatures toppling over the cliff face, flapping tiny wings in an effort to get airborne. There were no puffins here now. They won't be back until the spring. His father had told him that shortly after they're born, the adult birds abandon the hatchlings to their fate. To Per it seemed cruel but Søren had dismissed his son's sentiments as unmanly.

'Survival of the fittest, Per! It has always been this way in nature. You must make sure you're never weak. You must always be one of the strongest. You'd do well to remember that.'

'I never forgot it, *farsan*,' Per whispered the Swedish word for *Daddy*, as in his mind's eye he saw large clusters of baby black chicks bob over the wave tops.

'You are thinking about your father?'

'Yes. I am,' he answered. 'Where will he go when he dies?'

'He will come to Stasis like all others. He will be judged by his peers, as we all are,' Marcus replied stoically.

'I hope that cold old bastard gets sent straight to hell!' Per spat on the ground. The reverie and bonhomie briefly elicited, now gone.

'Hell is only a construct of man, Per. An actual place called Hell does not exist. It is a name given for what happens on Earth sometimes and to frighten young children. Men have always mixed up the message of the prophets,' Marcus rolled his powerful shoulders.

Per looked askance, 'So you're telling me there's no hell? No hell-fire and damnation?'

The Advocate didn't speak but moved his head slowly from side to side. He returned his gaze to the crashing waves, some several hundred feet below where they stood.

Per couldn't believe it, 'Fuck me, no hell! So what about this place called Gehenna?'

'Gehenna is not a place,' Marcus replied flatly. 'It's an instrument of destruction.'

The sudden knowledge that there was no hades roused the Swede from his gloom. 'Marcus, I have zero interest in going to the Host. I'm a creature of this world. I prefer it here.

Well not here, on this shitty little rock obviously, but back in civilisation,' he shouted over the noise of a siren gust.

'I'm a people person!'

That Per managed to say this without even the slightest hint of irony, amazed the usually tacit Advocate.

He strolled around the remote hermitage, hands buried deep in his pockets, stopping next to a small burial area. In a handful of inaccessible outposts such as this, a religion had clung on precariously during the dark ages. Scribes copied scripture, beautifully illuminated, onto vellum manuscripts. Their skilled hands inked animals and complex patterns on every page.

Here in this very place, small bands of scholarly monks, painstakingly translated the sacred texts from ancient Greek and Latin, and being mere men, added a few words and ideas of their own. Per wasn't aware that his direct ancestor had also landed on the Skellig - The Earl of a Viking raiding party which sacked the monastery and murdered the Abbot.

Marcus had planned to tell him about his relative – knowing well he would be impressed by his warrior lineage. However as he was being such a petulant prick, he thought better of it.

'Do you think they'd let me come back? That's what I really want,'

Marcus stared long and hard at Andersson as if studying a singularly unique being. 'To be honest, I don't know the answer to that. I must admit it's not a common request.'

What about this?' Per was pointing at a flat granite headstone inscribed with the names of two young children who had perished on the Rock, both sons of a lighthouse keeper.

'What an unimaginably stupid place to raise a family,' he chuckled.

Marcus lunged at the Scandinavian, grabbing the taller man by the lapels. He tugged the screaming Per to the cliff edge and tossed him over to be dashed on the sharp rocks below. But it was only what the Advocate imagined himself doing. Instead he bit down on his lip, *You have no empathy for your fellow travellers, Per Andersson. You risk much.*

Having had all he could take of the Swede, for now, Marcus yelled, 'It's time for us to go.' Then he vanished inside the doorway of the largest of the stone huts.

What if I just stay here and don't follow him, what would happen?

But Per was smart enough to realise this was not the time of year when boats made their visits. He would be stranded, the island his prison. He would most likely starve to death or die from exposure.

Of course when he died he would go right back to Stasis and find himself once more in front of that ugly grinning bastard - Marcus Agrippa. He couldn't win.

He took one final glance up at the giant limestone fingers that stretched above him towards the heavens. He took a deep breath and followed through the portal.

The jurors had received a message to assemble in Room 5. At the allotted time they arrived to find the Advocates already waiting.

'Welcome to you all,' Maryam gave to each, a warm greeting. 'Tomorrow morning after your breakfast meal, you will assemble here for your Judgment in the celestial chamber. We've asked each of you to come here today in order to clarify the process and to further explain what is expected of you... Marcus.' she pointed towards her colleague. Marcus stood up straight and read from a document that he was holding.

As they listened to his words, there were clear signs of growing tension. Mike repeatedly ran his hands through his hair. Abigail tapped her foot in time to silent music that her mind was composing. Nader held his face in his palms, desperately longing for one last smoke. While Miyu sat, anxiously interlacing and unlocking her fingers. Of all these souls only Per and Monique sat impassive and stony faced.

Marcus continued, 'The Judgments will proceed in the following order.' He read from the prepared list – 'Per Andersson. Miyu Tanaka. Michael Roberts. Abigail Perdue. Nader Khoury and... Monique Dumond.'

Nader let go a long exhalation. He'd been unconsciously holding his breath. So this was it, all were reminded that their time on Stasis was nearly up. Tomorrow is the Judgment Day.

Maryam resumed speaking, 'When you enter the chamber at the appointed time, please take your seats from left to right in the same order as your names were called by Marcus.'

'On each seat you will find a slate and a piece of chalk.'

'Very high-tech!' Mike wisecracked, in an attempt at levity, but no one reacted.

'When your name is called, you will seat yourself in the Judgment chair in front of your peers,' Maryam explained before her colleague once again took over.

'At this point, your Prot will be revealed to you. This part of the proceeding may be uncomfortable for some. However you will have a chance to speak afterwards and if necessary, launch a defence against anything that was said to your detriment.' Marcus continued, speaking calmly in even tones but the stress in the room had clearly been ratcheted up. 'No questions will be allowed at any time from the jury. This is most important. Remember it,' Marcus looked directly at Mike.

'At the conclusion of all testimony, when all have been heard, you will be asked to record your vote. But do not display what you have inscribed, until instructed to do so. You will not seek to view what anyone else has written,' he warned. 'You will keep your slate face down until such time as you are called on to reveal your verdict.'

Beads of sweat were cascading from Nader's brow and even the normally unflappable Mike felt trepidation when considering the enormity of what they were being compelled to do - to pass Judgment on another's immortal soul. It was a daunting task.

'At the conclusion of all six testimonies, you will be called one by one to reveal your vote.' Marcus had resumed his instructions.

'To record your decision on the worthiness of the life lived by each soul, you may inscribe only one of the following choices...'

Now Maryam began speaking, this routine was carefully choreographed and something that both Advocates had completed on thousands of occasions. Nonetheless they performed their duties with a calm and solemn efficiency, well aware that all the assembled souls in Room 5, were hanging onto each and every word.

'In the case of a soul, who in your opinion after all given testimony, has lived a life that amply demonstrated, evidence of compassion, empathy, mercy, charity and most importantly love, you may inscribe the word Heofon.'

'In the case of a soul, who has not demonstrated sufficiently the aforementioned qualities but who nonetheless showed characteristics of goodness, who applied kindness and responsibility and who demonstrated promise in their ability to improve further, you may inscribe the word Reborn.'

Anxious eyes peered nervously around the room at each other, making impassioned pleas for mercy on their own behalf. Then Maryam got to the crux, 'In the case of one, who has proved bereft of these essential qualities and who has debased their soul with repeated acts of violence, depravity or the wanton taking of human life, you will inscribe the word Gehenna.'

That lone word struck a succubus terror, draining the blood from each of the six. Here everlasting life was at hand but could also be annulled. And as it was to be based on actions that had already taken place, there was nothing that could be done but wait and hope.

Maryam gave them a reassuring smile attempting to soothe the visibly frayed nerves of the majority. By now even the Scandinavian and the feisty old surgeon were looking troubled.

'Also in attendance will be the Presiding Justice. In the current rota, this will be Gideon.' The role of the Justice is to facilitate the hearing.

Gideon had been a judge during his time on Earth. Abigail recalled from what little scripture she could remember. *I hope he was a fair one.*

'There will also be the Protatori,' Maryam added. Mike was bursting with curiosity to know more about these people, but he knew better than to ask, and kept his own counsel. Nader was befuddled, he would much rather be judged now, to have it over and done with. All this waiting was insufferable. He wiped another fall of moisture from his brow.

'In conclusion, the Arc or Arcs - for it is not unusual for two or more to attend - one must remember that their word is absolutely final. Okay any questions?' Maryam asked.

Mike's hand shot up, 'What happens if someone is going to the Heofon. When does it occur?'

'Almost immediately,' Marcus interjected. 'You will not be returning to your cells.'

Maryam confirmed, 'After all six verdicts have been cast you will each be brought through that door.' Maryam pointed to the plain, unadorned doorway at the back of the room.

'The Protatori, what are they like?' It was Abigail's turn.

'Well it depends,' Marcus shrugged. 'Protatori di Luce means 'Bringer of Light.' The Italian vowels rolled off his tongue and had the effect of softening his tone. 'They'll shine a light into the recesses of your soul and discover all your secrets and nasty indiscretions.' Marcus clumsily attempted to inject a little bit of humour but none of the jurors were in the mood.

'Marcus!' Maryam chided her colleague.

'Sorry, ahem...where were we?' he coughed into his hand, 'Ah yes, the order was tasked directly by the Creator, so they can be a little overzealous in their appetite for the truth. Therefore be warned, they can be tricky, if you have something to hide.'

Maryam ended the meeting.

'You won't know which Prot you've been assigned until they stand up, but by then you'll already be in the chair. We have spoken in private with each of you, about what we think may happen. Stick where possible to our advice and good luck to you all.'

There were silent nods of agreement across the floor.

As six very anxious souls prepared to leave the chamber, some to return to their cells, others to walk in the gardens, all were preoccupied with the same thought - *What will happen to me tomorrow?*

Before leaving Per addressed the Advocates and to Marcus in particular he said, 'You did tell them that I choose to go back? I don't want to go to the Host,' he stood tall and proud with his arms folded across his chest. 'I am here against my will, Marcus, and I want my old life back.' Maryam glanced at her colleague who rolled his eyes in irritation.

'Okay then, if I can't have it back, then at least give me a new one. I want to get back to the Earth!' He flashed a most insincere smile before vanishing out of sight into the corridor. Maryam found the whole thing quite amusing.

'The nerve of that guy,' Marcus fumed.

'Oh come on Marcus, you've been doing this long enough to know there are thousands like him, who pass through the Stasis blocks.'

The Advocate sighed, 'Yes of course, you are right, Maryam.'

And she was indeed correct. On any given day on Earth there are some 150,000 deaths as a daily average. All of these pass through one of the Stasis portals. Added to that each day the Heofon oversees an average of 300,000 births. Close to a third of that total are souls being sent back to be reborn. Every single day.

Of course that means a hefty case load for all who work on Stasis. With the vast rise in the population of the Earth, Maryam had been arguing diligently for an increase in the number of Advocates. Something the Arcs had promised to consider.

Maryam gathered up her files and headed for the door. 'I'm off to my next meeting. See you later. Oh I almost forgot, there's a meeting of the Sacred Council taking place. Most of the *Revered* will be here, so be on your best behaviour, okay!'

'Yeah okay,' the former Roman legionary replied. He tapped his fingers on the desk and decided to pay an old friend a visit.

Miyu Tanaka had found herself a new hideaway on Stasis, The Great Library. The world famous library of the Abbey of Saint Gall was designed by a soul who had once been reborn. Peter Thumb managed to recall what he had seen in a dream, and replicated the Great library of Stasis, in all its decorative splendour. Miyu learned of this from the friendly librarian, an elderly Chinese gentleman. She had loved the Mirador most of all, but she had begun to stay away as she was afraid to encounter the peculiar old French woman. The things she had to say were strange and unnerving. Something about her prophetic words made her feel particularly anxious.

Miyu adored books and here there were countless volumes and manuscripts. Enough books for whole lifetimes of reading. Li Er had been the curator for a very long time and he knew the location of every single book by heart. The long-lobed Li Er was delighted with the young girl's presence. So many new arrivals hung around fancy, high-end places like the Mirador - forsaking the simple pleasure and harmony of a perfect library.

The Japanese youngster parsed the great books in a state of wonder and recorded her thoughts and observations in a notebook that she was rarely without. She loved to roam between the tall rows of hand carved shelves, running her fingers across the spine of each bound and catalogued volume. She had so much love for books and writing.

Miyu's academic development was not quite formal, having been forced to quit school much earlier than most of her peers. However her sharp intellect and constant reading resulted in her attaining considerable knowledge. On the flip side it had also fostered an element of rich fantasy in the mind of the impressionable young domestic.

Li Er had been the custodian of the Stasis Library for many centuries. When he was asked to take this position for an unstated duration, he had accepted. He had seen so many souls pass through the doors of his library. A compassionate and learned man, he knew a good soul when he met one and this sad-eyed young woman was certainly a good prospect. The wisdom to see was something that came with the passing of years, and Li Er had achieved a wondrous age. Despite this ability however, he had failed to see a glaring flaw - Miyu had suffered fragile mental health and in the last months of her life she had begun to hear voices.

She smiled at the old librarian, she would be happy to stay awhile in such a magical place, this splendid hall of learning.

Monique, was walking in loops around the obsidian stone, quietly mumbling to herself. She was startled to hear a greeting called from behind her. Turning she saw the Advocate Marcus approaching.

'So Johanna, where shall we go?' Marcus used her given name, only in private.

'I'd like to go back to the same place. One last time, please.'

'After you Madame,' Marcus reached out and opened a seamless doorway, almost invisible in the black rock.'

'Thank you,' Monique said, stepping through the doorframe that stood in Stasis and alighting in the busy square of Marien-platz -Saint Mary's Square. The heart of the city of Munich, is the main square in the old town. The city's name derived from the old High German *Munichen* meaning - by the monks place. It was named after an old order of Benedictines who founded a settle-ment on the broad river Isar, north of the Alps.

Monique looked up at the gilded golden statue of the Virgin Mary, atop a crescent moon denoting The Queen of Heaven. It crowned the eleven metre tall Mariensäule column, from which their narrow portal opened out.

'Saint Mary's Column! How apt.'

Marcus manoeuvred his large frame with some difficulty through the slender opening. Conveniently they had arrived at exactly midday, as all eyes in the square were focused on the Neues Rathaus. Its famous Glockenspiel was chiming and its charming animatronic figures were holding the crowd's attention. Marcus stepped down gingerly between two of the figurines that guarded each corner of the plinth. Each *Putto* a symbol of what the city had once overcome. The Lion represents War, the Cocka-trice - Pestilence, the Dragon - Famine and the Serpent - Heresy.

Marcus' strong arms made light work of lifting the frail doc-tor safely to the ground, before he gingerly clambered over the balustrade. The Roman officer scrambled after Monique who was clearly delighted to be on familiar ground. She quickly blended in amongst the throngs of sightseers.

'Ah Munich, my great love,' Monique declared. 'You have no idea how young it makes me feel to be here.'

Marcus did not say anything but walked a pace behind the old lady who was heading in the direction of the gothic new town hall. Monique twirled, a wild look of excitement sparkled in her eyes.

'What fun I had here when I was a young woman, Marcus, oh the important people, the power, the glamour," she sighed. 'You would have been impressed with me then. They were the very best of times.'

The Advocate thought of another empire that he was more familiar with. 'You'll have to tell them about what you did, Monique.' Marcus reverted to her current identity.

'Oh, but must I?' she pleaded. 'And do indulge me Marcus and call me Johanna while we are here. I've always preferred it to dreadful Monique.'

'Okay, Johanna, but you will have to testify to your crime. There is no other way,' he said sternly. 'You know the Prots will bring it up.'

'I'll think on it,' she swirled and danced to music only she could hear. Impervious to the sniggers and stares of onlookers she continued stepping and twirling about, her arms afloat in mid-air, dancing with a partner that no other could see.

To hell with them all, she thought. *We shall party while we can.*

The younger, prettier Johanna had so loved her time in Bavaria. It seemed so recent that it had left an indelible impression on her, but now she had the inescapable feeling she might not ever see her beloved Munich again. So she kept on dancing and she intended to stay dancing until the music stopped for her.

Marcus Agrippa, her reluctant Advocate, looked on. *Her dancing days may be over sooner than she thinks.*

ten

Maryam was intent on catching up with Mike who she found sitting by the lower fountain - a deliciously ornate creation complete with chariots and maidens porting urns. He was there with Abigail and Nader Khoury.

Abigail was still somewhat unsure about the fisherman, but Mike had kept insisting that Nader was a good guy and that she should give him a chance. He did look different lately. He seemed to have softened somehow, become less suspicious of the others and slightly more talkative. For the moment she was prepared to give him the benefit of the doubt, but she struggled to shake off her own lingering suspicions after the surly first impression he had made. Mike had been telling Nader about what Monique had said.

'The Adam and Eve story - that's just metaphor. It wasn't a rib that Adam got. It was a tiny piece of the Creator instead - the soul. When a newly minted soul goes into the world, it's like a seed that's been sown. Instead of sunshine and rain, it requires knowledge and love to grow. When it fills up on these, its capacity expands exponentially and returns to the Host, hundreds of times more powerful than its original state.'

'She says our souls are reaped like a crop at harvest time,' Abigail added.

Nader was agog, 'Ebn El Sharmoota,' he cussed in Arabic

'Yeah, son of a bitch,' Mike agreed.

'Do you believe her?' Nader asked.

'I don't know what to believe? I think she's maybe not quite right in the head. You know what I mean?'

'Mike!' Maryam called down to the trio. She was standing on a ridge that overlooked the fountain. 'Mike, something is happening right now that I think you might like to see.'

'Oh really, what's that?' Mike was instantly curious.

'Your funeral, Mike. It's taking place right now.' The three souls breathlessly made their way up the embankment, towards Maryam.

'I know some people find it overwhelming to see their own cer-emony. But your colleagues are putting on quite a show. They're giving you an impressive send off.'

'Yeah I'd like to see that, Maryam. Is it okay if my friends come too?'

'Mike, I'd rather not, if it's okay with you? I'm going to head back to my cell. I've an important meeting tomorrow,' Nader joked. But the reality was that Nader Khoury was acutely reminded that his own human body was lying unrecovered on the seabed, his family unable to give him a proper Muslim burial. It surprised him how unsettled this made him feel.

'Yeah, sure buddy, not a problem. Catch you later, yeah?' Mike turned to Abigail, 'Are you coming?"

'Yes, I think so,' the Englishwoman replied.

The Advocate led the way to a room located back in the block. 'This is our auditorium, one of several.' Maryam politely held the door open for Abigail and Mike.

'After you, please.'

Inside, it resembled a small theatre with four concentric lines of polished-pine chairs, all facing towards a large curved screen. 'Please sit,' Maryam said, taking a seat alongside Mike. 'The images you're about to see will be in real time, are you ready?'

Mike took a deep breath, 'Yeah let's do it.' He braced him-self for whatever was to come. The theatre lights dimmed and an image began to appear on the screen, at first a little bit fuzzy but then within seconds becoming resoundingly clear. Mike was the first to realise what they were witnessing.

'Jesus H Christ, it's our ladder truck!' Mike looked at Maryam, 'I'm sorry, I didn't mean to cause offence.' But Maryam did not look concerned or offended.

On a bright-blue skied New York day, a large fire truck was fully visible, progressing slowly through streets lined with onlookers. On its deck was a specially adapted carriage on which a dark oak casket carried the last remains of firefighter Michael Roberts. The coffin was draped with his nation's flag and had Mike's leather helmet placed on top. On either side of the truck marched an honour guard replete with white gloves and number one dress uniform.

'Wow, pretty neat guys!' Mike cried, who at first was enjoying the spectacle. Behind this converted hearse was another sight to behold. More than 1,600 firefighters, men and women of Mike's department marched four abreast in long lines of navy blue. A lone piper walked a few paces ahead of the cavalcade, playing a lonesome lament. In front of the honour guard was a grief-filled gathering of family and close friends, headed by Mike's father Joseph and his older brother Francis.

'Jeez, they must have left him home on special leave,' Mike explained in hushed tones that his brother served with the military overseas. The screen shot zoomed in. 'Dad!' he groaned quietly. It was tearing Mike apart to see his father march behind a coffin yet again.

I just wish I could tell him that I'm okay. That everything's alright for me. Tears were perilously close to rising above the puffy-rose-levies of the young fireman's eyes. They were also flowing freely across the cheeks of his new friend, Abigail.

'No man should ever have to bury his child,' Mike said, 'My Dad, he's had to do it twice. That's not fair!' He felt a blistering surge of anger arise up inside, he glowered at Maryam. Her expression remained unruffled. Mike wanted to yell, 'Why are you doing this to him? My Dad's a good man.' But he held his tongue. After all none of this was her fault. Mike knew that. She was a demonstrably kind lady who had done everything to make him feel comfortable since he'd arrived in Stasis.

Maryam lowered her gaze from the screen to the young fire-fighter. 'It may seem heartless to you, Mike. I can only tell you that your father will almost certainly go to the Heofon when he passes. It's not my decision to make, of course, but I have seen his file and you're right, he is a good and decent man. You should be proud of him.'

'So why have they put him through this, Maryam? Why? His wife, his only daughter, and now his son too! That's too much for anyone to bear.' The New Yorker wanted an answer.

'I can only say that when he goes to the Host. He will be with your mother again. And with you, should you go there, and I hope that you will Mike,' Maryam patted the young man's arm. 'If you do, then you will know everything, you will understand it all. When it's your dad's time he will remember nothing of his current pain, great though it is. The Host of Souls is the healing salve for all the suffering in the world.'

Abigail Perdue on seeing Mike's father immediately began thinking of her own dad, Jacob. She scolded herself for putting him to the back of her mind. In her excitement at discovering an afterlife, it had consumed almost all of her waking thoughts. But now seeing her friend's funeral, she grieved for Mike's dad, for the pain of his loss and she also mourned for her own poor father. The visible expression of a life shattered, plainly evident on the face of sixty three year old Joseph Roberts. He was trying hard to keep it together, despite the crippling wave of emotions that wracked his once strong body.

Joseph was of course so proud of his son, who died on duty, trying to save the lives of others. Nonetheless at this moment he was utterly and completely bereft. Mike was his little boy, in spite of the fact that he had towered over his dad for many years.

'Why did they have to take Mikey?' he mumbled to himself over and over. 'Why take my little boy too?' Joseph Roberts' once implacable faith in his God, was now hanging by the flimsiest of threads.

'I can't watch anymore of this. I'm so sorry, Mike,' Abigail rose quickly and wiped at the wet lines that streaked down her face. She made her way from the auditorium, out into the Elysian Fields. Finding the nearest bench, she flopped down and immediately burst into tears. Mike stayed put, unable to rip his eyes away from the rows of black boots, polished to a lustrous sheen. Moving together in lock step - his firefighter brothers and sisters formed up behind his company truck in a mark of respect for their fallen comrade.

Mike himself had once been part of an honour guard for a fallen brother. But he never for a second thought he would be the next to go.

Nader had returned to his cell and as was his habit he began pacing around the room. There was not much he could do, his Advocate had said, but to fall on the mercy of the Arcs. He had made some real bad choices and those chicks were coming home to roost. He thought about his early days in Beirut. A good family life and a bright future looked distinctly possible. But oh how subtle fate spins around and points in a new direction, where woe-begotten men are compelled to follow.

His father's decision to accept the refinery job and to move his family to Algeria, became the catalyst for total change in the Khoury's world. The teenage Nader had always been a good student. He understood the necessity of working hard to get on in life. Effort was inextricably linked to positive results, but the murder of his father -Abdullah - by rebels, completely stymied any chance he'd ever had. It was simply not to be. Allah did not will it so. There was only one choice available to him. He would assume his role as *head* of the family. He would provide for their needs, his mother and his two sisters. Doing whatever it takes. He didn't complain. He just rolled up his sleeves and got on with it.

Nader married young, increasing the demands on his limited income. He had done so many things wrong but believed that he had matured in recent years and had settled down to his responsibilities. Nader doted on his children and it was with an eye to their future that he first took the 'easy' money. But once in, it's near impossible to get out, if one was so inclined.

The people who operated the smuggling ring where not the kind to overlook any perceived slight. To refuse later would be to have out his own family in harm's way, something that he would never contemplate. The best he could do, through all of this unsavoury business, was to conduct his end of the bargain with dignity. What happened to the people later was not his concern. He could not afford to think of them and he didn't - well not until he arrived in Stasis, where for now, an endless parade of unnamed faces appear in his mind – a vulgar plethora of poverty stricken souls, who had only the desire to live a better life.

He still had no idea if any of the people in the lifeboat had survived. He was certainly sure that anyone who had gone into the water was drowned. Captain Nader Khoury understood that he must accept and face the consequences of his actions.

Per had spotted the anguished form of a woman, weeping on one of the many benches that dotted the gardens of Stasis. *A damsel in distress, no less.* Per immediately hurried to comfort her. *A little bit of Per to soothe away the pain,* he joked.

He confidently approached Abigail, who had begun to compose herself.

'I'm sorry to see you so distressed. May I help at all?' He sat down alongside without waiting for an invitation. 'Come now, it's not so bad here, is it?' his soft tone maximised to imply a sense of compassion, a quality in which he was utterly lacking.

'It's not about this place, I just miss my Dad.' On the mention of her father, her emotions got the better of Abigail again. Per produced a Kleenex from his pocket and gently wiped the tears from her eyes. 'Thank you,' she murmured between heavy sobs.

'It's alright. Why don't we take a little stroll, it will help you feel better. Besides we haven't been properly introduced,' he stood up and offered a manicured hand.

'Okay,' she replied, and took his hand hesitantly. Per liked the feel of the English woman's skin, smooth but not too soft. There was strength in this girl he believed. 'Abigail is such a pretty name,' he lied. In truth he thought it drab and old-fashioned, lacking any sense of colour or vitality. But he did notice that little Abigail was not without her charms. She had a nice slender figure but was also sufficiently curvaceous in the right places,

A good rack too. Well-put-together Little Abbie has a very decent chassis.

'So tell me a little bit about yourself,' the smooth talking Swede fired the opening salvo of his well-practised patter. Abigail began recalling the major events of her life, her family, the death of her mother, the rise up the ranks through various youth orchestras, until she finally landed a coveted seat at the Philharmonic. She had up until the time of her death, been on top of the world. Abigail rather soon copped that this guy was vaguely distracted whenever she spoke, as if he was just going through the motions without being the slightest bit interested in the actual topic. Abigail Perdue was on this occasion at least, quite a good judge of character.

As they strolled on through the gardens, that topic deftly moved onto a subject much closer to the Scandinavian's heart – Per. It was a tour de force, his first million made while still in his twenties, wife briefly...kids briefer and then Per, Per, Per!

Now Abigail could not deny that this man was devilishly handsome, very tall, piercing blue eyes and he obviously kept himself in very good shape, for his age. She could see how some girls could go for that, but this guy was completely in love with himself. There was clearly no other thing he would prefer to talk about. *If he was made of ice cream, he would lick himself,* she suppressed an impish smile. But Per, sharp as ever, had noticed.

'Ah, you're smiling again, that's good Abbie. I'm so glad I could help to cheer you up.' Misreading the signals, he placed an arm around Abigail's shoulder.

'You know there's really no need to be lonely here, honey. Especially, as we have these fine, new heavenly bodies.' He raised an eyebrow suggestively.

Abigail slipped her shoulder free from the tall man's grasp, but he was quicker to react, clutching her tightly by both arms. 'Come on now little Abbie, you're not so shy are you?' Per was determined to have his way, whether Abigail liked it or not. He had been too long without a woman. Overpowered, she could feel his hot, stale breath rasp against the side of her face. Abigail freed her arms just enough to grab tight onto the Swede's shirt. She pulled him closer to her chest. Believing she had relented - as he knew she would - he smiled in anticipation of the moment. But one second later an expression of sharp shock and pain crossed his face and his eyes began to water.

Abigail Perdue had taken several self-defence classes, essential she believed, for any young lady who had to make her way around the seedier neighbourhoods of London. In that split second when she pulled him to her, she'd raised her right knee up with a powerful jerk. It connected her patella with the yielding, tender flesh of his now painfully swollen testicles. Per took a sharp intake of breath, dropped his hands automatically to belatedly protect *his jewels* and felt the full brunt of a sickening wave of nausea. Abigail took the opportunity to escape her assailant and moved back in the direction of the Stasis complex.

Per shouted after her through gritted teeth, 'What's the matter with you bitch? You a lesbian, or something?' Abigail stopped in her tracks.

'Indeed I am Mister Andersson, but even if I wasn't gay, I'd have more sense than to be interested in a Neanderthal such as you!' She spun on her heels and went on her way, feeling suddenly a whole lot better.

Unbeknownst to Abigail, the spectre of a barrel chested man stepped out from the shadow of a large oak tree. 'Everything okay Mister Andersson? Anything I can help you with?' Per was on his knees still cupping his manhood, 'What the hell are you looking at?' He rose up and hobbled in the other direction and making his way slowly and gingerly, he swore.

I'll pay you back on Judgment day.

'What the hell indeed! Good for you Miss Perdue. Good for you,' Lou chuckled.

'Okay, okay, I'm coming. Will you please stop that infernal racket?!' Marcus had been grabbing a long overdue nap in the Advocates room, snoring loudly in a reclining chair, he was none too happy to be woken abruptly by insistent loud knocking. He raised himself up slowly, his joints stiff, lactic acid in his calf muscles causing an incipient cramp. He tucked in his shirt and answered with bad grace. He was surprised to see Nader Khoury standing there. The man clearly agitated was almost hopping on his toes.

'What do you want Khoury?' he asked querulously, wiping sleep from his eyes.

'Forgive me for disturbing you, Marcus. Lou told me I might find you here.'

Marcus just stood there staring, unable to believe his bad luck to be woken from such a pleasant dream for this. 'And..?' he asked grumpily.

'You see, I have been visited by the Prophet.' Nader's voice quivered.

Marcus stretched out his arms and let rip an impressive yawn, he turned back towards the comfort of his armchair, saying, 'Which one?' He didn't invite Nader in, just left the door ajar, which Nader took as invitation. Nader closed the door behind him. Marcus was already sprawled back in the chair, legs akimbo.

'I'm sorry?' Nader did not immediately grasp the question.

'Which Prophet, Khoury? We have lots of them pass through here.' Marcus growled in bad humour. He did not appreciate having to repeat himself. He was immensely tired and although he liked Khoury, he wasn't in the mood for him now.

'*The* Prophet!' Nader repeated, wondering what was wrong with this stupid man.

Marcus looked back at him uncomprehendingly through bleary eyes.

'*Our* Prophet.' Nader tried again, bowing his head in reverence as he spoke.

'Oh!' Marcus perked up a little. 'Why didn't you just say so?'

'I...I did,' Nader mumbled.

'Never mind, so what did he want?' Marcus asked. He was mildly curious. The revered didn't often visit with penitent jurors.

'I was sitting in my cell, thinking about my family, when I looked up, he was there before me. In all his magnificence.'

'You were probably only dreaming, Khoury.'

'Of course, I admit it's possible I was dreaming, but if it was a dream it was very vivid.' Nader was still utterly stunned by his experience.

Marcus knew that quite a few souls who arrived in Stasis found the experience too much to handle and some became gradually unhinged or delusional. Could be that the fisherman was one of those. Although he did recall a bulletin, something about The Creator's plans to reach out to mankind again. Rumour has it that another will be sent to the Earth soon - to remind those who would wisely choose to hear. Of course Marcus knew that in Stasis 'soon' could mean anytime in the next 1,000 years. He cringed, knowing only too well how men have responded to the other messengers, quite often with staggering brutality. No man knew this better than Marcus.

Nader was still talking while just staring into space, almost trancelike...

'.....told me to have courage tomorrow. That the truth will prevail and not to fear or hide from the truth as it is the only path to Allah. I was so moved. I was really nervous about facing the Prots but I'm no longer afraid. The Prophet will watch over me,' Nader was smiling as he recalled this momentous event. Then the smile cracked and tears rolled freely across his heavily lined face.

'I miss my children, Marcus,' he blubbered. 'I miss my wife, my family. My greatest task was to protect them and in this I have failed.' Nader Khoury had never let another man see him cry, but he couldn't hold it back. Yet no man would see it this time either. When he stifled his sobs and wiped his eyes, he looked up to see Marcus was soundly asleep, his large head thrown back, mouth open, occasionally muttering something in an incomprehensible language. There was even a small dribble of drool leaking out from the corner of his mouth.

Nader laughed with genuine relief that his friend has not witnessed his loss of face. He had not belittled himself in his eyes. He got up and left the room quietly without another word.

eleven

JUDGMENT DAY

Abigail moved her head in gentle rotations, easing the tension that had kept her from restful sleep. Her Day of Judgment finally arrived. The full ramifications of the life she had lived would be put before others, who would now have the power to condemn her soul or to grant eternal salvation. Abigail was surprised at how nervous she had become as the hours counted down to her final appointment in Room 5.

She was certain that she could rely on Mike to support her and she feels she could count on the votes of Miyu, and possibly Nadar too - thanks to Mike's influence. Yet she could not know how the old doctor would vote. She also realised that her recent encounter with the seedy Swede meant he was unlikely to do her any favours. *But that game plays both ways*, and she too would have her say in what happened to him.

However the order of Judgment had already been announced and as he was to go first, it would come down to Abigail to make the opening move.

What if I support him with my vote? she agonised, *Then he goes and double crosses me?* The possibilities were multitudinous and truly maddening.

'Screw him,' she said. If she got the votes of Mike, Miyu and Nader, then surely it wouldn't matter which way that snake and the doctor voted. It could even come down to Arcs.

The name 'penitent.' That was another detail that Marcus included. They would be referred to as penitent, while in the chamber. Abigail was certain that even the most hardened of criminals would be wobbling at the knees at the thought of what was to come.

On the night stand adjacent to her bed sat a bowl of freshly cut, lightly poached pear, and a large cup of cappuccino, both untouched. This was usually her breakfast of choice, but on this occasion she couldn't bring herself to place even a single morsel between her teeth. She rose, walked to the bathroom and washed her face, taking her time. She examined the girl that stared back at her from the mirror. She was not unattractive and she had lived a very fortunate life. She knew this. Abigail had gone through every detail of her life that she could think of, every significant moment, cause and event that had shaped and informed her twenty-six years.

'Abigail Perdue, did you live well enough? Did you love enough?' she whispered but the answer she would have liked was not forthcoming. She was confident that she has not done anything barbarous except for the one incident of which she was so unsure, but Maryam had prepared her well for this. Nonetheless it was too late now to fuss over things in the past. She dressed quickly, took a deep breath before plunging into the unknown. She realised she was leaving her cell for the very last time. She was sure going to miss that cello, which she'd placed reverently back on its stand.

Waiting, outside Room 5, were Mike Roberts, Per and the gloomy doctor. Mike embraced Abigail with a reassuring bear-hug, asking politely how she was doing and offering words of encouragement. Monique proffered a skeletal hand in greeting, but said nothing more than a simple, 'bon chance.' Abigail wished good luck to her too.

The Scandinavian gave only a sullen scowl in her direction before moving his blue eyes down to something more interesting on the floor.

'Can we not go in yet?' Abigail asked Mike.

'It appears to be locked.'

Morning all,' came a jolly voice from the end of the passage-way. It was the genial Lou, carrying a huge bunch of keys. *That's odd?* Abigail thought, she hadn't noticed a keyhole in the door of Room 5 before, but there was certainly one there now.

'Sorry to keep you waiting,' Lou said, as he selected one of the larger iron keys.

Lou pushed and the substantial bulk of the new door relented and opened. The room was in complete darkness. 'Just a moment,' Lou called out. 'I'll get the lights.' The grey-haired Attendant hummed tunelessly but seemed even more cheerful than usual.

Must like Judgment day? thought Mike.

When the room was illuminated it astonished the four peni-tents. All were struck speechless. Room 5 bore no resemblance to the place where they had their first meeting. The plain, unadorned chamber was no longer discernible as any sort of room that Nader had ever seen. They stood facing a parallel row of tall white stan-dards that fluttered lengthways on ornate silver poles, although there was no evident breeze.

The pennants ran straight at first then branched out after six yards or so to the left and right sides, forming a crescent shape, in which six empty seats faced a single white chair. Lou had caught their astonished stares and explained, 'Welcome to the celestial chamber,' he gestured with an outstretched arm that all should quickly move to their allotted place. On a small dais set behind the Judgment chair, were two benches. One was dead centre, with the other slightly to the right. This sombre setting was framed by a further row of billowing banners.

The Judgment Seat sat stark and imposing to the front of the juror's seats. Both improvised aisles lead to identical arched doors. But what was most remarkable to the jurors was that Room 5 no longer had any walls. Both the entrance and the portals were set against an open expanse of azure sky and slow moving domes of feather light cloud, like the type you see from an aircraft window.

Per sat back with a carefree expression on his chiselled features, betraying none of the anxiety that clawed remorselessly at his gut. Miyu felt tears well in her eyes which she resolutely kept lowered to the ground. Per glanced down by his leg where he saw a slate tablet and a single stick of chalk. He stole a look at the young English woman, just inside his peripheral vision, *Now you bitch, I'm going to have fun voting you down.*

He salivated at the prospect and found himself distracted from his more immediate problem of how others were likely to judge him. Per gazed around, mulling over which way he would vote. He could wait to hear their testimony and then decide, but he'd already made up his mind in most cases.

That shifty Arab and the dyke, they're both going to Hades, he reckoned. *The annoying American, I think we'll send him back, the gook girl and the old battle-axe too. So that means I'm sending no one to the Host today,* his malevolent thoughts provided him with scarce amusement. *To hell with them all, they probably don't deserve to go there anyhow!*

Mike sat ramrod straight, but he'd clenched one fist in the other to stop himself from fidgeting. His eyes gazed down repeatedly at the dark grey slate. To Mike, it was like waiting for an exam to begin. Abigail was quietly reciting prayers in an almost soundless whisper, prayers long unsaid but remembered from a childhood that was not so long ago. She spared a moment to include a prayer for her ancestors, her relatives who had gone before her, and those loved ones left behind. Abigail had chosen not to pray for most of her short adult life, a fact that she now bitterly regretted.

A sudden loud clank at the door revealed Marcus and Maryam. They entered with reassuring smiles and nods for each of their clients. Nader was especially pleased to see Marcus. His presence brought him a laconic feeling of calm. With his head lowered, the fisherman tried to muster any shred of courage that remained to him.

'Allah's will be done,' he quietly intoned over and over.

Monique sat staring into space, funnelling red coral rosary beads at rapid pace through paper-skinned fingers. Her face unworried but her hands betrayed her false serenity. Miyu felt her tears dry up, a sensation of tranquillity came over her, *Where is that coming from?* She glanced around to see who had spoken the words that had given her such peace. She was unsure of their origin, but she knew at once, that they were *divine*. She could not prevent a full smile from lighting up her features.

The voice had whispered to her in soft, gentle tones, 'Fear not my child, I am with you. You are in my care.' She couldn't tell if it was male or female, but it was undoubtedly kind. Miyu carefully watched her fellow jurors, but could not discern any sign that it was speaking to any of them. *Perhaps I've finally gone crazy?*

On account of all she had seen here on Stasis - so many wonderful and magical things - she guessed that the voice was probably real. She raised her face and glanced up at the clear blue sky and she physically felt it - a ray of sunlight brushed lightly against her face, she was not alone - the Room God was with her now.

Maryam and Marcus did not speak to any of their assignees but sat together at the Advocates bench, dressed in their familiar business attire but carried none of the files and folders that they were usually burdened with, by now they knew their clients intimately.

Nader observed the solid bulk of Lou, standing arms folded beside the entrance, a broad grin spread over his face. Although there were two empty chairs, Lou remained standing. He caught Nader's eye and winked in recognition. Nader had also noticed the rapt expression of Miyu, sitting just three places from him. *What in hell is she staring at?* he wondered, instantly regretting his not very tactful choice of words.

Is she having some kind of apparition? It struck him why he had thought it bizarre - he realised that he had never seen Miyu smile. *First Lou, and now Miyu? This cheerfulness must be infectious. May it be my turn soon.* But he waited in vain for his stomach to stop churning and for any sensation of joy. It only served to increase his suspicion that things may not go well.

Lou ported a large leather-bound book to the front of the dais - a huge tome that he placed reverently on the pulpit. Maryam had told Abigail in an earlier conversation that it was called the Book of Life and Death. All verdicts were noted on its pages before being sent for posterity to the Stasis Room of Records. As the Attendant moved back to his position by the door the natural light in Room 5 began to alter perceptively. All eyes was drawn to the same sturdy portal where Maryam and Marcus had entered, it opened once more admitting two distinct figures, one male and one female - an angular dark haired man with a sharp face and long aqualine nose was followed by a good-looking Asian lady, both were laden with a stack of files. *The Prots!* Abigail guessed correctly.

They took their seats at the Protatori bench and Jocelyn smiled unnervingly at the jurors. This was a ruse that Marcus had warned them about. Jocelyn's methods were often unorthodox and mind games were part of her repertoire. From behind the Prots came an older man, with a great long beard - the Presiding Justice, Gideon. He took his place on the bema, addressed them all in a fatherly manner and explained that he was on a raised platform only as it allowed him to see better. He had after all, reached a great age. It implied no other meaning or rank, 'All,' he said 'are equal in this chamber.'

Unheralded a bright phalanx of amber rays crisscrossed the sky. Mike thought it looked like something from an X-Files movie. But the reality was far greater in its significance. Hidden out of sight by the dark mahogany panels, whatever was the source of the shifting lights, appeared to move steadily closer. The arched portal opened once more, but without any help from hand or body. The temperature in the room fluctuated and a fleeting tingle of cold moisture gambolled upon the skin of all present. Nader was not looking at her now, but only Miyu seemed unperturbed.

Monique was the worst affected, biting nervously into her bottom lip, drawing blood, as if she dreaded what was coming her way.

A tall, blonde, man, or more accurate to say a form resembling a man, came through the portal. Donned in a white silk garment, draped down over slender shoulders, light did not fall on his features but appeared to shine outwards from an energy source within. Maryam stood, followed by Marcus, who indicated with an inconspicuous gesture that the penitents should rise. The blonde figure was seated, although in the more natural light of the chamber his hair was more silvery-grey. He was followed by another - a powerfully built black man - garbed in similar attire. His facial features gleamed like polished ebony as he made his way to the lectern.

A third figure alighted in the chamber, a female anthropomorphic form. Marcus and Maryam exchanged a look of genuine surprise. She had plaited dark hair, wore the same simple garment, but hers was lilac purple and tied at the waist with a thick cord of majestic silk. She ascended with graceful motion to her place on the right side of the Archangel Gabriel.

Nader was completely mesmerised by the beings before him, they seemed to radiate an authority that was unspoken and unquestionable. His Advocate had forewarned him that sometimes two Arcs may attend a Judgment, but there were three Seraphs here today.

Nader struggled to recall his childhood lessons, *Seraphs*, meaning literally, *The Burning Ones*, but he couldn't be sure. Each of the beings shimmered softly in and out of focus, the retinas sent their image via the bundles of optic nerves, where they appeared in his mind like a mirage in the desert heat, real yet unsure of their providence. Real they were and none could lift their eyes from these immortals of the Heofon. Maryam walked to the platform and bowed, a sign of respect returned by all three Seraphs.

'Welcome our children, all souls of the Creator. We are gathered here in the presence of the Host's representatives,' she said with devout reverence. 'The Archangel Gabriel - Chief of the Angels,' she proclaimed. The silver-grey crown lowered in acknowledgment.

'Michael - Keeper of the Book of Life and Death,' she called out. The Arc at the pulpit inclined his great head.

'Ananchel - the Angel of Grace.' Maryam continued, indicating the female Seraph who bowed towards the jury. Mike Roberts had never seen such a beautiful woman in all his life, the sight of her had prised his mind from his worries. Marcus on the other hand was rather surprised by her appearance. Ananchel was better known as the Arc's main scout. *Must have some new talent in her sights,* he mused.

'For the Judgment of the six penitent jurors assembled here on Limbus Stasis, Gideon will preside,' Maryam bowed her head courteously. The bearded man raised his right hand in recognition. Without any further ado, Gideon announced, 'Per Andersson, you will step forth and be judged.'

The Swede unfolded his long limbs to stand, as his Advocate, Marcus, stepped smartly forward. Marcus had done this task thousands of times, but nonetheless was always awed in the presence of the Arcs. He believed it would be easier to face a marauding band of Visigoth raiders than take the full direct gaze of an Archangel on his human form. Marcus indicated to Per that he should approach and be seated in the Judgment chair.

THE JUDGMENT OF PER ANDERSSON.

Per stopped in front of the dais and bowed to the Presiding Justice as Marcus had instructed. He strode to the chair with a lofty expression. Maryam couldn't help but be impressed by his composure, however fake. He lowered his long frame gracefully onto the Judgment seat but something changed the moment he adjusted himself into a more comfortable position. Per was overcome by a sensation of falling through space. He gripped the arms of the chair and clung on desperately, his face contorted in fear.

His false bluster completely dissolved. This simple chair had a very strange effect on some men.

The Archangel Michael turned a page in the book and nodded to the Protatori bench. Niccolò rose and approached the trembling man. 'Per Oskar Andersson, born in the city of Malmo, Sweden, to parents Søren and Frida Andersson?' he enquired.

'Yes.' The Swede grudgingly admired this man for how well looked, attired in a powder grey, immaculately tailored suit.

'You were a rather wealthy man I believe?'

'I had a fortunate upbringing with regards to material things and yes I made some money in my adult years,' Per replied truthfully.

'But yet you were a sad child, starved of affection by your father,' Niccolò stated.

Abigail gasped audibly when over their heads appeared an image contained within an invisible oval perimeter - ten feet in length and with perfect definition. All those assembled, could plainly see a boy, obviously a much younger Per, sitting alone in a room full of toys. Per was not prepared for this portrayal of his childhood and he hesitated.

'In your youth, you got into quite a bit of trouble, Per. You were expelled from a number of schools and in a last ditch attempt to provide you with an education, your family packed you off to an institute in Switzerland.' As Niccolò spoke, exactly what he had described was accompanied by a continuous stream of visuals, to which the eyes of the jurors were drawn like moths to the flame.

A very handsome, ash-blonde youth was seen, at times smiling, laughing on occasion but always retaining a look of oblique distance. Miyu discerned cruelty in his laughter. The Prot carried on, 'During your late teens, you were quite promiscuous in your sexual behaviour? You made three women pregnant, arranged and paid for abortions. Then in your twenties you suddenly got married?'

I married a German woman. It was a juvenile impulsive mistake. I fathered two daughters, Pia and Franziska.' At the mention of their names Per turned his attention away from the jurors to look at the projected image - a vision of two beautiful girls cast upon the ephemeral screen. Two children who had been left without a father's presence had at least been blessed with his exceptional good looks.

Per gulped, as he struggled to keep his self-control, 'Patti and I divorced within four years, but I continue in regular contact with my girls.' He gave an abashed smile towards the Protatori. It appeared to Niccolò, that this man, didn't appear to be contrite, but instead was reciting by rote. Niccolò abhorred insincerity. He didn't need to push on his questions, he'd just feed this proud fellow enough rope, allow him to coil it around his neck, then pull it tight, at the right time. *He'll discover the error of his ways!*

Although privately Niccolò prayed this man would not be for Gehenna, his unwanted record was a millstone on his neck. In a long career he'd had to send enough souls there for a myriad lifetimes. He had no desire to send more.

Why don't they get it? All it requires is a little kindness to their fellow man! he reflected wearily, but he still had a job to do and the integrity of the Host was paramount.

Miyu, Abigail, even Monique were transfixed by Niccolò, his patient demeanour as he listened to Per who had carried on talking animatedly, '...I moved to Australia and made a considerable fortune, which enabled me to indulge my passion for surfing and keeping fit.' Marcus snickered. He could hear the pride evident in the register of Per's voice, when he'd begun to talk about his soul carriage.

Miyu looked on, as this giant, white man squirmed in the chair, his life played out for all to see. He was plainly a conceited individual, but she felt mostly a sense of pity. He'd taken advantage of a lot of girls - young women, just like her, but he was also a human being, a person without love in their life.

The Swede, oblivious of her thoughts ploughed steadily on, '...Sadly during my final years on Earth, I had a succession of girlfriends, who I didn't always treat with the proper decorum.' Again Per stuck to the script that his Advocate had helped him to prepare. He paused for a breath. As he was about to resume, a devastating image materialised that stopped him dead in his tracks - Per as a young boy. He looked mortally afraid. An older man, possibly a family member, appeared in shot, he wore a twisted sneer on spittle frothed lips and as he approached the boy he began undoing his trouser belt.

Per visibly blanched.

'Is your treatment of women in any way connected to your sexual abuse, at the hands of your great-uncle, do you think?' Niccolò asked.

Per jumped up like a tightly coiled spring suddenly released, his face flushed deep red crimson. He screamed, 'Stop this now! Stop this abomination!'

He pounded his huge left fist in fury against the arm of the Judgment chair. The sound echoed across the room. Such was the impact, that for a moment Maryam feared that the *Chair of the Just* would shatter. Marcus moved swiftly to try to calm and if necessary restrain him. He put his hand on Per's shuddering shoulder but the Scandinavian angrily pushed it off.

'Per, please, the Prot is only trying to get to the truth. He is looking only for your honesty,' Marcus urged his charge to sit.

'Honesty!' Per sneered. 'I'm the most honest soul amongst this entire lot!' He pointed at the jury. 'Sure, I may be an egoist, I don't deny that. But look at these fools - all pretending to be something they're not!' His face darkened.

'I'm an atheist. I don't believe in or recognise any god and I refuse to be judged by you, in this place or any other place,' he pointed at the open mouthed group of penitents and then turning to face the Seraphim he shouted, 'Or by you!'

'Sit down, this instant.' Gideon demanded.

But Per was not for stopping. He stormed towards the Justice blustering 'I do not recognise the authority of this kangaroo court! I demand to be returned to the world immediately!' He ran a sleeve roughly across his mouth. 'Maybe I can't have my old life back, but you can at least give me another go! I don't belong here.

I am of the Earth. I demand to go back!' he thundered with arms folded across his chest like an oversized petulant child.

That video clip has really stirred him up! Mike thought, although he did feel some sympathy for the dude considering the sordid nature of what had unfolded on screen. The graphic images of molestation had now thankfully vanished.

Marcus was about to grab the Swede more forcefully, but the Archangel Gabriel warned him away with a look. The Seraph rose to his full height. Per trembled at the sight of the Arc, half in fear of what may happen and half as a result of being filled with the hurt brought on by such a painful reminder of a long supressed trauma. When the Archangel Gabriel finally spoke, his mellifluous voice exuded a calm authority.

'Per Oskar Andersson, you have refused the Judgment of this court and you unwisely reject the mercy of your Creator.' His eyes burned brightly as his gaze locked on Per, 'For most of your human life you have been an imprudent man - a man who has displayed little empathy for the lot of your brothers and sisters.' Per remained stock still and silent.

'Yet you are not an evil incarnate and I acknowledge through the power bestowed in me, that there remains in your soul, the slim possibility of rehabilitation. All is not yet lost for you, despite your many failings and your open rejection of our laws. I thereby instruct the Presiding Justice, to grant to you an immediate return to the Earth, to live once more as a man. But I formally caution you to live a better life. It is to be recorded, in the Book of Life and Death, that you are to be Reborn.'

Now it was his Advocate who struggled to hold his tongue, this cocky excuse for a man, was to be allowed a second chance. But before he could reproach the Archangel, he felt the hand of Maryam touch his. He knew instantly that he should remain hushed. Gabriel had spoken. His decision as always was final and irrevocable.

The Keeper of the Book then spoke. Monique was chilled by the warning given to the Swede. They were words she had heard before.

'Go from here Per Andersson, to your new life. A new beginning…and we hope that you will recover and accept the grace of your Creator, so that on the day when you are again called to the Judgment chair, you may finally enter the Host as Puresoul. If you do not change your ways, be advised, you flirt with eternal damnation.'

Per could not believe his luck, *I'm going back, hallefuckinlujah!*

'You may leave us now through this portal,' The Archangel Michael commanded as he directed the excited Scandinavian towards the closest doorway. Miyu recalled that no one had yet come or left by that archway. Per felt a surge of triumph.

He couldn't resist shouting, 'Amen, brothers and sisters, I'm getting out of this place.' He turned towards the exit that would bring him to his new life. *I was successful once, I can be again.* As he caught Abigail's eye, he mocked in low tones. 'Another time you dyke bitch,' then somewhat louder he added, 'So long suckers, enjoy your new boring lives! Whatever!' He got to the portal and noticed the Attendant, glaring at him intently. Per sneered, flipped him the bird, pushed the unresisting door and charged through.

Marcus roused himself from his severe shock and cried out, 'But the water of Lethe!' The Swede had already gone. It was too late now. The Seraph Ananchel smiled serenely and raised a single finger up to her lips, as if to say 'Hush my child. All is well'

In the chamber, the Archangel Michael was in deep conversation with Maryam and Marcus. They spoke only in the ancient language of Aramaic, but from what Abigail could guess from their hand movements, there may be an issue with protocol. Fingers were being raised, six, then five. She recalled Maryam had said, 'The Judgment requires a quorum of six penitents.' With Per gone, they were down to five.

Abigail had deduced correctly, the correct protocol to resume, is exactly what they were debating. Marcus argued that the Judgment could not be completed without a replacement for the Swede. He made a mental note to ask later, where that ass Andersson had ended up. The Advocate had never before seen a penitent be allowed to leave subsequent to their verdict and equally, he was totally surprised, to see a soul go back without the prior erasing of its memory.

There was a sharp knock on the door, Lou hurried to open it and was met by the smiling figure of Manny, He exchanged a friendly greeting with the Attendant and following behind was the figure of a small-statured Asian man.

'May I present to the chamber, Mister Tomas Esposito. I believe you may be short a juror,' Manny beamed.

Maryam walked directly towards Tomas. Taking his hand she greeted him warmly. 'Welcome to Stasis, Tomas,' she smiled.

'Has my son brought you up to date with the proceedings?'

'Yes, he has Madam,'

'Good. We have a quorum of six again. We may continue I believe. Please take a seat,' Maryam lead the man to his allotted place, formerly occupied by the departed, but not much lamented, Per. The Archangel Michael turned the page of the book and called out the name of the next penitent.

'Miyu Tanaka, step forth and be judged.' The quiet and timid girl walked purposefully across the room and took her turn in the chair.

twelve

THE JUDGMENT OF MIYU TANAKA.

It was Niccolò who once more was to 'bring the light.' The young woman seemed so tiny in the large seat, that her toes barely made contact with the floor.

Will Niccolò dive directly in or will he take it easy on Miyu? Marcus wondered.

You could never tell. The Protatori di Luce worked for brief, intense periods, rolling into one Stasis block after another. The current pair were both formidable proponents of their profession. They had studied the files and made their choice on which penitents to tackle. With the constant increase in new arrivals, they had to extract the truth quickly.

Most of the Protatori would have come through Stasis in its earlier incarnation. They were not malicious, however cruel their methods might appear to be. They insert their words like a sharp needle into a soul, poke it around and try to wheedle out any corruption that had infected it.

If Miyu was nervous she didn't show it. Abigail was full of admiration for the girl, who although quiet as a mouse, was durable. Miyu would not fold easily, or so she had thought. Niccolò leaned in towards the young woman and began.

'Miyu, may I call you Miyu?' She signalled her assent with a slight downward cast of her eyes.

'Miyu, when you were employed as a cleaner in the Sato's home, isn't it true that you stole things - items of jewellery and clothing. Things that you believed may not be missed.'

'Yes, I did,' Miyu's answer was barely above a whisper. 'But only small things. Nothing really valuable.'

'Were you in love with Akihiro Sato?'

'Yes I was. At least I believed I was,' Miyu mumbled keeping her head held low.

'Please speak up Miss Tanaka.' Gideon urged.

'Yes, I loved him.' Miyu answered again, only marginally louder.

'Did he love you back?' the Protatori pressed.

'I thought that he did, but it seems I was wrong,' Miyu stared down towards the floor. It was clear that she found it excruciating, to talk about herself in public.

'So if you loved him, as you claim, why did you set out to trick him?'

Miyu gazed up at the man in dismay. 'What?' she stammered.

'Your pregnancy, wasn't that a situation that you'd carefully planned?'

'No!' Miyu moaned.

'You wanted to ensnare Mister Sato, to force his hand to make him leave his wife of twenty years and to choose you instead. You tried to deceive him, didn't you?'

The Prot moved right up in front of the Judgment chair, towering over the slight figure of the penitent juror. But he had got too close. Miyu Tanaka kicked out, scraping her sandal with unexpected force, down the shin of her stunned inquisitor who yelped in pain.

'Miss Tanaka!' The Presiding Justice bellowed from his bench. 'You will conduct yourself in a proper manner or you will forfeit any chance of advancement.'

Marcus could barely contain his amusement at Miyu's action. *This girl has gumption, no doubt about it. Still she had better behave.*

'I beg the chamber to excuse my client. The Protatori did try to demean her honour,' Maryam said. 'Please remember that Miyu did lose a child, as a direct result of Sato's response.'

Niccolò was rubbing vigorously at the spot of discomfort on his shin. 'I apologise if I have given offence.' He graciously conceded to Maryam.

'Miss Tanaka, Miyu...' once more he took a conciliatory tone, but the Advocates knew well that he was just baiting his trap. 'You do know that the taking of life may prevent you from going to the Host?' Niccolò spread out his open palms in mock surprise, as if this shocking news had only just reached him.

'That is absurd Niccolò!' Maryam was on her feet again. She addressed the jurors directly. 'Culturally Miss Tanaka did nothing that her society would consider dishonourable. Seppuku has long been part of their tradition.'

'Her death-leap had nothing to do with ritual suicide,' Niccolò raised his voice.

'Both of you please, remember where you are,' Gideon cautioned, just as the two counsels were about to lock horns. Niccolò threw his adversary a disdainful look, as if he was weighing up whether to say something or not. He chose to speak.

'Miss Tanaka may be exonerated on a technicality of cultural acceptance, Maryam, but she cannot be innocent of taking her unborn child's life. That is a simple fact.' Niccolò had the gloves off now and it appalled Maryam.

Why does he always have to be so pernickety?

The Advocate responded, 'She did not cause a soul to pass.' Maryam was referring to the soul insertion - when the first breath of life is given - when a human child is born into the world. Prior to that there's but a proto-soul - a life spark. But she knew that this line was weak. Gideon asked, 'Any further rebuttal?' But there was no obvious defence to the charge. It was incontrovertible, but it was a low blow nonetheless.

'Not at this time.' Maryam slumped down on her bench and folded her arms grumpily. Marcus sat alongside, his tightly knitted brow graphically illustrating the cogs that were moving in his head, as he tried to see a way out for Maryam's client.

Miyu sat perfectly still, arms across her lap, her slim fingers rigidly entwined. Once more she heard the voice in her head. 'Be calm child, you have nothing to fear.' Miyu had no desire to unveil the full story of her life to anyone - living with her mother and sister and how her alcoholic father would frequently fly into a drunken rage, raining fists on her mother's head and pummelling his two daughters at the slightest hint of defiance. Miyu didn't shed a tear when an overindulgence of tainted saki, poisoned Katsuro Tanaka, and complete renal failure hastened his end. Niccolò had told the court that she had in fact felt relieved.

For a few years, her little family struggled by on meagre provisions but Miyu's sister had found employment for them both, cleaning houses in the posh Roppongi Hills. These extravagant homes were a different world from anything the Tanaka sisters had ever known.

A few weeks after she'd began, Mister Sato, a big company man, began to compliment Miyu on her work and on her clean appearance. It was a simple task for Sato to turn an innocent girl's head. He began calling home at unexpected times, sometimes early in the day while his wife spent long hours at her country club. Within weeks the affair had turned physical. Sato was small in stature and not especially attractive but his wealth and status made him as powerful as a god to Miyu. She like many young girls who become enthralled with an older male, wanted to please him in every way, a situation that Sato took advantage of with increasing relish.

Soon after, she'd purchased a home pregnancy test from a drug store. Twin blue lines materialised and had fostered hope of future happiness in her callow breast. It seemed to her only natural that on account of his wife being barren, Akihiro would surely discard her in favour of Miyu. Yet like so many in this sad situation the apparition was fleeting and the reality harsh. Instead Sato had dragged her by the hair, to the gates of his house and had flung her distraught and bewildered on the roadside.

Abigail had raised her hand to her mouth in shock when Niccolò described the young woman's death plunge from the top of the skyscraper to the ground below.

Mike Roberts liked Miyu, and although she didn't speak a lot, she seemed a sweet kid. To think of how scared she must have been, before jumping, made him feel nauseous. Working as a firefighter, dealing with jumpers and the messy aftermath was an occupational hazard. He would have gladly and without hesitation, used his powerful fists to teach Sato a lesson. Mike wasn't on the job back in 9/11, but he could never forget the image of that one falling guy. It was plastered all over the magazines. He looked over at this young kid and consoled himself. *That Sato guy's gonna show up here in Stasis someday and they'll know what to do with him.* He looked at the robust figure of Marcus and he had no doubt.

Unlike the courts back home on Earth, 'real justice' plays out here. Everyone's gonna get what they're due. You can bet your life on it. he figured.

The mysterious voice she had heard or imagined, had given Miyu the resolve and strength to see the process through to the end where she sat listening while the Prot had dissected and picked through the pieces of her short life, until finally, Gideon dismissed her from the chair. She was emotionally spent. Her Advocate Maryam helped her from the Judgment seat and led her back slowly to her allotted place.

Abigail smiled across when she finally caught her eye and Mike also gave her a thumbs-up, but her attention it seemed was caught up elsewhere for now. Next, it was to be Mike, followed by Nader, Abigail, then Monique and the new arrival Tomas Esposito.

THE JUDGMENT OF MICHAEL ROBERTS.

The Prot Jocelyn, turned on her heels and asked, 'Mike, do you recall the name of Andrew Granby?'

'Yes m'am I do.' Mike's throat felt dry and his voice cracked just enough to betray his discomfort on where the Prot might be going with this.

'Please won't you tell the chamber how Andrew Granby is known to you?' Jocelyn was pacing in slow deliberate strides back and forth in front of the jury.

'Andrew Granby was a Candidate firefighter at the Academy. We were in the same class group,' Mike gulped, as he realised where she was headed.

'Please tell us what you know about young Mister Granby?'

'I don't know really, there's not much to tell. He was with us for a number of weeks then he washed out,' Mike felt his hands tighten involuntarily on the sides of the chair.

Jocelyn continued pacing. 'Washed out? Hmm...I see. By that you mean he didn't finish his training, he didn't graduate, is that correct?'

'Yes m'am, that's correct he didn't. He quit three weeks before the end,' Mike replied.

'Mister Roberts, will you please inform us all, what colour is Andrew Granby?'

'Excuse me, I don't follow?' Mike said.

'It's a simple question, what colour, Mister Roberts? What race is Andrew Granby?' the Protatori raised her tone a notch.

'African American, Andrew Granby is black.'

'That's right Andrew Granby is a black man,' she smiled at the jurors.

Marcus leaned closer to Maryam and whispered, 'Jocelyn is really some operator.' Although he didn't care much for her personality, he had witnessed her in action many times. Marcus admired her skills as an interrogator. His colleague didn't reply she felt that Jocelyn looked far too pleased with herself. In that split-second she realised that she must have found some dirt on Mike, something that his file compiler must have missed.

'Do you know where Andrew Granby is now?' Jocelyn continued.

'No, I do not,' Mike answered grimly.

'Well I'll tell you, shall I? Andrew Granby is presently on Riker's Island serving fifteen years for aggravated armed robbery.' Jocelyn Wu pushed back a long silky black bang that hung over her beautifully sculpted face.

Mike lowered his head, 'I didn't know, I'm sorry to hear that.'

'Sorry indeed,' the Prot replied, a little too smugly.

Jocelyn stopped pacing and turned to face the young fireman directly, 'Andrew Granby was a respectable young man, whom you and your white friends forced out of the Academy.'

Mike's eyes flared open in disbelief at what the Prot had claimed. He had gone over his life with a fine tooth comb. He'd been understandably nervous when it was his turn in the chair, but he never saw this curve ball coming. He was unprepared. Now Jocelyn was moving in to expose him as something he didn't believe he was.

'In his despair at the loss of his job, Mister Granby got himself mixed up with bad folks and serious crime. I put it to you Michael Roberts that could be you are the reason that Andrew Granby is now incarcerated in prison?' There was a gasp from two of the penitents.

'Could you really be so primitive as to think that pigment can define a person?'

'That's not the whole story...' Mike tried to speak up but was headed off by the Prot who said, 'Have you considered that you might be racist?' She paused to let her words take effect. 'After all, you know they don't allow racists in the Heofon,' Jocelyn Wu winked at the ashen faced Mike.

'This is utter nonsense, Gideon. Jocelyn is dealing in supposition,' Maryam stood and addressed the Presiding Justice.

'Am I indeed? Well I do apologise, Maryam,' she was clearly enjoying herself. She cut an impressive figure and was a supremely able Prot.

'Mister Roberts, do you know what this means?' She again turned her attention to the penitent and made a motion with her hand. Palm faced inwards, fingers held out straight, she ran her hand from her eyes down past her mouth.

'M'am...I...let me explain.'

'Answer the question, do you know what this gesture means?' Jocelyn said while repeating the hand movement.

'Shade! It was the sign that was used to indicate a coloured person,' Mike faltered.

Abigail turned to look at Maryam. She found it hard to believe what was taking place, she certainly wouldn't have figured Mike for a racist.

'A gesture that is code for a coloured person, I see. Why was there a need for such a signal?'

'Because you'd be fired if you used that...you know...word?' Mike kept his head down.

'That word? Which word is that exactly?' Jocelyn licked her lips, waiting.

Mike looked up, he was shamefaced but his courage had returned. 'I will not utter it here or anyplace else. I don't like to use that word, it makes me uncomfortable. The colour of a man's skin is completely unimportant to me.'

Good for you, Mike, Maryam smiled.

'But you have used this sign, haven't you Michael?' Jocelyn repeated the hand motion. 'It's better to get things out, Mike. It's good to accept what we are.'

'But I'm not that, at least I don't believe so.' He felt the hot flush on his cheeks.

Jocelyn turned towards the jurors, her upturned hands moving up and down in slow calculated drama, as she continued to question Mike. 'Andrew Granby was driven out of the Fire Department by a mean cohort Michael, by grimy hand signals, foul comments and hatred. Your part in these sordid events, appear to be those of a racist?' Jocelyn Wu stared at the penitent defiantly. Nader felt a chill run down his spine. His friend Mike, was in serious trouble.

Maryam took the floor. 'May I respond? What you are shamefully omitting Jocelyn, is that while yes, Andrew Granby was subjected to dreadful bullying by several of his classmates, Mike was not one of the main perpetrators.' She walked towards the young firefighter and whispered in his ear. Her words were met with a lowering of his head and a solitary nod of affirmation.

Maryam addressed the jury, 'Yes, regrettably he did make that...sign. He is not proud of it, but to put it in its correct context, Mike was within a peer group of thirty seven young males and eighteen young women. Young men as you well know are prone to doing stupid things.' Miriam wheeled back to face her young charge. 'This young man is no exception to that. He wanted to fit in. He felt intimidated and he went along with the minor jokes but I stress, at no time did he ever confront Andrew Granby directly, in such a disrespectful manner. He is certainly not a racist.' Maryam resumed her place.

Jocelyn was undeterred, and returned right back to centre stage. 'Well let's see about that, shall we?'

'Mister Roberts do you recall your part in the rescue of a window cleaner in November last year?'

Mike took his time, he remembered it well. It was his first save and every firefighter remembers his first save, he cautiously replied, 'Yes, I certainly do. We had got an alarm call to a building up by Astor, just past the Alamo, you know that famous sculpture they call *The Cube*? Well our company Engine 33 and Ladder 9 were first on scene. We got orders to carry out a height rescue.'

'A height rescue...sounds fascinating.' Jocelyn cupped one elbow while raising her index finger to her ruby lips, as if lost in deep thought. 'Some men were in serious peril were they not?'

'Indeed they were. A window cleaning crew got into difficulty, they were working on a rig where the support chains were old, rusty and not well maintained. Two of the wires gave out on one side of the platform. These two guys slid right over and were hanging on by their fingertips,' Mike paused. He could see their scared faces, hear their pleas for help, as if it was only yesterday. The look in a man's eyes before he dies, you never forget it. Your mind plays it out like a card in a roller deck. He gathered himself and continued the story.

'Sadly one man fell to his death, but we managed to rescue the other,' Mike puffed out his chest a little. He was proud of his team's work that day.

Jocelyn feigned confusion. 'Oh? One man fell to his death you say?' she smiled at Mike, it gave Mike a creepy feeling. He imagined her curvaceous mouth, curled up like a shark smiling at its next meal.

'Yes, that is correct,' Mike braced for what was coming next.

'Is it also accurate to say that the man, you didn't save, was a black man?'

'Erm...' Mike hesitated, he looked across pleadingly at his Advocate, who didn't show any sign of emotion, Maryam sat stock still, stony faced. 'Yes m'am that is true,' he sighed. Mike's eyes narrowed. He understood the Prot's angle just in that moment.

'So the man you chose to help, was a white fellow. Was his life was worth more to you than the black guy?' Jocelyn snapped the trap shut.

Maryam shot to her feet, 'Oh come on Gideon! The Protatori has no basis for this outrageous accusation! It should be purged from the record.' She looked furious.

A pained expression came over Gideon's countenance as he said. 'Jocelyn you will explain yourself now, or you will apologise to the penitent.'

'I'm sorry, let me be more precise. On that November day, when your company responded to the Downtown area, please enlighten us with your version of what happened next? And be aware of the sanctity of your testimony.'

Mike cleared his throat and glared at the smug Prot. This lady was spinning a web of untruths, trying to provoke him. He needed to tread carefully or his feet would get stuck in her snare. 'Responding to the alarm call, my squad made our way to the roof of the building. The men were hanging from the apparatus around the 15th floor. We hightailed it to the roof, made fast the ropes - that is to say, we secured our line rescue equipment and we rappelled down there, lickety-split. There was myself and Tommy Burns.'

Mike took a deep breath before continuing. If ever he needed to exercise self-control, it was now. 'On the way down, Tommy's belay device got jammed up. He couldn't drop close enough to the rig. It can happen. That left just me alone,' Mike's tempo of speech began to slow, as he recalled the events of that fateful day.

Right about that same moment, the court Attendant Lou, had quietly made his way up behind Maryam, unobserved. Everyone's gaze was fixed firmly on the young man sitting in the Judgment chair. Lou placed a hand on the Advocate's shoulder and whispered something in her ear. Anyone who had been looking would have noticed an almost imperceptible smile emerge and the slightest nod of her head. She raised a hand up to her shoulder and tapped gently on Lou's fingers in appreciation.

Mike continued his testimony, 'When I got down to the rig, it was at a very precarious angle, perhaps sixty or seventy degree slant. The two guys were clinging on as best they could but it was real cold, they couldn't hold on and I could only take one.'

'So you helped the white guy,' Jocelyn repeated. No one dared breathe, for in that infinitesimal period of time, there was absolute silence in the room.

'Yes, I mean no, I couldn't reach the other guy...I just couldn't!' Mike was losing it.

'Seems to me, Mike, you have an aversion to coloured people. Could it mean that you saved the white man and left James Jones, a father of three, fall fifteen floors to his death?'

Mike Roberts wasn't trembling in fear, he was furious. He had played that rescue out over and over in his head many times. The guy he saved just happened to be the one closest to him. He made a snap decision. It had nothing to do with race. It never even entered his head, until now. But as he recalled the memory of that day, it was causing him to question his own motives. *There's no way... a racist, surely not?*

Two of the female jurors clasped a hand over their mouths. The case against Mike had taken an unexpected twist and was looking grave.

'I invoke Moses Law in this case.'

At first no one was sure who had spoken, but Maryam raised her voice as she walked to centre of the room, towards the Archangels sitting on the bema, and proclaimed once more,

'I invoke Moses Law in this case.'

There was a type of silent consternation going on. None of the penitents had any idea of the significance of what had just happened but it was clear to them that Maryam had done something rather extraordinary. Gabriel, Michael and Ananchel exchanged knowing glances. It was Niccolò who composed himself first.

'But Gideon, Moses Law hasn't been invoked in the celestial chamber for more than 500 years,' he stated.

'He is right, Maryam,' Gideon looked down solemnly from the dais.

'He is right, but that doesn't mean it cannot be invoked,' she turned her gaze towards the Archangel Gabriel.

'Gabriel with respect, the Creator made the direct stipulation that in any contested point of a Judgment that concerns the matter of the death of a human being. Then Moses Law can be petitioned for.' Maryam crossed her arms and held her ground. Every pair of eyes in the room was now locked on the Arc.

Maryam continued, 'I will explain for the benefit of the assembled jury and for the accused penitent, that Moses Law allows for the soul of the deceased person, to be summoned back from the Host, if there that soul resides, and to return to this chamber to give sworn testimony. I believe that his soul is indeed in the Heofon and as such I call for James Jones to give evidence as is my right.'

Niccolò was gobsmacked. Gideon looked to Gabriel for guidance. The Archangel affirmed his agreement with a single nod of his head. The Presiding Justice called out 'Lou, is this soul in the Host.'

'I believe he is,' Lou answered with a wry smile.

'So be it. The soul of James Jones is called to give evidence when we resume this case tomorrow,' the Presiding Justice ruled.

'This can't be, Gideon,' Jocelyn piped up.

'My decision is made!' Gideon declared.

'I must object,' Jocelyn was plainly not happy with the turn of events.

'I will speak with you later Jocelyn. We will recess for now.' Gideon rose.

'But that will delay the timeline Gideon. We will have passed the Seventh Day.' Jocelyn protested weakly.

'This is Stasis, Madam Protatori. Limbus Stasis. You know well that we have all the time in the world. We have all eternity if needs be,' the old Judge said.

The Protatori conceded and retired to their bench.

Mike Roberts had little idea what had transpired, but he could see from the big grin on Marcus' face and how he was congratulating Maryam, that whatever had occurred, it had happened in his favour. At least he hoped it had. What James Jones will have to say, well that's a different matter. But for now a feeling of exhaustion and enormous relief washed over him. Before the jurors were dismissed, Gideon announced that they would resume for one more Judgment, at sunset - The Judging of Abigail Perdue.

The jurors left the chamber and headed for their cells or some favourite part of Stasis. Nader was hanging back hoping to speak with Mike, but the young American was still heavy in conversation with both Advocates. Most likely they were explaining to Mike, the implications of Maryam's strategy. Nader sucked in a large swallow of fresh air as he strolled out into the Elysian Gardens. *Oh what I'd give for a smoke.* The session had been tense and his nerves felt at their limits.

'Pssssst...hey Captain Khoury over here,' a disembodied voice called out.

Nader looked around but couldn't see anyone.

'Behind you!'

Nader recognised the voice. He turned to find Lou, holding out a very welcome sight.

'So what would you give?'

'Lou,' he gasped. 'You can get these in Stasis?'

'Anything that can be got on the Earth, can be got here also - if you know the right people,' Lou laughed with gusto and offered Nader a cigarette from a slightly crumpled pack.

'Let's go around here out of sight. I'm trying to cut back. I promised Maryam and she'll scold me something bad, if she catches me lighting up again.' Lou led the fisherman to a semi-enclosed courtyard, heavily obscured by lush foliage. 'This is my smoking spot,' Lou chuckled, as he lit his own cigarette, before offering the book of matches to the rather startled captain.

Nader pulled hard, drawing deep the mixture of toxic chemicals and smoke into his lungs - they spluttered their distress with a cacophonous cough in response - while other receptors luxuriated in the nicotine hit. 'Oh man I needed that. Shokran, Lou!' Nader offered his thanks in Arabic.

'Don't get too used to it young man. They won't take kindly to you ruining a new set of lungs. After all you won't be keeping that body much longer,' Lou advised. Both leaned back against the wall, enjoying their illicit pleasure.

'I really appreciate this Lou, but I hope that it doesn't cause you any problems.'

'Oh don't worry yourself about that Captain Khoury. It is after all traditional to offer the condemned man a last smoke before his execution!' Lou's brow furrowed and his eyes set deep as he turned his head towards Nader - eyes which seemed to have taken on a darker, more sinister aspect. Nader's cigarette dangled from his lower lip, almost straight down at a right angle, his jaw slacking in shock at Lou's words.

Lou let fly another blast of raucous laughter, 'Man, you should see your face, Captain Khoury. I'm just kidding with you son.' It took a couple of moments before Lou could fully restrain his chortling, slapping his meaty hand repeatedly against his midriff. 'My oh my.....'

Nader drew nervously on his cigarette again. He had smoked it much too quickly, right down to burning his fingers. The joke had rubbed too close to the bone and had taken from his dubious pleasure.

'Forgive me Captain Khoury,' said Lou. 'I know I shouldn't fool around like that, but sometimes I just have to give in to my darker side.' As the older man blew out perfect concentric rings of smoke and smiled wickedly. Nader noticed the fingers of this new skin were free from the blemish of nicotine yellow and brown stain. 'How strange, the things we do to our bodies,' he remarked.

'What's that you say?'

'Oh just how happy we are to put poisons in our bodies, when they are made in the image of the Creator,' Nader replied.

'Oh no my friend, you've got it wrong - way wrong,' Lou coughed. 'It's not this fleshy old thing,' he was pinching a section of his skin on his forearm. 'None of this is in the Creator's image. This is just your soul carriage - it's just meat, blood and bone.'

'But I thought that...'

Lou cut him off. 'Nader, your soul is the image of the Creator, not your body.' He offered another smoke to the captain who accepted graciously before taking his leave of the anxious fisherman.

'I had best get back to work, going to be a big day tomorrow. Won't be surprised if it brings in some mighty important spectators,' he repeated as he walked off towards the pathway, talking to himself. 'Moses Law, hmmm...that will sure stoke up some folks around here.' Nader finished the second cigarette and went back inside in search of Mike.

In Room 5, Maryam and Marcus were taking stock on Mike's life. *How did she miss this accusation?* Mike was going to need to ask himself some hard questions. *How did the file compiler miss it too?* At the moment of death, a soul departs its carriage and docks back in Stasis. It travels swiftly and unseen outside of the light wavelength that the human eye can perceive. Humans especially the religious ones, have the misconception that they are watched over all of the time by the heavens. But's that's impossible, with over seven billion beings on the planet. It also isn't necessary. Why? Because each soul records every event in its life, like a little black box on an airplane - all of the experiences, every transgression or good deed, it's all there - stored away. They extract it out here on Stasis. It isn't the human mind that stores the memories - it's the soul.

The brain calls them up from the soul in the same manner that a file complier can call up memories when they log the details of each life and condense it into a bound file for the Advocates. Somehow this racism thing had gotten missed.

Maryam knows that can happen. That's why you need the Prots to get to the bottom of things. Jocelyn is very thorough at her job. She probably took a look, interpreted the scans herself and dug around a little. Maryam kicked herself for not being better prepared. She had never liked mistakes.

Painstakingly they went back over Mike's life, for the hundredth time. Maryam asked him about any incidents with people of other race. There was only one that he could recall. The problem for Mike was that he really didn't know any coloured people. Where he lived the families were primarily Irish, Polish, Germans and Italians, now he thinks about it, it was a staunchly white neighbourhood other than Jorge Diaz, the little Hispanic kid on Fourth Street.

The only black people he had any knowledge of were his sporting heroes - the athletes, the football and basketball players - but you don't get to hang with those guys on your street.

Perhaps the most telling incident happened when he was nineteen. He and Davy Maguire had been stood up against a wall at knife point by some gang bangers. They took what little money they had and for fun cut a deep gouge in Davy's face which had left him with a prominent scar. Perhaps that day Mike had been scarred too; the gang members were all black.

'That's it,' Marcus interjected.

'Huh?'

'You got held up by some black dudes, and now you're suspicious of all blacks, is that it?'

'No…I don't know?' Mike blustered.

'You have a slight prejudice Mike. Not very strong thankfully, but it is there,' Maryam tried to calm things a little.

'I never knew! Honestly!' Mike choked up.

'People are always a little suspicious about what they don't know or understand Mike. The important thing is to recognise it then do something about it. You need to get out and see things for what they really are. I've seen how well you and Nader get along. Bet you wouldn't have thought it possible beforehand,' Marcus said.

'I guess. Look I am sorry,' Mike was genuinely contrite.

'I know you are Mike, I know,' Maryam patted his shoulder. 'Why don't you go get some rest now? Big day tomorrow, yeah.'

When Mike left the room, she said to her colleague, 'That boy's no racist, he's just immature, but a lot depends on what James Jones is going to say when he gets on the stand.'

THE JUDGMENT OF ABIGAIL PERDUE.

The sun had set on Stasis and it was Abigail's turn in the chair.

The young Englishwoman crossed the room and was seated. She was alarmed to see the figure of Jocelyn, rise and follow suit. Abigail had paled when she remembered how she had given Mike such a torrid time.

Jocelyn bowed her head towards the Arcs and to the Presiding Justice. Gideon motioned that she should commence. 'Is it fair, Miss Perdue, to say that you are a spoilt little rich girl?'

Wow! Straight for the jugular, Marcus winced.

Abigail felt flushed with embarrassment, but remained poised. She addressed the Prot in a deliberately even tone, 'I would agree that your description would not be far from the truth.'

'So you'd admit you were a rich daddy's girl, who had everything far too easy.'

'Oh come on Gideon.' Maryam called from the Advocate's bench, without rising, 'That's not probing, that's harassment.' She was well used to Jocelyn s tactics, to immediately unnerve and unsettle the penitent in an emotional blitzkrieg. 'The Protatori are expressing opinion not fact.'

'Moderation Madam Wu, please!' Gideon ordered.

Jocelyn clasped her hands and her smile was the picture of insincerity.

'Well let's get straight to the nub then shall we?' she continued. 'What does the name Ruth Rosen mean to you, Miss Perdue?'

'Ruth Rosen was my cousin - my first cousin,' Abigail answered truthfully. She was prepared. Her Advocate had said this was sure to come up and they'd covered it in great detail.

'Don't let them rattle you,' Maryam had urged. 'It will be difficult, but you can do it.'

'Why do you refer to Ruth Rosen in the past tense? Why use the word *was* and not *is*? She is still among the living is she not?' Jocelyn was toying with the penitent.

'Yes I believe she is alive. I used the past tense only because I am not of the Earth anymore, Ruth is in my past, not my present,' Abigail replied calmly.

'Oh come now Miss Perdue, Ruth is very much in your present,' Jocelyn's smile evaporated, she paused and resumed with a devastating blow.

'Ruth Rosen, your first cousin, she is alive. But not in the full meaning of the word. Isn't that so Miss Perdue?' The arrow hit its mark. Abigail felt the first of the tear drops, collect in the corners of her eyes.

'Please tell us about the night of Ruth Rosen's eighteenth birthday Miss Perdue. I'm sure that you can recall that night.'

'I...I...I mean we...' Abigail hesitated. The Prots had got to her.

Come on girl, pull yourself together, Maryam urged.

'We were out celebrating Ruth's birthday, we took in some clubs, had a few drinks.' Abigail's eyes were beginning to glaze over, a single tear streaked plainly down her alabaster hued cheek.

'Then what...Miss Perdue?'

'My friend Stephanie and I, we decided that we'd do some-thing crazy. We had bought cocaine and pushed Ruth to try it.' Abigail's hitherto even tone now fractured as she recalled a long suppressed, intensely painful memory.

'Isn't it funny how we subconsciously move from *I* to *We*, when we want to divert attention away from ourselves or apportion some of the blame on another. It is a very human trait,' Jocelyn sighed.

'I'm sorry...what?' Abigail mumbled.

'*We* decided....*we* pushed,' Jocelyn's tone grew more severe.

'Ruth Rosen had up until that fateful evening, no interest in drugs. You on the other hand dabbled on a handful of occa-sions. You were accustomed to this weakness of the wealthy. You encouraged your cousin to try it. You accompanied her to the stall in the restroom and showed her how to inhale...isn't that so?' Joc-elyn pushed the knife home.

'Yes it is,' Abigail surrendered all effort at defence.

'Without your egging on, she would never have tried drugs... isn't that so?'

'Yes, that is so,' Abigail whispered.

No Abigail, no! Come on you got to fight back! Mike was out on the edge of his seat. His heart was breaking to see his friend in such a pickle.

Maryam stepped in, 'Jocelyn that is purely speculation. What Ruth Rosen would have done in the future is complete conjec-ture.' Gideon agreed and instructed the Keeper of the Book to strike the comments from the record.

'Where is Ruth now? Jocelyn changed tack.

'She's in a nursing home, south of the Thames,' Abigail took on a haunted look.

'That's right, she is in a nursing home and has been confined there for a number of years...and why is a woman in her mid-twen-ties, in a nursing home?' Jocelyn prompted her to continue, but Abigail was unable or unwilling, so the Prot finished, 'Because Ruth Rosen had a catastrophic reaction to a mixture of cocaine and alcohol. Her body went into shock and she suffered seizures and cardiac arrest.' Abigail despite her preparation had caved. What Jocelyn had told the court was the sad and unfortunate truth.

'Poor Ruth, a young girl with her whole life in front of her, now takes food intravenously - she has locked-in syndrome as a result of her drug cocktail. Did you know Miss Perdue that alcohol and cocaine when taken together are not processed individually by a human liver? No? They combine to form a super drug called Coca-ethyline,' the Prot explained. 'This is what caused your cousin's heart to fail and subsequently parts of her brain to shut down due to oxygen starvation,' Jocelyn turned and pointed at Abigail.

'And you did this to your own flesh and blood Abigail Perdue. You stole her life, yet you sit here thinking you are worthy of the Host?'

'No...I do not feel I'm worthy.' Abigail shrank in the chair. She cast an abject figure.

'You will be fortunate if they don't send you to Gehenna,' Jocelyn scolded and returned to the benches. Maryam rushed to Abigail and took her in her arms, her sobs came fast and furious and her body shook in uncontrollable tremors. She kept mumbling 'I'm sorry Ruth, I'm so very sorry.'

'We offer no rebuttal at this time,' the Advocate demurred. 'We ask for a short recess.' Gideon agreed with the request, feeling nothing but compassion in his old heart for the young woman before him.

Abigail, now back in her cell, wept until there were no more tears left to fall. She got up from her bed and soothed her red puffy eyes with a splash of cold water.

My poor dear Ru, my poor sweet girl.

She had genuinely mourned the fate of her cousin and it was a substantial loss. True, she had not died, but what remained was only a vestige of what had once been a vital, energetic girl. They had been friends since early childhood, her aunt Sarah was a regular visitor to their house and her eldest daughter, Ruth, would always accompany her. Abigail and Ruth were firm friends but as the Perdue's were the more affluent side of the family, it was Abigail who could most afford to sail closest to the wind, in her great hurry to grow up.

Ru on the other hand, was what Abigail considered, 'A conscientious old soul in a young body.' She studied hard, determined to make her own place in the world. Abigail thought she needed to shake things up a bit, have some fun. So for her upcoming birthday, Abigail had asked Stephanie, to call up her dealer. It was supposed to be harmless merriment. What Jocelyn had said, was in one important facet entirely accurate - without the pressure from her older cousin, Ruth would never have taken drugs. But she idolised Abigail, who convinced of her own invincibility believed that her dear cousin was indestructible too. She wasn't, and the result was calamitous.

But far worse and what had not been revealed, was that Abigail in an attempt to evade responsibility had brazenly portrayed Ruth as the habitual user - the one who had encouraged them to try it. It was a fabrication, perpetrated on a helpless girl who could not defend herself: Ruth's condition meant she could not speak or communicate. It was the fear of being caught in a lie – of her family's disdain and the completely natural inclination of the young to run for cover that made Abigail Perdue push all real thought of Ruth to the dark recesses of her mind. That was until the dream had returned and today when Jocelyn exposed her misdeed and her true nature.

Tomorrow she would confess. Abigail would not ascend to the Great Host. The realisation was devastating, *What if they send me to Gehenna?* Even if she deserved to die, the thought of it petrified her.

To escape the spiral of negative thoughts, she resorted to the one thing that was always able to give her succour - music. She picked up the majestic cello, ran her splayed fingers up and down its spine, the feel of the burnished wood so smooth and cool to the touch. It comforted her. The occasional tuck and catch in her throat now the only sign of her anguish, she began playing, this time the movement *Prayer*, a staggeringly beautiful arrangement from *Jewish Life*. It had taken her months of practice to perfect and oh that difficult middle section.

Abigail inhaled through her nostrils, delaying each outward breath a while as the cello's bass notes resonated through the room with its sonorous, languid vibrato.

Abigail dipped once more back into her formative years to the accompaniment of her virtuoso touch and elegant bow work, each note gave voice to Bloch's masterpiece. And as the final tone decayed she whispered words her mother had taught to her many years ago, the words of wise King Solomon, 'All is vanity and a chasing after wind.'

As before, the healing of music and words had stoked a nascent repair of Abigail Perdue's worn and derelict spirit.

On the way back to their cells, Nader began talking to Mike. 'I think you did really well in there, Mike. You were really brave. I've no doubt that Allah will bring you into the Host. You certainly will have my support.'

Mike slapped his buddy's sturdy back and said, 'Thank you my friend. That was the hardest thing I ever had to do. To tell you the truth I'm more than a little worried about this accusation.'

'Tell me this Mike. Imagine you had three daughters. Then one day the eldest comes home and says, Father I have fallen in love with a Chinese man. The next day your second child comes to see you and says, Papa, I'm going to marry a man from the Lebanon.' Khoury was grinning mischievously, while Mike wondered where this was leading. 'Then on the third day, your youngest child – whom you love the most – tells you she wants to marry some black guy. How do you react?'

Mike took his time and said 'Well, as long as all three guys were good to my girls, then personally I wouldn't have a problem with it.'

'See! You have nothing to worry about. This accusation is groundless,' Nader spread his palms wide and shrugged. 'Don't worry brother.'

'I'm not so sure, Nader. When you sit in that chair, I don't know how to explain, it just compels you to spill your guts.'

'Well then I'm in big trouble too. I've done many things to be ashamed of. I have not led a righteous life,' The fisherman remarked with a furrowed brow.

'Nader, forgive me, but who the fuck has? The Dalai Lama, maybe. Ghandi or some saint? Most of us, we fuck up. But do you know what? I think they get that here. I think they understand that we are far from perfect and that surprisingly they love us for it, despite our faults.'

'I hope you are right, Mike. I so wish I had a cigarette,' Nader's fresh exposure to nicotine was bringing on diabolical cravings.

'You can't buddy, those things will kill you. Don't you know that?' Mike laughed. And in their shared laughter both men felt the bond of friendship strengthen between them.

Meanwhile Monique had cornered the newcomer - the Filipino seaman - Tomas Esposito. She was filling his head with her conspiracy theory and making a case for the penitents all sticking together, 'We should stick together, that is definitely what we should do,' she urged.

The quietly spoken Tomas was taken aback by the whirlwind of words that came from what he had mistakenly thought was a quiet old lady. He could clearly see now that Doctor Dumond was a forceful and combative personality.

The Arcs had convened in a small antechamber adjacent to Room 5, leaving Marcus and Maryam alone. 'So what happened to that playboy dipstick, Andersson?'

'Now, now, Marcus, have a little compassion,' Maryam rebuked playfully.

'I'm sorry Maryam, really. But he has to be one of the more taxing souls, to have crossed my path for many a year.'

'He has begun a new life. Let's hope his more humble surroundings will rub off on his character.'

'But why not wash him in the waters of Lethe, before sending him back?'

'Because his soul is badly corrupted, Marcus,' she explained. 'For it to have any chance of redemption, it needs to have some realisation of the consequences of poor choices. He probably won't have a total recall, but enough to prompt a considered response. If it fails, then it is likely to be his last chance. I hope he makes it.'

'You are far too merciful sometimes. I don't hold out too much hope for him. Did you see what he did to Lou before he left?'

'Of course, but his insolence is learned behaviour, it is not hardwired yet.'

On account of the delay in the proceedings the jurors were informed that a special banquet had been laid in their honour and they would take supper as a group on their final night in Stasis. There was a solitary knock on the door and Monique let herself in. Not everyone was happy to see her. Miyu for one was glad that the only available chair was furthest from her. Monique apologised for her tardiness.

Abigail and a few of the other jurors also had helped themselves to a little wine and its effect was starting to loosen tongues. She suggested a parlour game - an idea which was enthusiastically received by most. They would each tell the others one secret about their lives that they had never spoken of before.

Around the table it went, with each person unloading a secret or a burden they had carried around with them for too long. Tomas was the only one who resisted, the others let it pass, not wanting to make him feel uncomfortable.

Abigail's secret had been her sexuality, she'd never come out to her family. Mike's story was entertainingly embarrassing and had produced loud whoops and peals of laughter. But it was Monique who had brought stunned silence to the diners, when she told them she'd lived before and remembered some of her experiences, but when pressed, she point-blank refused to reveal who she had been.

Finally it was Miyu's turn. She looked up at the ceiling and in her soft voice, a barely audible whisper said, 'I tricked Sato.'

Later, when their supper was ended and having eaten and drunk their fill, the festivities came to a close. None would sleep well on their final night on Stasis. Some were haunted by scenes from their past. Some had vivid dreams that woke them up in a torrid sweat. Others gave up the ghost and didn't try for sleep at all, but sat there contemplating their final hours. What comes next? None could tell.

Abigail Perdue was one of those who couldn't find peace or comfort. As well as her own situation, she thought about her new friends. Of course she realised that she barely knew them. *Oh my God, Miyu! She planned her pregnancy! The little minx and all of us full of sympathy for her.* You can just never tell with people.

Like all of us humans, Miyu Tanaka was a far more complex creature than she first appeared. Nonetheless Abigail liked her very much.

And Mike! She remembered how easy his banter with that creepy Swede. The accusations against him had tarnished her good guy opinion of him somewhat, *Throw enough mud and I guess some of it's going to stick, but a bigot? No, I don't think he really is.* She spent long hours figuring it all out, right up until the dawning of the day.

Arising with the sun, the jurors dressed and made their way to Room 5.

When they entered the chamber, it was already alive with activity. Lou's prediction had been correct. There were a number of new faces sitting in the gallery behind the Protatori bench.

The Prots and Advocates were at the places and the jurors took their seats. Last to arrive were the Arcs and Gideon.

'Good morning,' Gideon addressed all present. 'Tomas Esposito, step forth and be judged.'

THE JUDGMENT OF TOMAS ESPOSITO.

The Filipino seaman gracefully made his way over to the Judgment chair. It was clear that he was nervous. When his Prot began questioning him, he spoke much too quickly to be properly understood. Marcus approached and calmed him. His rate of speech then slowed to a more intelligible degree.

Niccolò circled the room taking pot-shots but Tomas answered well.

Tomas Esposito had always been poor, he had always had to struggle, yet there was no discernible anger in the man or self-pity at his situation. In fact he came across as resilient and resolutely cheerful.

The closest the Prince could get to a reaction was when he accused the Filipino of being resentful and jealous of the people he served: the wealthy and those more fortunate than he. Mike could see the tensing of the body, the arteries engorged and throbbing in his neck, Tomas denied that he had been any of these things.

'Then you were not jealous, because you could feel nothing! When your wife died you became a hollow man. You gave up on life, cared for nothing, felt nothing.'

There is a line that when crossed, sees a badly frightened man become no longer afraid. When the Prot mentioned his wife, Tomas stepped over that line and just kept going. He stood up from the chair and pointed at the Prot, his eyes narrowed and he unburdened himself of the question he had been waiting for more than twenty years to ask. It began first as an impassioned plea but rose quickly in intensity, as rapidly as the rage that was erupting in his chest. 'Why?!' he all but screamed. 'Why did you take my wife? Why did you hurt her? You see everything here! You know everything! So you knew she was my world. She was not a bad person, she never hurt another soul and yet you still took Gloria away from me? His eyes burned with fire as he repeated his accusation to the Arcs.

'Why do you take people so young? Good people who are loved. It's just not right! It's not fair. You are murderers!' he yelled. Tomas was trembling, his hands clenched, the knuckles turning white.

Marcus looked on quietly contemplating what he was seeing, this mere human daring to confront three powerful Seraphs. It took all sorts of strange things to produce courage. Some people like the American, did dangerous jobs for a living. They took calculated risks and they were brave. But real courage is demonstrated by people who although terribly afraid, still manage to stand up and fight back.

I think the Arcs are impressed by this quality, he guessed. The Seraph's certainly did not display any overt hostility to the seaman. They just observed impassively and listened as he cursed them and all religion.

Niccolò faced the juror and looked him directly in his eyes. 'People die every day, Mister Esposito, all over the world. It is just the way things are.'

'But you leave people behind who feel half dead inside. Why could you not take me as well? What did we ever do to your God?' he cried.

'So you confess to being a non-believer, Mister Esposito?' Niccolò was undistracted from his role.

'You left me with nothing to believe in,' he said. 'You took everything.'

'But you believe now, don't you? Now you are here in Stasis.'

Tomas shrugged in defeat. 'What choice do I have? What choice did any of us have?' Tomas eyes turned towards his fellow five jurors.

'We are only like playthings to you,' he spat the bitter words out, but it was his final parry. His anger now spent, Tomas' tired face fell and his hands dropped to his sides in unison. Abigail rushed from her seat to comfort the poor man while the Archangels looked on.

'A brief adjournment please, Gideon,' Marcus requested.

'Yes of course,' he agreed. 'We will recommence in fifteen minutes.'

Most of the jury were glad to get out of Room 5, at least for a few moments. Tension hung heavy in the air, ratcheted up a few more notches by the Tomas' unexpected outburst. Abigail had escorted him out into the gardens, guiding him to a bench where he thanked her for her kindness. He asked if she would allow him a few moments alone in order to gather his thoughts.

'Sure, Mister Esposito, no problem. You take whatever time you need,' Abigail smiled sympathetically. She walked back towards the Stasis block and at the entrance she bumped into Nader, on his way out.

'Well that was certainly intense,' he exhaled, 'I didn't think the little guy had it in him.'

'That poor man,' Abigail said. 'It must be really something to have so much love in your heart for one person.' Abigail's expression grew sad as if she remembered something now lost to her. The fisherman had noticed. 'Did you leave someone special behind?'

Nader's tone was noticeably more gentle, he was making a special effort to be kind, which surprised her.

'Yes I did,' she sighed. 'We'd been planning to go on holiday together.' a sorrowful look crossed her pale features.

'I'm sure that he misses you very much.'

'She,' Abigail replied.

'Pardon?' the Fishing boat captain was confused.

'My lover is a she, Nader, not a he,' Abigail hooted with barely supressed laughter on witnessing his discomfort. Only then did she remember that Nader had gone to the restroom, when she'd revealed her secret. He hadn't heard. 'Her name is Katie.'

'Oh? I see,' Nader lied. He was in fact completely astounded. *This woman is gay? I would never have guessed.*

He wondered how this news would go with the Arcs. After a few seconds of protracted silence, Abigail moved to the whereabouts of their mutual friend.

'Have you seen Mike anywhere?'

Nader, glad of the chance to move off topic, responded in an over-eager manner. He blustered that Mike had been cornered by the old doctor in the corridor. 'She's browbeating him about a voting pact.'

'I'll head back in then. Maybe he is in need of rescue.'

Captain Khoury nodded in agreement. But he believed that it was he, who needed most to be saved.

thirteen

THE JUDGMENT OF NADER KHOURY.

The abrupt confession by the fisherman, that he was involved in human trafficking, brought gasps from Abigail and Miyu and reproachful looks from the doctor and the Filipino.

Mike felt sorry for his new friend. This revelation could really hurt him.

The Judgments had resumed and all had again assembled in the court. Nader had been commanded to step forth and be judged and his Prot, Jocelyn, wasted no time in laying into him. She had quite a lot of material to choose from.

She had begun by asking about an incident during Nader's younger years. He had happened across a prominent religious figure who was forcing himself on a young girl, but he had pretended to see nothing and never spoke of it again. When Jocelyn pressed him about why he had not intervened, Nader simply said, 'I was afraid.'

His counsel rebutted by explaining that the mullah was a man of power and influence in his community, whereas Nader was a newcomer and a foreigner. He would have signed his own death warrant if he'd caused trouble.

'You know that Gehenna has seen plenty of mullahs, rabbi's and priests, who had pretended to be men of faith. They came seeking their reward in the Heofon, but we gave it to them here instead,' the Prot remarked, glowering at Nader, despising his cowardice.

Jocelyn then threw down her ace - Nader Khoury was a human trafficker. She began reading a list of names, it went on and on and on. She asked the fisherman if he was familiar with any of them? When he answered no, she really let fly.

'Those are the names of people who died as drug addicts, prostitutes, people who were murdered, exploited and abused. The thing they have in common - You were their Charon, you were their boatman who took them to this fate. You were complicit in their degrading!'

The Advocate Marcus looked on nervously, his broad fingers repeatedly running over his strong jaw. However to his credit Nader made no attempt to sugar-coat anything. He proffered no excuses. He sat up tall and told his story warts and all.

Monique clucked her tongue. She had been convinced this Arab was a shady character and now she was proven right. *Maybe it will take some of the heat off me,* she thought. *Human trafficking's not something the Arcs will look kindly on.*

Jocelyn was on a roll and not about to stop now. 'Not only were there many who went to a premature death, there were also many more who suffered mental illness and loneliness,' she added.

Loneliness - the new buzzword in Stasis. More caustic to the soul than any would have imagined. In the last fifty years, more and more souls were coming in with something up until then, rarely seen. Their mass blemished and bloated, not by their mis-deeds but from their despair. Loneliness they'd found was toxic to a soul. The top minds in Stasis were set to work, to discover the reason for this disturbing trend. Their findings, it was rumoured, were why a meeting of the Sacred Council had been called.

We humans build bigger and vaster mega cities, and in the midst of all these vast crowds, people have been never more alone. The old are discarded, their knowledge wasted. The young left fearful and anxious. Loneliness is the sickness of mankind's future. A disease of the soul. Something has to be done.

Where did it all go wrong in the sophisticated West? Where the affluent hide behind high gates and security cameras and ultimately die alone, unappreciated and unnoticed until the heat makes their corpses smell like putrid garbage.

Marcus was ripped from his thoughts by an elbow in the side from Maryam and the sound of his name being called. It was Gideon.

'Advocate Marcus......Advocate Marcus, do you wish to offer a rebuttal.'

'Indeed I do, Gideon, yes.' Marcus unfolded his heavy limbs and got up from his bench. He approached Nader, who looked shattered from his time in the chair. He hadn't warned him about what he was going to say next.

'Nader Khoury has been described to you by my esteemed colleague - he nodded towards Jocelyn - as a merciless human trafficker - and she's right. He is!'

Nader shot up in the chair, *What type of defence is this?*

'Well he is the second part at least, a smuggler of people. But Nader Khoury is not without mercy, ladies and gentlemen. Far from it.' Marcus looked directly at the jury.

'Five years ago, Nader was making one of his illegal runs, when a passenger died on board his boat, a young woman who had a baby cradled in her arms. At the time the Captain was approaching the Italian coast and those on board were getting ready to jump.'

'What would you do in his situation? None of the women would agree to take the child, Nader was desperate. There was one man who came forward, he wanted to take her. But there was something about his expression that ran a chill down Nader's spine. Captain Khoury believed he was in the presence of evil. He had no proof on which to base his gut-feeling. It was a hunch nothing more, but there was no way that this man was getting the infant.'

Nader took the baby into the wheelhouse and swaddled it in some blankets. Then as he guided the boat as near to the shore as he could safely go, the man appeared at the door and made a lunge for the child. Nader met him with a fierce blow. He picked up the demon and tossed him over the side. It's only a pity that the blow did not kill him. We may have seen him in Stasis sooner than we did. Three years later, he arrived, a serial abuser who stole children and sold them for profit.' Marcus remembered him being swiftly dispatched to Gehenna.

He continued his story to the attentive jury how, when Nader got home, he persuaded his wife to care for the child and they raised it as their own. 'Mina is Nader's daughter now, but she is not his blood. His actions saved her life that day. Not to forget the children and the woman he saved before he drowned. During your deliberations, you would do well to remember this.'

Abigail Perdue looked at Nader Khoury and saw him through new eyes. She was not alone.

THE JUDGMENT OF MONIQUE DUMOND.

'We have now come to the final Judgment,' Gideon announced.

'Monique Dumond, step forth and be judged.'

The shrew-faced woman rose slowly from her chair, fussed over her jacket then made her way across to the seat. She was turned out immaculately as always. Abigail could see a glimpse of the dashing figure she must have cut in her younger days. The advancing years had worn at her Patrician features like the blows of a relentless sea, eroding her beauty until it was all but vanished. Nonetheless the woman exuded a certain poise.

Yet Abigail had not warmed to her. Monique remained aloof from the group, only speaking to the others occasionally, to warn about Stasis and to press for their vote.

She's creepy and a little bit nuts, Abigail figured.

Monique lowered herself carefully into the chair, straightening the hem of her twill skirt. Her voice came out reedy and nervous punctuated by the occasional raspy cough. There is no illness that afflicts the human body on Stasis, so Abigail presumed it to be an affectation or perhaps her nerves were troubling her. Certainly she seemed unusually apprehensive.

Niccolò was to be her Prot and at the beginning he played her along with kid gloves. It was almost a love-in. His questions allowed her to present her best side, her work and the advancement of medical science. It was easy to discern that pride ran deep in the doctor.

But then came the fall.

'Doctor Dumond may I ask you, has there ever been any indiscretions on your part, during your marriage?'

'I must confess that over a period of several years in the latter-stages, I did maintain a physical relationship with a work colleague. When my husband Albert discovered our liaisons, I fear it contributed greatly to the decline in his health.' She wiped nervously at her eyes, but no tears were evident.

'My dear Albert sadly passed away some seven months later, from a mystery illness.' Monique lowered her head in a show of contrition. The Advocate Marcus stared slack jawed not believing what he had just heard.

She couldn't go through with it! Damn her to hell, she couldn't do it, he fumed. *She has omitted the most crucial part of her testimony. She can't get away with this?*

He looked over aghast at Maryam who returned a look of acute surprise. Monique resumed her perjured testimony; she never remarried and immersed herself in her work and with helping others. Again Marcus was left to ruminate over the sheer chutzpah of this old woman. She was definitely going for broke in her attempt to swing the jury. It annoyed him that she, of all people, was getting such an easy ride. Niccolò was returning to his bench, saying, 'That is all for now.'

A glimmer of hope flickered in Monique's trenchant eyes.

'But wait...' he turned back. I almost forgot. 'Monique Dumond, you killed your husband, did you not? Or is it your direct intention to deceive this jury?'

Her face flushed with anger, 'It was a mystery illness, nothing was proven. They were unable to diagnose,' she fired back her retort.

'It was poison Madam Dumond!'

Sweet mother of the divine! Mike thought. *This day gets more and more interesting.*

Doctor Dumond was then completely exposed by Niccolò. He read aloud from a document handed to him by Jocelyn, how Monique regularly applied minuscule, nearly untraceable amounts of botulinum toxin. A protein and neurotoxin produced by the bacterium clostridium botulinum. It is the most acutely toxic substance known to mankind and used in the manufacture of Botox, a substance which millions of people voluntarily inject into their skin, in a futile attempt to hold onto their youth.

Marcus used to laugh, rather unkindly, at some of the souls who arrived in Stasis with their exaggerated bee-stung lips and unwrinkled brows. That was until Maryam chastised him for it.

Niccolò continued, 'In your role as a Senior Researcher, Doctor Dumond, you had ample access to supplies of the non-synthe-sised Botulinum Toxin. And as it accumulated in his system, over a protracted period of lethal exposure, poor Albert died a quite horrible death,' he accused.

The jury looked first at Monique who had her face clasped in her spidery hands, then at the Prot, then back to the doctor, now unmasked as a murderer.

But Monique was not finished yet. She flashed a look of pure malevolence towards Niccolò. 'I had to do it! He was a witless dullard! He threatened to divorce me if I didn't end my relation-ship with Nicolas. He threatened me....Me?! After all I had done for him.' Her eyes blazed and her retort bore a final barb.

'Would any of you, who have a heart...,' she looked at the jurors, '..unlike you heartless creatures,' she directed her scorn at the Arcs.

'Would you have condemned me to an entire life, not worth living, to a boorish, fool of a man? If he had divorced me I would have been scandalised. I had no other choice,' she cried. But the fire went out of her eyes, the fight in her gone. She slouched in the chair, defeated. Abigail Perdue looked across at this poor lost soul with something akin to pity.

'We have come to the end of the Judgments,' Maryam announced. 'But before we proceed to the closing arguments, I would like to show you all someplace very special.'

With the session concluded, the Advocate asked the jury to follow her out of the chamber and into the corridor, where she stopped at the furthest door. Marcus had come along too, leaving the Arcs to their deliberations.

'I believe this is something you will all find interesting,' Maryam said, opening the portal. Behind the door, the penitents were astonished to see rows and rows of enormously tall wooden structures - like the most massive library imaginable but with each shelf divided into numerous cubby holes of about two inches square. This grand room ran as far back as the eye could see.

There must be hundreds, perhaps thousands, Abigail was awed by the scale involved.

'What are they for? What are all these millions of little boxes?' Nader asked.

'Billions!' Marcus replied.

'Go look and see,' Maryam encouraged.

Each of the jurors walked along a single row with their Advocates following close behind. It was apparent that each tiny box housed a small slip of paper.

'Choose one,' Maryam instructed 'Do please return it after, to exactly the same place where you found it.'

Miyu slipped her hand into a randomly chosen cubby and retrieved a slip of vellum paper. Inscribed on it was someone's name with one word written directly underneath.

'Moshe Weinmann,' she called out in surprise, then, 'Heofon.' *Well done Mister Moshe, whoever you were. You made it to the Host,* Miyu smiled.

Mike Roberts retrieved another, 'Peter Laidlaw, Reborn,' he exclaimed, his voice full of wonder. Abigail asked why her chosen box had two slips of paper. She took both in her hands. The first said, Robert Barr, Reborn. The second said, Maria Esteban, Heofon.

Nader joined in, 'Mine has two also. What's that about?'

Maryam explained that it was the record of the journey of the same soul. 'The first slip refers to the soul's first life on Earth,' she pointed at the papers that Abigail was holding. 'The soul that lived as Robert Barr was sent back to be Reborn, this time as a woman named Maria Esteban. She made it home to the Heofon,' she explained.

'This is The Room of Records,' Marcus said. 'In here is detailed the record of every human that has ever lived and died. And also the verdict that was recorded at their Judgment.'

Tomas was shocked to read the two slips that he had chosen, it chronicled that the Soul was Reborn whereas after the second incarnation it was condemned to Gehenna. *An errant soul,* he shuddered.

Monique looked at the name on the slip that she had chosen, the name inscribed on it read, Johanna Magdalena Ritschel, it stated Reborn, as the verdict.

She dropped the vellum paper on the floor as if it had burned her skin. Then she bent down, picked it up and stuffed it hastily back into its slot. The Advocate Marcus, stood arms folded at the end of her row, watching her intently.

fourteen

THE CALLING OF JAMES JONES
FROM THE GREAT HOST.

A large crowd had gathered for the most anticipated part of the day. Lou had brought in extra chairs and it was now standing room only. Prior to the verdicts, there was an important piece of business to conclude. The soul of a former window cleaner, James Jones, was summoned from the Heofon to appear before the jury, where he would give testimony relating to the accusation made against Mike.

A vibrant hum of conversation permeated the room. Then Gideon called for silence.

As he did, the door opened. A Puerto Rican man of about forty entered. He appeared calm but a little uneasy, as if unused to his new skin.

'Please take a seat Mister Jones,' Gideon welcomed the arrival from the Host.

As James Jones was not on trial, he would not be questioned by either the Prots or the Advocates. This star witness would only be addressed by the Presiding Justice.

'Mister Jones, it goes without saying that you will remember the day of your passing from the Earth.'

'Yes sir, I sure do.'

'Do you recognise the young man seated across from you?'.

'I believe I do,' he said. 'He's the young fireman who came to save us.'

'But he did not save you, did he?'

'No, sir, he did not,' The man answered.

'Could he have saved you Mister Jones?' Gideon asked.

'I do believe he could have, yes.'

A surge of whispers broke out in the gallery. Mike's face drained of colour.

'So he chose to save your colleague rather than you because you are a black man?' the justice said.

'No sir, I didn't say that. He saved my friend, because he was closest to him,' James Jones replied truthfully. He was closer to him than to me, that's all.'

'But you said that he could have saved you.'

'Yeah, I guess he probably could. But then my friend would have died. So there really was no win for him.' The soul from the Host smiled at Mike. 'The boy just went for the nearest guy to him. That's what I believe happened.' James Jones nodded solemnly

'So you don't believe that this young man is a racist?'

'Whoah! I know nothing about that sir. Maybe he is. Maybe he ain't,' he paused. 'I just know that I didn't die on account of him. It was just my time that's all.'

'Thank you for your testimony Mister Jones,' Gideon dismissed the witness.

'My pleasure,' James Jones looked across at Mike and said, 'It's okay son, it wasn't your fault, no way, no how.' He walked across and shook hands.

Lou escorted him from the chamber. Passing Jocelyn he winked mischievously and whispered, 'Not today Jo, not this one.' There was barely time to catch breath before Gideon called time on the verdicts.

'Here we go,' said Mike.

THE VERDICTS ON THE QUORUM OF SIX.

Once all six jurors were accounted for and seated in their place. Maryam said, 'I would like you all now to place your slate on your knees. When you are asked individually to present your verdict, I would request you to hold it out in front of you, so that all can see clearly. I understand you are all rather anxious, so we will begin immediately.'

THE VERDICT RECORDED ON THE SOUL OF TOMAS ESPOSITO.

The Archangel Michael's deep voice reverberated around the room, 'With regards to the soul of Tomas Esposito, how say you?'

Maryam bowed her head in the direction of Miyu Tanaka, who slowly and methodically inscribed her verdict. Maryam asked her to raise her slate and she did so, turning it out for all to see. She had inscribed the word, Heofon.

Miyu turned smiling to look at Tomas, who grinned back and nodded in gratitude.

Next it was Mike's turn, once more the slate was inscribed with the word, Heofon.

Another bout of happy grins is exchanged between most of the Penitents. Things were going well so far, for Tomas.

Next to go was Abigail. She gave a dramatic exhalation of breath before declaring her decision, to send the soul of the Filipino seaman to the Heofon. Three down and only two to go. No matter how the remaining votes went, Tomas was almost sure to be declared as Puresoul. Provided of course, that the Arcs agreed with the verdict.

Nader Khoury displayed his vote. It said Heofon.

Only Monique had a different verdict, she had inscribed the word Reborn, on her slate. Monique had no particular reason for disliking 'that little brown fellow,' as she called him, but she wasn't in the mood to be generous.

Then the Archangel Gabriel spoke. His voice not as sumptuous as Michael's but it had nevertheless a pleasant value. 'Tomas Esposito, it is the verdict of the jury of your five peers, by a count of 4 votes to 1, that you be sent to the Heofon. We, as the Creator's representatives, concur with this decision. Let it be recorded that you are Puresoul, bound for the Great Host of Souls, at the conclusion of this hearing.'

Tomas was brimming with happiness. Mike Roberts could not restrain himself from punching the air and shouting an ebullient cheer, 'Whooo hooo!' And despite the state of tension in the room, it was a reaction that provoked only smiles from Marcus and Maryam.

Abigail and Miyu both clearly delighted by the verdict, broke into spontaneous applause.

THE VERDICT RECORDED ON THE SOUL OF MIYU TANAKA.

The Archangel Michael recorded the final judgment of Tomas Esposito in the Book, and then called out, 'With regards to the soul of Miyu Tanaka, how say you?' Miyu lowered her eyes to the floor not bearing to look. Tomas went first, on the slate held out in front of his slight frame. He had inscribed the word Heofon.

Mike on the other hand had struggled hard with his decision regarding the young Japanese girl. She had after all taken her own life, but he acknowledged that she had particularly difficult circumstances. He had thus inscribed the word Reborn.

Abigail had felt enormous compassion for little Miyu and even though she was not as innocent as first thought, she had written the word Heofon as her verdict.

Nader felt he could not in all good conscience send this girl to the Host. Understanding the gravity and sanctity of this decision, he wrote Reborn.

So with four verdicts in, Miyu had two votes for the Heofon and two to be Reborn. The final verdict was down to Monique. With no sign of emotion, inscribed in spidery handwriting, a six letter word Reborn. Maryam stepped forward saying, 'Thank you for your verdicts.'

The Archangel Gabriel looked on the young girl and declared, 'Miyu Tanaka, the jury of your peers have recommended that you be Reborn.' Miyu raised her head and exhaled the tension out of her body. But the Arc was not done, 'We have decided, that your soul will not be Reborn today. You will spend some time with us in Stasis, where an appointed role may soon become available. We are perhaps in need of a new custodian for our Library.'

'It is true,' a voice came from out from the gallery. It was the Librarian, Li Er. 'I have waited a long time for the right soul to come along. My bones are old and tired. It is well overdue that I return to the Great Host. I believe that this young soul will make a suitable curator,' he nodded towards the girl, who smiled back enthusiastically.

Miyu was over-joyed. She bowed towards the Arc, acknowledging her acceptance of his decision.

The Archangel Michael, Keeper of the Book of Life and Death entered the verdict.

THE VERDICT RECORDED ON THE SOUL OF MICHAEL ROBERTS.

'With regards to the soul of Michael Roberts, how say you?' The rich baritone of the Keeper of the Book, rang through the chamber once more. The cheerful Tomas, clutched up his slate, inscribed with the word Heofon. He smiled at Mike, who was very pleased. Miyu also had voted for the Heofon, as did Abigail, as did Nader. Mike could not resist giving two thumbs up to his friends. He looked to each in turn, silently expressing his gratitude, to each of these kind souls. Then it was Monique's turn. To everyone's surprise she had also inscribed Heofon.

Monique shrugged. The young American was brash and loud but it was clear he was some sort of boy-scout type. Hence she had concluded that since she must offer some mercy, he should have it. Mike Roberts threw back his head in relief and whispered, 'Thank you.'

The Archangel Gabriel cast the final verdict, saying, 'Michael Roberts, any who lays down his life for another saves the world entire and is demonstrably Puresoul. We concur with the verdict and at the conclusion of this Judgment, you will be bound for the Great Host.'

Mike was going home to his mom. Overcome, he screwed his eyes shut and rubbed at the tears, as the Keeper recorded the verdict on his soul.

Three verdicts had been recorded and two already bound for the Host. It was shaping up to be an auspicious day. It was at least for Mike and Tomas who would within moments ascend to paradise. I should know not to speak of omens here, but sometimes the old faith still lingers in the language.

I had of course no idea of the unexpected surprise that was in store for me. It never had crossed my mind. Three more souls then to receive their verdicts and then it will be done. Of the three awaiting, one was unlikely to go well. It simply couldn't happen, not after all that had transpired, not after the mercy and compassion that had been so graciously and in my view, *naively* extended. The verdicts on Abigail, Nader and Monique, were all that remain to be heard.

THE VERDICT RECORDED ON THE SOUL OF ABIGAIL PERDUE.

This was to be the first time that the Filipino had deviated from his earlier pattern. Tomas had hesitated but for Abigail he had - not without some misgiving - recorded the word Reborn.

She seemed to him a very likeable young woman. However he felt he could not condone what had happened to her cousin and that perhaps she needed a little more time. He did feel bad, knowing that Abigail had already voted for him to ascend. Abigail bit on her lower lip when she saw his vote.

A tiny spark of anger ignited and left her aggrieved, *I voted in his favour and he screws me over!* But it quenched and passed quickly. She was prepared for the worst, but human nature also meant she'd been hoping for the best.

At least he had not inscribed Gehenna.

Miyu soon put a smile back on the young woman's face. She had determined that Abigail should go to the Heofon. She was confident in her decision. Abigail felt the first wave of relief. Mike had no doubt that she was Puresoul – she should be sent to the Great Host of Souls, so another vote for the Heofon.

Just Nader and Monique to go, Abigail was pressing hard on her knuckles, feeling none too confident in the outcome.

Nader had deliberated for the longest time with this one, for him it had been the hardest choice and it was one that troubled him greatly. *She's not ready for the Heofon.* Yet he had gotten to know a little of this individual and he knew she was certainly not a bad soul. In his opinion, the very best he could do, was to vote Reborn. Abigail was dejected. It showed clearly on her face.

Two votes each for Reborn and the Host, with the casting ballot going to Doctor Dumond. Her breath held fast. At that moment, Abigail Perdue did not feel it would go her way. She was right. Monique turned her slate to the front with the slightest crease of a smile, as if somehow she'd got some dubious satisfaction by blocking the passage home of this young soul. On her slate she had inscribed Reborn.

I'm not going to the Heofon, Abigail cried quietly to herself, crestfallen. She brought her hands to her eyes, but she understood that under the circumstances, it had been an unrealistic goal. Reborn was the best that she could have hoped for, but it had been impossible not to dream about what might have been. For now the thought of being born again held certain trepidations for her.

The Archangel Gabriel pronounced, 'Abigail Perdue it is the verdict of the jury on a count of 3 votes to 2, that you be Reborn and...'

'Wait!' Mike Roberts had leapt from his chair, 'Stop please, take me instead. I will go back in her place. Abigail is Puresoul, I know it! She should be in the Host. Please, I beg of you!'

Abigail ran her palms over her tired and strained features. *Typical Mike*, she laughed bitterly, *Always coming to the rescue, no matter how lost the situation*. And in that moment she felt nothing but love for this brave young man. The Keeper of the Book glowered a fierce warning at Mike, 'Be silent and resume your place!'

'I would like to speak for this child.' A measured, gentle voice came from behind the jurors.

The jurors twisted in the chairs to see who had spoken and Abigail was aghast. It was the Patriarch of Limbus Stasis. He had been watching the proceedings from the gallery, seated quietly alongside the Attendant, Lou. He approached Abigail, offered both hands and she automatically raised hers to meet them. 'I know this girl as one of my tribe. I have a request of her. We have an Advocate's role we would like her to fulfil.'

The Archangels Gabriel, Michael and the Angel Ananchel, bowed reverently.

Abigail's eyes opened wide in surprise and her mouth dropped open.

The Patriarch said to Mike. 'Your offer to take this young woman's place is a generous one, I fear you do not realise how munificent. But it is unnecessary. She will return to the Heofon in due course. Will you accept, Abigail?'

'Yes, of course,' she replied.

The Archangel entered the decision of Abram, Governor of Limbus Stasis. Maryam led a trembling Abigail back to her seat. She was not shaking from fear, of which there was a complete absence. She trembled with pure emotion.

THE VERDICT RECORDED ON THE SOUL OF NADER KHOURY.

'With regards to the soul of Nader Khoury, how say you?' The voice of the Archangel Michael called out, reminding all, there were still two Judgments to conclude.

Tomas saw in Nader Khoury a troubled man, a man who struggled with his principles but not evil. Nonetheless he had been directly involved in the misery of trafficking. Once more, he could not in his heart, give a vote for the Heofon. And as such he wrote Reborn.

Nader took a deep breath and braced himself for the other verdicts.

Miyu being next also recorded Reborn. She also had qualms about what the fisherman had been up to. *Maybe I'm going back?* Captain Khoury figured. *I need only one more vote.*

Mike Roberts looked his good friend straight in the eye, turned his slate out and declared for Heofon. Nader raised his hand to his heart, signalling his eternal affection for his American friend. Abigail had really wanted to declare a verdict of Heofon, but she realised that she wanted to do it more for Mike than for herself. Nader had been mixed up in a lot of dodgy stuff during his time on Earth, but she had gained enough humility here to understand there are very few without fault. *Heofon or Reborn, which to choose,* she hesitated. A voice in her head said, *He screwed you over, it's payback time.* She ignored it, but still her vote was Reborn.

Perhaps Nader would be the type of person who would make a good Advocate, she thought. He certainly seemed quite a similar personality to Marcus. Mike was disappointed with her vote, although he did his best to hide it, whereas Nader Khoury did not react. He just sat there in silence, looking on, kneading his hands in frustration. *It could be a lot worse,* he reckoned.

Monique had far too much disdain for a man she believed to be surly and untrustworthy. She'd felt vindicated when his smuggling activities were uncovered and brought out into the cold light of day, for all to see. As such she had no trouble in choosing to send the Arab to – Gehenna.

There was a distinct cry from several sources when Monique showed her verdict.

It was the first time in this quorum of six that any of the souls had opted for the destruction of another. But Monique sat stone-faced, looked directly ahead and had no doubts about the righteousness of her vote.

Nader was genuinely shocked. *This same woman had been urging us all to take part in a voting pact, to send all to the Heofon, and now she wants me destroyed?!* His eyes burned with rage, as he stared across at the bat-faced crone. *Maybe it will be okay, I have three votes to go back, I just need the Arcs vote now. I would settle for that,* he concluded nervously.

A hush descended as the Archangel Gabriel said 'Nader Khoury you have received the verdict of the jury. Three are in favour of your Rebirth, one believes your soul should be in the Heofon and one feels that you should be destroyed in Gehenna.'

Before continuing with his decision, the Arc looked at each of the jurors in turn, 'I thank each of you for your verdict. Nader Khoury, there is no doubt that you have made many bad choices. You have not lived well and we would ordinarily agree that you should be sent down to be dismantled.' Nader could barely breathe with the tightness in his chest.

'Nevertheless, the moment you made a choice to save four young lives, you redeemed almost every bad choice you had ever made. This was your reprieve.'

Nader looked on stunned, almost traumatised, as the Arc resumed speaking. 'That one act of faith, laying down your life for others unknown, has saved your soul. As the representatives of the Creator, our verdict does not concur with the jury. You will not be Reborn, but will work for a time, here on Stasis, as a new Advocate of Souls.'

Nader's ears were ringing with the shouts of delight from his companions and the emotions that were assailing his senses.

He was staggered, in a state of utter disbelief, after all he had done so much wrong, and yet he would stay on as an Advocate, 'All praise to Allah, the ever merciful,' he mumbled. Nader, for the second time, felt warm tears sting his face, his redemption was almost complete.

THE VERDICT RECORDED ON THE SOUL OF MONIQUE DUMOND.

This is the one I had been waiting for. If she had adhered to what I'd told her to say, then just maybe, the outcome - although not good - may at least have been bearable. In this difficult case I can honestly say I had to put aside my personal animosity and my own belief in what should happen and put the interest of the soul foremost. It was my job after all.

When the din had finally died down, the Keeper called the last name, 'With regards to the soul of Monique Dumond, how say you?'

Tomas had been won over by the doctor, although he was dismayed to learn that she had murdered her husband. All considered he just didn't have it in him to condemn a soul, however bad, to Gehenna. As such Tomas inscribed the word - Reborn.

Monique mouthed a nervous 'Thank you,' to the seaman.

Miyu, had also felt great pity for the old woman. She had worked hard all her life, studied for years and had achieved much. That she'd committed a terrible crime was not in doubt, but it must be balanced by the fact that in her work she had helped many people. As such Miyu Tanaka chalked her verdict down as Reborn.

Monique did not visibly react this time, but instead kept her gaze fixed directly ahead. She was so close now, she could feel it. *Just one more vote!* Maybe she would see Munich again.

Mike had been appalled when he'd learned that this doctor could stoop so low as to murder her husband. *His life must have been hard enough been married to this stuck up bitch, besides she also tried to stitch up Nader.* He tried to reinforce his opinions, but it was fruitless. He could not write what he felt he should. Thus the American also voted Reborn.

With three ballots cast, it seemed almost certain that Monique would get a second chance. *I'm there!* she presumed, *I have the three votes I need!* A premature elation was beginning to rise inside the doctor, but then she remembered, *Gabriel!*

Abigail did not deviate from the direction of the voting. She didn't have the heart to hurt her, no matter how much she distrusted this woman. She also recorded Reborn as her verdict. Nader Khoury - the soul whom Monique had wanted to condemn - without ceremony held out his slate for all to witness, it said Reborn. She had a clean sweep of all five votes, unanimously in favour that Doctor Monique Dumond, should begin a new life.

Marcus snickered, *All five in her favour,* scratching his head in astonishment at what was unfolding. He could hardly believe it. *Humans! What a weird bunch we are, unfathomable, capable of all sorts of twisted horrors and then such misplaced mercy, unbefuckinlievable!*

Doctor Dumond appeared elated in as much as her withered countenance could elicit. Perhaps, just perhaps, she has another chance at life. *The next time would be better. They cannot ignore the vote of all five jurors, surely!* She had convinced herself.

The Archangel Gabriel sat forward on his bench raising his voice for all to hear. 'This cannot pass!' he boomed. Monique's lower jaw dropped in fright, all eyes in the room were focused on the presiding Seraph.

'Monique Dumond, you have been judged by a jury of five peers. Considering your crimes they have been more than merciful. However, we do not concur. You are a recidivist criminal, an errant soul of the worst kind and can only be treated as such,' the Arc stated.

'For the benefit of your fellow jurors,' he added. 'I will explain that the Protatori are restricted to refer only to your most recent life. They cannot comment on any others. We, however, do not have such restriction,' his expression turned grave.

Mike raised a hand. He was terrified of interrupting the Arc, but was compelled to speak. Gabriel nodded his assent. 'Can you please tell us why we are being over-ruled?' he asked bravely.

The Arc didn't reply, instead he pointed towards The Keeper of the Book of Life and Death, who thumbed through his large volume, stopping on a chosen page, he read, 'The soul before you, Monique Dumond, has walked the Earth once before.' All of the jurors recalled Monique's little secret, confessed at their last supper.

'Then she was known as Johanna,' the Arc said.

'Given the spark of life in Berlin, Germany, in 1901. She was born as Johanna Magdalena Ritschel. Years later she was to marry a high profile Nazi minister. She became a notable figure in her own right. Johanna died by her own hand, in the same city of her birth and first came to Limbus Stasis in 1945. For most of that life, the soul before you went by the name of - Magda Goebbels.'

'Holy mother of...' Mike just stopped himself in time.

The slight figure of Monique Dumond slumped defeated, as the facts of her previous life were read out for all to hear.

'Johanna Magdalena Goebbels in Stasis, was found guilty of the murder of her six children; Helga, Hilde, Helmut, Holde, Hedda, and Heide aged between four and twelve years,' the Arc kept reading.

'I told you then, it was those Doctors, Stumpfegger and Kunz who killed my children, It was not my idea, I loved my children dearly.' The old woman was suddenly on her feet and animated in a furious barrage of defiance.

The Arc calmly responded, 'Herr Doctor Kunz administered the morphine that put them to sleep and Stumpfegger cracked the cyanide between their teeth. But they followed your orders, yours and your husband's.'

'What choice did we have? The Russian monsters were on our doorstep,' she shrieked. 'They would have defiled my beautiful children. There was no future for us without the Führer.'

Abigail and Mike were dumbstruck. Could it really be that Monique had been Magda? And that she'd murdered her own children. The woman was unpleasant for sure, but this was next to inconceivable for them both.

The Archangel Michael continued reading aloud, 'Your step-father was Jewish and he'd loved you dearly. He perished at the Buchenwald camp, but you never tried to help him, Johanna. You were sentenced to Gehenna - as was your husband - by a jury of your peers.'

'Holy shit!' Mike leaned across to Abigail, 'Can you believe this? Sentenced to Gehenna!' Abigail sat open-mouthed in a state of disbelief.

The Arcs eyes burned now almost luminously incandescent, 'You appealed directly to the Godhead. As a mother, they looked on you with compassion and had mercy on your soul. Your husband was doomed for his crimes, but it was commanded that you should receive one more chance.' At that precise moment you could hear a pin drop in the chamber.

'In this subsequent life - as Monique Dumond - a life you have also defamed. You have proven again to be an irredeemable soul, incapable of remorse,' the Arc said.

The soul known as Monique, took on a terrible aspect, her face scrunched up in fury. She looked around frantically, like a cornered creature, her eyes darting from side to side. An horrendous keening sound emitted from her throat.

She began hissing and cursing in tongues. Maryam was heart-broken. She looked on at this pitiful creature and felt nothing but sadness. But then she remembered those difficult years, a terrible time to be in Stasis. Almost completely overrun by the endless lines of people - women and mothers - who tramped into 5, telling their tales of persecution and State-sponsored murder. Millions selected for killing on the ramp of the Death Camps.

They went down under the ground, to breathe the foul gas, forced to take their beautiful children with them. It was such an appalling time to have worked here. *No,* she decided. Her pity should be reserved for those innocents who perished. *The sentence would be just.*

The Archangel Gabriel stood and declared, 'Monique Dumond, you are to be taken to Gehenna.'

Abigail and Miyu both raised their hands to cover their mouths, visibly in shock. The men looked on astounded but said nothing as the old woman ranted in fury. Seated at the bench, a dejected Niccolò sighed, 'One hundred and one, straight.'

Monique was about to launch herself again at the presiding Arc when she felt a strong grip on her left arm. It was the Attendant, Lou.

'Lucifer will escort you to your final destination,' Gabriel said.

The horrified doctor looked askance at the Attendant – 'Lucifer!' she cried.

Here they call me Lou, for short,' he grinned.

Unexpectedly, Monique lashed out with demonic strength. She caught Lou with a terrible blow, tearing chunks of skin from his face with claw like nails. The personality of the penitent had been subdued by the demented soul, now gone fully rogue - it was fighting for its survival. It ran in circles seeking a way out of the chamber, but was faced by a Seraph on three sides and Lou on the other. The snarling prisoner probed for the route of least resistance and made directly for the Angel Ananchel. The Seraph displaying neither fear nor surprise, raised her palm outwards, a sudden sharp juddering blast blew the jurors from their seats. On the floor of the chamber, Abigail writhed in agony, hands clasped across her ears, the noise jarring, deafening and painful. She rolled over in time to see that the Seraphim's fingers extended towards Monique, now suspended in the air, her arms hanging limp like a rag doll.

Restrained by supernatural force, Lou had time to bind Monique's carriage and insert a large syringe into the muscles of her neck. The Seraph's lowered their hands and the shuddering noise stopped abruptly.

The afflicted soul crashed to the floor, momentarily unconscious, it did not struggle against its bonds. Marcus and Nader had both ran to help Lou, who straddled the creature as he carefully pocketed the hypodermic.

'Suxamethonium chloride, it's a neuromuscular blocker,' he grinned impishly. 'You just gotta love science!'

The errant soul was no longer Johanna, Magda or Monique. In its total contamination it had suppressed and abandoned all need of personality. Lou hefted the soul carriage, gripping under the armpits, he ordered Nader to lift at the legs. Although Monique had a slight frame, the debased matter of her soul weighed much heavier than her form. Marcus opened the portal and Nader and Lou struggled through. Abigail went to follow but was grasped by a firm hand. 'That door is not for you,' Marcus said firmly.

'Where are we now?' Nader asked on passing through the portal.

'Coming down from the Mount of Olives, about to enter the Valley of Hinnom,' Lou replied. 'A place where the followers of Moloch sacrificed children to appease their false gods.'

'The Holy City of Jerusalem,' Nader sighed. They descended down into the valley by the south east corner of the old city walls. 'Where is this Gehenna?' Nader was blowing hard under the load but the old Attendant seemed physically unaffected.

'Inside Belshazzar's Gate.'

'I've never heard of such a gate?'

'That's because no one knows it's there,' Lou smiled. 'Mortals cannot see it.' Lou led the damned soul to the foot of the city wall. He stopped at the rock face and ran his fingers across the stone. An image began to form, burned in a fiery gold. It said אנמ, וְיסרפו ,לקת ,אנמ

The soul, once called Monique, had begun to recover some function, hissed and spat, 'What does the writing on the wall say, tell me now?'

'Mene, Mene, Tekel, Upharsin,' the Attendant said, facing down the wicked creature. 'It's from the Book of Daniel. It says that you've been weighed, judged and been found wanting.' A section of the stone wall rumbled nosily inwards, leaving a dark gap no more than three feet across. Inside this ancient space were two doors of dark wood. Their handles tethered by a coil of sisal rope and held in place by a mummified claw. Lou patiently undid the knot.

'So long Johanna,' Lou said. 'By the way, all of your children were reborn. Half of them have since passed to the Host. They expect the other three will follow soon. They all have lived exemplary lives.' The personality of the condemned fleetingly reasserted control, *My dear children.*

Staring up at the Attendant it made a final plea for clemency, 'You were the Morning Star, Lucifer. Let me pass and I will be your disciple for all eternity. We will find others who will follow you!'

The sclera of Lou's eyes glowed fiery red, 'I was once ambitious and burdened with pride. My fall from grace was hard and brutal, cast down into the depths of the pit. But I repented with all my heart and mercy was extended, even to me. Yet now you would try to tempt me!' He growled. 'Begone from our sight! Time to throw out the trash.' With effortless strength, he flung the debauched soul inside and slammed the door shut.

It inhaled deeply. Nothing happened.

If this is Gehenna, why has nothing happened? it wondered. The sky was still the same, the breeze touched on its face. It looked all around, there was nothing but tranquillity. Several moments passed and nothing had changed. *Was it really all just a bluff?* It cackled a harsh laugh, full of contempt. No sooner had the laughter passed from its lips, a great lake of fire shot up and encircled it. The condemned soul cowered and took a step back, agitated and afraid. Just as suddenly as they appeared, the flames receded in a whoosh, leaving only a gargantuan bed of little skulls and skeletons - the bones of the children who had been burned here by the Canaanites.

The eyes of its soul carriage contemplated the monstrous scene strewn before it, but felt neither pity nor remorse for the victims. It felt only fear for itself. The only one who could have intervened, now looked on, saw its reaction and sighed, *the Judgment was correct.*

An ear-splitting noise first distant, now came closer, The Great Host passed over the creature's head, heard but unseen, its voices unleashing an inconsolable wail. The sense of absolute loss was overwhelming – the severing of the covenant and the final separation from the Creator, without which a soul cannot survive. A fissure spread across its mass in a spider web of cracks, from which a searing light burst through. The soul self-immolated in its own skull. The flesh avulsed from its bones, disintegrating into a fine powdery dust that was whipped up and consumed by a great burst of fire that engulfed all of Gehenna.

The fire raged briefly at incredible temperatures, then extinguished. As did the life of a soul, that no longer existed.

As they ascended from the valley, the atmosphere was sombre, as if coming from a funeral. The destruction of a soul was a grievous loss for all. Lou said to Nader. 'I've heard it's been decided to reach out to mankind again. Many souls are at a perilous time of despair and are disconnected from the Heofon.'

'What will they do?'

'Give them hope.' Lou said. 'They will offer the world empirical proof of the existence of the immortal soul.' The Attendant smiled knowingly as he opened the portal that led back to Stasis. Before stepping through, he turned to the fisherman and said, 'They worship new false gods now. Disposable ones – they call celebrities.'

fifteen

On returning to the chamber, Nader was relieved to be far from Gehenna. The Advocate Maryam stepped forward and addressed the remaining jurors, 'This session is now concluded. I wish to congratulate those of you, who will now move on to the Great Host of Souls. You will not be disappointed. Many of your loved ones and ancestors, who have gone before, await you now.'

'Wait, our business here is not yet done.' It was Manny who spoke. 'There is one more soul to be judged.'

'Immanuel, what soul do you speak of ?' Maryam asked.

'The soul of Marcus Caelius Agrippa,' he answered.

The Advocate Marcus was flummoxed. He had not been expecting this.

Maryam turned to Gabriel, saying, 'But we require six for a jury. There are but five souls remaining.'

Manny walked to the line of chairs and sat down in a vacant seat. 'I have also walked the Earth as a man, I believe that entitles me to be one of the jurors.' The Keeper looked at the Archangel Gabriel who considered the conundrum. He merely shrugged and nodded his assent.

'As you wish.' The Keeper of the Book said, 'The soul of Marcus Caelius Agrippa. Step forth and be judged.'

THE JUDGMENT OF MARCUS CAELIUS AGRIPPA.

As Marcus sat in the Judgment chair, he remembered the same unease he had felt nearly two millennia before. *You never get used to this.*

'For the record, I Maryam, shall be the Advocate for Marcus Caelius Agrippa.'

Marcus looked at each face ranged before him and filled his lungs with a deep breath. It was Niccolò who stepped forward. He sneered as he approached, 'Agrippa, for too many centuries, you have dragged your sorry ass, around Stasis.' At the Prot bench, Jocelyn giggled.

'You should have been flogged then burned in Gehenna, but they took deep pity on you,' The Prot said. Marcus was grim-faced. He didn't need reminding of his great wrongdoing. He had lived with it every day since.

'And worse!' Niccolò bellowed. 'You have appalling dress sense, your shirts are permanently stained, and you snore like a train!'

What is this about? Marcus was bemused. He looked around the chamber and saw that many of those assembled were smiling and barely supressing laughter. Only the Arcs maintained their usual composure.

'There have also been rumours that you get into brawls?' Niccolò said, his hands held wide, feigning incredulity. 'I really don't think it is wise or safe to keep you around anymore Agrippa. What say you?' Niccolò pointed at the Jury.

None of them knew what to do? They stared wide eyed at Manny, looking for direction. Manny reached for his chalk, picked up his slate and wrote the word Reborn, which he displayed to all. Abigail got it now. She also wrote Reborn, as did all of the other jurors who had begun to slowly cotton on. Gideon addressed Marcus. He was also smiling.

'Rebuttal by the Advocate?' he called.

'There is no defence. He is guilty of all that's been said,' Maryam chortled.

'Well then Agrippa. Get out of that chair,' said Gideon.

Maryam took Marcus' hand and squeezed tight. 'It is time Marcus. I agree, you have indeed been here long enough,' she said by way of encouragement. The former soldier got up and stepped away from the Judgment chair. Marcus was sure now, that his fate was to walk on the Earth again, something that he had longed to do many times.

'Life as a little boy all over again,' Marcus guffawed to himself, but the idea clearly both excited and terrified him.

'If I may?' Manny asked to approach the bench, the Archangel signalled that it was appropriate and he leant forward to hear what the young man had to say. The Arc's eyes widened in surprise as he heard Manny's words and a solemn hint of a smile crept slowly across his sculpted features. The Arc called out in a clear voice, deep and resonant, 'Marcus Caelius Agrippa, you have been judged by a jury of fellow souls. Their verdict is that you be Reborn and walk again among men.'

A spontaneous round of applause broke out in the chamber. Marcus has clearly made a lot of friends during his time on Stasis. Even the normally aloof Protatori joined in.

'However...' he continued. 'You will not start in a new body. Instead you shall return in your present form, at your current human age of 33 years. You will resume your life and carry out the work that will be requested.'

Now it was the Advocate's turn to stare in astonishment. 'Go back as I am?' he muttered. Marcus did not have any idea if there was any precedent, but he did know that in all his many years in Stasis, he had never witnessed such a thing. This time it was Manny who spoke. He approached the bemused Advocate, embraced him, and placed his hands on both shoulders, 'My friend Marcus, have faith in our plan for you. Go and live simply as a man once more- as a man called Marcus Cael.'

Your memories will not be erased by the Lethe. You will remember all things that transpired here. The souls need a new reminder, go live your life amongst the men and women of the Earth, Marcus

Cael.' Manny bade him farewell and Marcus dropped back onto his bench, scarcely coming to terms with what he had been told. In just a few moments, he was going back - just as he is now, *but to where? Where will I go?*

For a very long period of time I have had the opportunity, maybe I should call it the privilege to observe and to study what we refer to as human nature - what is it that makes us do what we do? The mechanics of our life on the Earth are set: our carriage becomes irretrievably attached to its soul and the New born or the Reborn who were doused with the waters have no memory of an existence outside of their body.

They cannot recall that their human form is just a thing, destined like all things on the Earth to decline and decay. They cannot countenance the natural and inevitable separation of the two by design. For many the only logical conclusion is that the death of the lesser one is the end of life. But they're wrong. It is only the end of this Earth-bound life. Yet many who believe in an afterlife, beyond the realm of the physical body, are in today's world taunted and goaded, accused of ignorance or believing in a fairy tale.

The human body and its soul although symbiotic are not equals - the soul being immortal, it will exist for eternity unless it is deemed to be soiled - the body designed to return to basic matter and to be recycled into the Universe where nothing gets wasted. An integral part of its miraculous design is that from the moment of insertion, both the soul and its carriage are intractably bonded. The body wants only to live, it is programmed to survive and it will attempt to do this no matter the condition of the soul. I'm not privy to the thoughts of designer regarding this dichotomy nor would I ever question their logic, I state merely the conclusion from personal observation. This condition is what makes the Archangel's marvel when on the rare occasions that the soul gains the upper hand and overcomes the body - when a human surrenders his life so another may live. It is a sacrifice that trumps all others.

Manny has said that he will come to visit me during my time on Earth but has not as yet revealed his purpose for my rebirth. But I am grateful for this second chance. I will wait with great anticipation, for that day when he will call, as I live my days as Marcus Cael.

The Keeper of the Book of Life and Death recorded the verdict on the former Roman soldier and then all three Seraphim departed the room, their sacred task complete. Now only the five jurors remained in the Judgment chamber plus the Advocate Maryam, the former Advocate Marcus and the Attendant whose given name had been Lucifer.

Maryam approached each of the souls in turn, embracing them and offering her congratulations. Nader meanwhile approached his friend Marcus and shook his hand vigorously. 'I'm so very happy for you,' he said.

'And I for you,' was the reply.

'Marcus, why does she do this work? She is the...'

'You are like her children,' Marcus cut him off, 'What kind of mother would not try to help her children?'

Maryam arrived at Nader's side. 'Nader, as you can see, there has been an opening. I would like you to take Marcus' place, with me here.'

The fisherman spluttered, 'I don't know how to do that thing with the hand, the thing that brings calm?'

Maryam laughed and took his hands in hers and said, 'Do not worry Nader, I will teach you, it's just pressure points.' Nader just smiled and nodded his agreement.

Finally the Attendant Lou, called, 'It's time to clear the room, everybody please. I have to prepare for the next quorum. Stasis is always busy, yes siree!'

Maryam shook Mike's hand and pointed at the door on the far side. A look of concern flashed across his eyes. It was the same door that Monique had been taken to Gehenna. 'Have a little faith Mike,' Maryam said. 'That door has a different purpose for everyone.'

Mike hugged Abigail and Miyu, shook hands with Tomas and then embraced his good friend Nader. 'See you on the other side brother,' Mike said slapping Nader's broad shoulders.

'Inshallah – May God will it so,' he replied.

Mike Roberts stepped cautiously towards the doorway, placed his hand to open it and turned the handle slowly. Before stepping through, he looked back at the souls who had accompanied him on this most epic of journeys and felt a deep sense of love. He entered and the portal swung shut behind.

He stood there waiting but nothing happened. *Am I here in the Heofon?*

A vision materialised before his eyes as if a mirage, he was on a street, a familiar street. He could see his house, but like it was years before, from his childhood, a house brimming with love and optimism. In the garden there's a tree swing, and a young woman tending to her roses. *Mom!* Mike was astonished.

He was startled by a voice beside him, he turned to see the man he knew as Manny, smiling broadly, 'Welcome home Mike. What are you waiting for? Go on! They've been waiting all this time for you.'

Mike grinned at Manny, then his feet broke into a run. He heard a sound, a familiar voice unheard for many years but instantly remembered – his mom's voice. 'Mike! Mike I'm here!' She was waving now a huge smile on a young woman's joyful face. For in the Heofon you may appear as you wish. Hundreds of other voices joined in, acclaiming his return home.

In mid-stride Michael's skin fell painlessly from his bones, his human form disintegrated and the dust was swirled around by the enormous orb that passed overhead.

The Puresoul of Michael Roberts ascended into the Heofon to be warmly welcomed by the many souls who had gone before him, all of whom rejoiced for being in his company again.

Gloria was waiting for Tomas Esposito when he entered, 'Where have you been?' she said, her slightly lopsided smile breaking into a huge smile, their love resumed once more, as they ascended together. Twenty years of unbearable pain washed away in an instant.

Marcus shook hands with Lou and Nader. He wished Miyu well in her new job and Abigail too. He stopped to speak a final time with Maryam. He embraced her in a great bear hug lifting her petite frame easily and spinning her through the air. Both were laughing.

'Did you know about this?'

'Immanuel may have said a little something,' Maryam replied. She was immensely happy for her colleague. She would miss him dearly but he had earned another chance. She spotted Abigail waiting on the fringes of their conversation, self-consciously rocking up on her toes.

'So big man, before you go, as she's going to be helping out here for a while, it might be a good idea to show Abigail some of the more important workings of Stasis,' Maryam suggested.

'Indeed, the behind the scenes tour, the backstage pass, why not?' Marcus held his hands out wide. His unexpected news had put him in a gracious mood. 'After me, if you please,' he gestured to Abigail 'It's time you saw the Light Room.'

Abigail her natural curiosity piqued fell into step with the big Roman. 'You seem very happy to be going back.'

Marcus turned to look at her, his expression incredulous, 'Of course I'm happy, woman! I have a chance to redeem myself. I've been watching souls trundle merrily to the Heofon for centuries. I admit, it makes me a little jealous. I'm no different than any other soul here. I want to go home too!' he grinned. His good spirits had quickly returned. They passed the entire way through the block before arriving outside a large metal door.

'This is where the magic happens!' Marcus reached into a wall-mounted box, passing Abigail a pair of sunglasses. 'You'll need to put these on or you won't see shit in there...' he stopped mid-sentence and said, 'Forgive me, I sometimes forget myself.'

Abigail giggled. 'Must be really bright in there?' she said, putting on the wrap around shades.

'You'll see.' The Advocate turned the large radial lock in an anti-clockwise motion and pushed the heavy door inwards. He gestured for Abigail to enter. The Light Room at first seemed to have an inappropriate name. It was pitch black inside.

'I can't see a thing!' she said nervously.

'Hold up your hand Abigail, then wait a moment,' Marcus' instructed her from behind.

'Crikey!' she cried out. Abigail could see her hand in a multitude of whitish purple colours. She marvelled as she twisted it back and forth in front of her eyes.

'This is how the Angels see,' Marcus stepped inside and closed the door. 'I'm not much on the science, but they tell me that, the human eye only has a range of 390 to 750 nanometers on the electromagnetic wavelength, which leaves only a billion or so wavelengths that we can't perceive.'

'Wow, I didn't know that,' Abigail was impressed.

'In the Light Room there are a whole load of colours that humans can't see, mostly infrared, gamma and ultraviolet. Some people with a genetic mutation called Aphakia can pick up some of the ultraviolets - like the painter Monet when he had a lens removed in his old age - but mainly it's the animal kingdom, cats, dogs, butterflies even.'

Marcus pointed towards the back of the hallway. Abigail's eyes were becoming accustomed to the beauty of this unseen world. They walked together towards a long, narrow viewing window.

'We can't go inside,' Marcus cautioned. 'Only Seraphim can handle souls.'

Nothing in her human life or even her short stay on Stasis could have prepared her for what she saw next - countless cords of tubular strands were bending and undulating back and forwards in an erratic dance, like some crazy headed Medusa. They reached out from the edge of a precipice where the cords where anchored and sheltered beneath a cavernous roof. At the top of each strand was a violet-white tulip shaped cornet.

'What is that?' she gazed in awe. From out of the dark sky came hundreds of pinhead shards of a most brilliant light, travelling at incredible velocity, like a field of shooting stars. As each one got closer the strands whipped forwards and their tulip mouths opened its petals and cushioned a pulsating speck. None missed their target. They shut closed again in the blink of an eye before the cornet detached from the cord and propelled up into one of thousands of volutes in the ceiling. Immediately another cornet grew in its place.

'You're looking at newly arrived souls. You came here in this manner, as did I.'

Abigail was dumbfounded she had no idea if what she was looking at was biological or a machine, maybe even both. Marcus caught her expression, 'It's called the Nepesh Locus -The Soul Cradle.' Abigail was overwhelmed by the enhanced light spectrum that was confounding her brain. 'What does it do, where do they go next?' Abigail was intensely curious.

'I'm really not the best person to explain this,' Marcus sighed. 'In its cradle each soul is weighed, basically.'

'But why?' Abigail pressed her face against the glass.

Marcus explained, 'The soul at creation has almost no weight, but when it is soiled by wrongdoing, its density increases. It absorbs the blemish like a thumb mark on a peach,' he said. 'The more the damage the more layers it penetrates. Conversely, acts of kindness and love can heal the wounds.' Abigail found herself at a loss for words.

'Like I said, I'm no expert but I've been told that they use an instrument, something like a Super-Interferometer. They can analyse the light particles for absorption or emission of sin, When the cradle shoots upstairs the memory data is logged by the file compilers - usually younger Seraph's, then prepped for re-entry to a shiny new body all ready for Judgment.'

Marcus grinned, 'Press the button on the stem of your glasses. It will give you a close up.'

Abigail did as commanded just in time to see a magnified view of a newly arrived soul. It quivered and vibrated like a pulsar before landing in its host. Tempted, she peered over the top of her sunglasses and could no longer see anything in the Light Room. 'An invisible world - yet it exists!' The thought made her very happy.

When they got back to Room 5, Lou had the room prepared. Only Nader and Maryam remained. Miyu had been in a hurry to get to her books. She had so many to care for now.

'So what did you think?' Maryam asked Abigail.

'The Light Room, oh it's beyond any words.'

'Maryam, I guess it's time for me to get going,' Marcus said, and for a moment it seemed to Abigail as if he had tears in his eyes, as he spoke to his mentor.

'Don't worry you big oaf,' Maryam said. 'You know we will meet again, when you come back the next time,' she smiled.

'I have no idea what I am expected to do?'

'You'll be fine Marcus. You will know what to do at the right time. Tell those who will listen, about what you found here. What they can expect if they are kind.' She took his strong hands in hers.

'You've worked hard for a second chance, so take it with a happy heart.'

'Thank you Maryam.' And with that Marcus Agrippa walked through the arch, emerging through the portal into a great city. He was a human once more. A man called Marcus Cael. He had no money and only the clothes on his back. But he still had his memories and he would find his way.

Nader meanwhile was handed a couple of leather bound files and his new boss asked 'Ready to go to work?' Maryam told Abigail that she could use her old cell, and of course the cello was still there waiting to be played.

City of Mumbai, India. Present Day.

A new born baby cries out. The young midwife stoops to clutch it up but recoils in horror. The family have not been blessed on this occasion. The child cries even louder until another, more experienced woman, swaddles and cleanses the greasy white vernix from the folds of the skin.

Gentle female hands raise the trembling child up for cursory inspection.

Beautiful and ugly in the same carriage.

The breath of life has been imparted from the Heofon and a new life begun. Born into a sprawl of shanties, shacks and slum tenements, called Dharavi. This garbage strewn slice of the Mega city of Mumbai, covers just one square mile and is home to a scarcely believable one million souls.

The new father looks down on his child once more and feels shame in his heart, for believing him cursed by the gods. This tiny newborn with its cleft palate and withered left hand will struggle to survive in the Dharavi slum. Such little room for pity, for the deformed and the weaklings, born daily on its overcrowded narrow streets, carpeted with crud and foul water.

But there is a vast and deep wellspring of goodness here, more than a modicum of which, runs in the veins and the beating heart of this kind father, a simple man, who has no way of knowing, that this brittle soul has returned to the world.

So cruel on the surface that a child must exist on the charity of others. Still the Heofon moves in mysterious ways, as this devoted Baba makes a silent vow to Vishnu, to love and safeguard his crippled son. Yet the most difficult part, comes now: to survive past the first five years amidst the raw sewage and heavy metals that course through the street canals of this shadow city, where cholera and other diseases abound. This child is already off to a vulnerable start.

In the normal course of human development, a newly born infant cannot see clearly at birth. But unknown to those who gaze at him, this *special* child sees all with perfect acuity. Inside this tiny infant's frame, the seeing eyes of a soul that - once the proud possessor of a strong and virile body - look up at the circle of unfamiliar brown faces, spots his shrivelled arm and remembers the blow he struck the Judgment chair. His unabated screams will last long into the night. But perhaps now, the soul once known as Per, has finally found the limitless love of a father, something that he'd always craved. And also a real shot at going home.

In time we will see, but for now, I guess only Heofon knows.

The last thing she can recall was lugging groceries up the many steps to her flat, when a ferociously blinding headache split straight through her skull. Now she is here in this strange place, outside Room 5. She knocks hesitantly before entering and is met by a bright smile on a dark weather-lined face.

'Welcome to Stasis. My name is Nader.'

'I know you didn't expect to be joining us today, but don't worry, please take a seat. Your Advocate, Abigail, will be with you soon.'

CPSIA information can be obtained
at www.ICGtesting.com
Printed in the USA
LVOW08s1814290318
571634LV00004B/907/P

9 780692 491553